Winter Trees
A Marigold Manor Story

Kim Stokely

Bellevue, Nebraska

Kim Stokely
Bellevue, Nebraska 68123
www.kimstokely.com

Publisher's Note: This is a work of fiction. Names, characters, places, and incidents are a product of the author's imagination. Locales and public names are sometimes used for atmospheric purposes. Any resemblance to actual people, living or dead, or to businesses, companies, events, institutions, or locales is completely coincidental.

Cover design by Bruce Skinner @ Hyperion Photography, Carver, MA

Book Layout © 2014 BookDesignTemplates.com

Winter Trees/Kim Stokely. -- 1st ed.
ISBN-13: 978-1500954666
ISBN-10: 1500954667

For Maureen Nichols,
who has worked in Assisted Living facilities
for over twenty years.
Your dedication and stamina amaze me.
Your friendship and encouragement inspire me.

All things are possible to those who believe, yet more to those who hope, more still to those who love, and most of all to those who practice and persevere in these three virtues.

—BROTHER LAWRENCE

CHAPTER ONE

The day began like a typical Monday. I slept through my alarm, spilled coffee on my first outfit, and hit every red light on the way to work. The ashen color of the Nebraska sky melted into the gray-black slush piled along the side of the road from a snowfall two days ago. It did nothing to improve my sour mood. When the sun finally did break through the clouds, it sat at the perfect spot to blind me as I pulled into the parking lot of Marigold Manor Assisted Living. To top it off, I found my office door unlocked and George Franklin standing behind my desk wearing nothing but his boxers, dark socks, and dress shoes. You'd think that'd be my biggest worry, but it wasn't. The fact that he seemed to be talking on the phone scared me more. I could only hope he hadn't gotten an outside line and called China.

I stepped into my office. "George? What are you doing here?"

He placed a hand over the mouthpiece of the phone. "Gladys, darling, you know you must call me Mr. Franklin when we're at work." His baritone voice still held on to the Southern drawl he'd acquired growing up in the Carolinas.

"We have to maintain appearances." He went back to his phone conversation. "Please, tell corporate I'll be on the next flight to St. Louis."

Although I've never liked my given name of Virginia Elizabeth, I can assure you I've never thought of myself as a "Gladys." With my tall frame and red hair, I've always thought I should be named something more exotic, like Rene or Jasmine. I satisfied myself with the nickname "Ginny." I closed the door and hung my jacket up on the coat rack, taking note of George's robe draped over one of the rungs. At least he hadn't walked down the hall in just his skivvies.

"Gladys?" George hung up the phone and grabbed my mug. "Coffee?"

"Coming right up, Mr. Franklin." I figured it was better to humor him today than try and bring him into reality. I'd let Karen, the head nurse, know what'd happened. Maybe she could up his dose of Aricept.

As I walked back through the lobby of Marigold Manor, several residents called out greetings. I waved at Bernice and Agnes, who played cards at the corner table. Mary sat in front of the fireplace, staring into the flames with a serene smile on her face. The fireplace stood in the middle of the lobby and opened up on either side. In the far corner of the front half of the room sat a baby grand piano bathed in sunlight from the large picture window. An overstuffed love seat covered in a hideous cabbage rose pattern dominated the sitting area, flanked on either side by two wing-backed chairs. Frank and Bill sat in them with their noses stuck behind newspapers. Bill peered over the top of the page and gave me a wink.

"Hey, good-looking. How are you today?"

"Fine Bill, and you?"

"Still on top of the sod, so I must be doing something right." His face lowered again behind the paper.

I continued into the dining room, where Samantha and Rachel sat at the table next to the coffee machine. Sam looked resplendent in her fuchsia jogging suit and matching lipstick. Even her hair had taken on a pink tinge this morning. Rachel pushed her wheelchair back. Her polyester floral house coat barely covered the top of her legs.

"We were supposed to have sausage patties today." Rachel glared at me. "Not links."

I got out two Styrofoam cups and poured coffee for me and George. "I'm not in charge of food. I only do activities."

Rachel grunted. "No one will do anything around here. You all pass the buck. I want some action! We said at the last food committee meeting we wanted patties, not links. And here we get links." She pointed a bony finger at the offending pork products on her plate. I found it strange that her fingers remained skinny while the rest of her gained weight.

"I'll talk to Chester." I sighed and took the coffee into the kitchen. "*Hola.*"

Chester, the cook, glanced up from where he stood wiping off the counter. A first-generation American born from two Mexican immigrants, he spoke perfect English but indulged me in my desire to retain the small amount of Spanish I'd learned in high school. Besides, the rest of the kitchen staff spoke only Spanish, so I needed to try and keep up my vocabulary.

"*Hola*, Ginny." Chester waved his dish towel at me. "*Como estas?*"

"*Cansado.*"

"Tired?" Chester frowned. His mustache crept down around his mouth like a fuzzy caterpillar. "It's only Monday!"

"I know, but they're already complaining."

Chester scowled. It was cute the way his eyes squinched up and his mouth puckered. "Aye yi yi. Is it Rachel again? About the sausage?"

I nodded. "You've heard?"

"You're the third person she's sent in to tell me. I told her, the food service was out of patties yesterday. I've already got them on order for Friday." He threw the towel on the counter. "She'll have her patties by Saturday. I'll have Maria cook them special for her."

"*Gracias.*"

"*De nada.*" His deep brown eyes twinkled and he waved a finger at me. "Don't stay out late tonight. Then you won't be tired."

I stuck my tongue out at him and headed back into the dining room. Chester knew I wasn't out late. The whole facility knew I had no social life. It had been two years since my fiancé had died, and I had yet to be on a date. Susan, the administrator, had ordered me last Friday to RSVP for the Christmas party, or rather the *holiday dinner*, next month. It would be my first real outing since Mark was killed in a car crash. I wasn't looking forward to it.

Rachel gave me the evil eye as I left the kitchen. I took a deep breath. "Chester's on it. You'll have your patties by Saturday." I hurried off before she could complain some more. I called to one of the med aides as I made my way back to my office.

"Sandy, can you help me with George? He's commandeered my desk."

The petite blonde groaned. "Give me a minute. I've got Margaret Ann in the bathroom. I'll get her then come down to you."

"Thanks."

〰

Frank Leno lowered his paper so he could watch Ginny walk back to her office. The girl's red hair lay in a thick braid down her slender back. It swayed as she moved. "If I were forty years younger . . . ."

Bill, one of the few men in this facility who still had the sense God gave him, chuckled. "If you were forty years younger, you'd still be too old for her, you old goat."

Frank sighed and did the math. He'd be thirty-six. Maybe that'd still be too old. But some women liked older men. They saw them as more mature, better providers. He'd made a great life for his wife and four children, spending twenty-eight years in the Navy, retiring as a rear Admiral. He'd had another career as a school superintendent while pulling in his Navy pension. When he'd finally retired, he'd been able to collect on a state pension as well. Yes sir, he'd done well for his family. Frank's gaze roamed around the lobby of Marigold Manor. *And now I'm here.*

Agnes Pendleton caught his eye and gave him a smile. Frank smiled back. He'd been a rover all his life. He liked women — all kinds of women – young, old, skinny, or fat. He liked being around them and making them laugh. He blamed his Italian blood, the tradition his grandfather imparted of putting women on a pedestal. That and his rugged good looks made him a magnet for women, even now, past his prime. He may have put on a few pounds, but he still had most of his teeth and a thick head of deep-gray hair.

Agnes blushed as he stared at her. He looked away. *No, Agnes I don't want to start anything with you.* He might like women, but he did have his standards, and at ninety, Agnes was a little too old and a little too gone for his liking.

He checked out Agnes's card partner, Bernice. Now, she wasn't half-bad. She was only in her eighties and still had most of her marbles. Frank shook his head. *Who am I fooling?* He folded his paper and tucked it under his arm.

Bill's bald head popped up from his paper. "Leaving?"

Frank nodded. "It's nearly nine. My daughter has her grandkids web cam me on Mondays."

"Web cam?" Bill swore under his breath. "You know how to do that?"

"You gotta keep up with the times, my man." Frank tapped a finger against his temple. "Only way to keep the brain working right." He waved to his friend and headed to the elevator. As he waited for the cab to arrive, he thought about what he'd said to Bill. It was true. The one thing he feared the most, especially after living here for a year, was the thought of becoming like his wife had: bedridden, not knowing who he was, who the kids were. Not even remembering how to eat. What kind of life had that been? *Please, God. Don't let me end up like her.*

"You plan on taking up residence here, or you actually going to ride the thing?"

Frank looked down at the rotund woman in the floral housecoat and scowled. Rachel Johnson was one ornery, crazy, old loon. "Morning, Rachel."

"Don't 'Good morning' me. Get in the elevator, or move aside so I can go up."

Frank entered the cab and pressed the "door hold" button to give Rachel a chance to wheel in. He smiled at the thought of pressing the "door close" button instead and watching the door try to slice the old crone in two.

"Press the button, you fool. Or, are we just going to sit here on this floor for the rest of the day?"

Frank pressed the second floor button and sighed as the doors closed.

Sandy, the med aide, arrived in my office after I'd given George his coffee and pretended to "take a letter" to corporate. She told him that one of the VPs had called an emergency meeting in the boardroom. I helped him put his robe back on, insisting that he needed to wear his jacket to the meeting, and we led him out to the dining room. The visual clues of the tables and silverware, as well as the smells from the kitchen, were usually enough to bring George back to, if not reality, then at least acceptance of where he lived. His wife came in as I brought him another cup of coffee.

Helen approached the table. "I'm sorry, dear. They came to give me a whirlpool this morning. He was still asleep when I left. Has he been much trouble?"

I shook my head. "He seems to like my office. Look for him there if you ever lose him again."

Helen sighed as she watched her husband stare blankly out the window. "I'm sure it reminds him of work. The corporate life was all he knew for so many years." Her pale blue eyes moistened. "It's one of the few things I think he remembers."

The woman before me stood straight but I could see the burden that weighed her down. I'd sat with her one afternoon as she'd told me her story. George had married her in

Germany after WWII and brought her home to help with his parents' farm while he attended college. She'd left all her family back in Europe, and although they had three children, it had to be difficult to be without extended family when struggling with a disease like Alzheimer's.

Helen smiled at me. "I'll take care of him, dear. You do what you need to do." She placed a hand on her husband's shoulder. "George? Are you all right?"

He jumped at her touch. "I need to find a phone. I need to call my wife."

I could see the pain in Helen's eyes. "She called earlier. She's gone out to the hairdressers then over to Carol's house." Carol was their youngest daughter. George seemed to calm at the mention of her name.

His eyes searched Helen's face. "My wife knows I'm here?"

"Yes, George." Helen sighed and sat down opposite him. "She knows."

Once George was settled, I ran up the hallway to the activity room to get it ready for "Sittercise," our half-hour daily exercise program for the residents. They could remain sitting in their chairs and wheelchairs, but we used weights and stretch bands to help them keep some of their muscle tone and mobility. Harsh sunlight streamed in through the windows in the back of the room, it reflected off the several inches of snow and the windshields of the cars in the parking lot. A brisk Nebraska wind whipped through the pine trees that lined the facility's driveway. I was glad the snow had arrived early this year to cover the brown mud and barren trees left from autumn. As I watched, an elm tree outside the window seemed to shrug off its snowy coat, leaving its branches to wave aimlessly in the wind. It looked like a hand— a giant hand trying to grab hold of something to support it against the forces that sought to rip it from the ground. I shivered and adjusted the blinds so the sunlight wouldn't bother the residents with sensitive eyes.

Sam strolled in, steering her walker like a shopping cart. Her kids had found her a bright purple one, and it fit her exuberant personality.

"Howdy, Ginny."

"Morning, Sam." I smiled again at her fuchsia ensemble. "I sure do like that color on you."

"Pink's always been a favorite of mine."

"Well, it becomes you."

Sam groaned as she swung her walker around and sat. "My advice to you, darling: don't grow old. It's for the birds."

"We'll get your blood pumping this morning. That'll make you feel better." I placed a one-pound weight and exercise band at every chair.

"I don't think I believe you, but I'll try it."

"We'll play some hangman after that, get your brain working, too."

"You're a slave driver."

I laughed and left the room to round up some of the regular attendees who either needed a daily reminder or help coming down. The mottled blue and pink carpet whispered under my feet. I barely noticed the oil paintings of mountain streams and English cottages as I pushed Margaret Ann's wheelchair down to the elevator. She mumbled something under her breath.

I leaned down, bringing my face even with hers. "I'm sorry, Margaret. What did you say?"

Her brown eyes held a depth of sorrow I could only begin to understand. "Don't you get tired of being with old people?"

I pressed the button for the elevator and knelt by her side. "Nope. I never do." The doors opened, but I didn't move. "I like being with great people."

Margaret Ann let out a snort of disbelief, but her mouth softened into a small smile. "You'd do better with kids your own age."

"People my age aren't half as interesting, or fun, as you are." I patted her hand and stood to roll her into the elevator.

I had always felt more comfortable with older people, but never more so than after Mark died. Not one of our residents was immune to the grief of losing someone they loved. Husband, wife, sibling, or child. They understood my pain. I'd only been a volunteer then, helping out when I visited my grandmother, but these wise people had wrapped me in hugs of consolation and given me what no one else had been able to: acceptance. They didn't pressure me to "get on with my life." They didn't continually ask me how I was doing. They allowed me to grieve and showed me in a thousand little ways that they understood my sorrow.

∿

"Don't get me wrong," Bill said as he and Frank rode the elevator to the second floor after lunch. "It's not that I mind that gospel music, but it's the way some of those ladies sing it."

"I know," Frank said. "Half of them are deaf, and they're out of tune. Like drowning cats."

"Exactly." Bill hobbled out to the hallway as the doors slid open. He gestured toward the couch in the upstairs atrium. "You want to sit here today?"

From downstairs, the residents began an off-key rendition of "Just a Closer Walk with Thee." Frank groaned. "Let's go to the game room. It'll be quieter."

Bill leaned heavily on his cane, grimacing as he walked toward the glass-enclosed game room. A soft-serve ice cream machine hummed in the corner. Styrofoam bowls, plastic spoons and cones sat next to it. A variety of sprinkles and toppings lay nearby. Frank and Bill sat at one of the three Formica-topped tables along the far wall. On the other side of the room, a bookshelf held stacks of board games and puzzles. A pool table, dart board, and a miniature shuffle board table filled in the rest of the space.

"You want to play some checkers?" Frank asked.

"Sure."

"I'll grab us a set." Frank rapped his knuckles on the table as he stood. He found the game in the bookshelf and brought it back. "It's cold out there today."

Bill grabbed the red pieces. "Is it?"

"I went out to get some milk this morning. I think we'll get more snow soon."

They set up the game in silence. Frank nodded to indicate Bill should go first. He slid a red checker forward a square. "The nights seem longer."

"We're getting close to the equinox, the shortest day of the year." Frank made a move.

"All the days seem short now."

"What do you mean?"

Bill advanced another piece. "Time's going by too fast. There's a lot I'd hoped I could do before I died, you know?"

"Like what?"

Bill stuck out his lower lip as he contemplated either Frank's move or his question. "I'd always wanted to go back to Europe. I wanted to see Germany now, without the bombs and the blood. I bet it's a beautiful place."

"I was in the Pacific theater." Frank jumped one of Bill's pieces. "I have no desire to go back. Too hot."

"Isn't there something you wish you'd done?"

Frank stared at the board. "I always wanted to go to Rome. I wanted to see the Vatican and St. Peter's Basilica." He watched as Bill made another move. "Wouldn't you love to see the Sistine Chapel?"

"That's the one that guy painted on his back, right?"

"Michelangelo. It took him years."

"Why didn't you ever go?" Bill asked.

"I never had time. Work seemed too important."

Bill nodded. "My wife and I didn't have the money for a trip like that. That's what I thought, at least. Now I wish we'd maybe not bought the new cars. I would have liked to take that trip."

Frank crowned one of Bill's checkers. "There's still time. I'd go with you to Germany if you'd come with me to Rome."

The bald man made a dismissive noise. "No use now. I couldn't walk around like I'd want. I can barely make it around here."

Frank shrugged. "So, we get you a wheelchair. I'll push you."

"You'd get sick of me."

"Let's do it. Let's plan a trip for the spring."

"You think we could?"

"Why not?" Frank moved one of his pieces into Bill's territory. "King me."

His friend stacked the checkers. "It would be a hoot, wouldn't it? Two old goats like us wandering Europe?"

"You let me know when you want to go, and I'll start planning it."

Bill jumped two of Frank's men. "I'll think about it and get back to you."

〰

It had been a long day, even for a Monday. A resident fell at lunch and had to be taken out in an ambulance. A volunteer had called in sick, which meant I'd had to do manicures that afternoon. I sat at my desk, trying to plan out the calendar for December, when the phone rang. I knew Patty, our administrative assistant, had left early for an appointment, so I answered it.

"Thank you for calling Marigold Manor Assisted Living. This is Ginny. How can I help you?"

A tenor voice answered. "Just the girl I wanted to speak to."

"Who is this?"

"It's Dan. From St. Andrew's."

"Father Dan." I smiled to myself. I'd known him since he and I were kids. I still couldn't believe he was a priest. "How are you?"

"I wanted to give you a heads-up. Father Timothy is out of town this week visiting family. I'll be filling in for him on Wednesday."

"I'll let the residents know." I tapped a pencil against my desk. "Stop by the office when you're done. I'd love to see you."

"Will do. Gotta run."

We said our goodbyes and I went back to revising December's calendar. I was ready to pull my hair out trying to make room for all the carolers, schools, and churches that wanted to come in over the holidays. Don't get me wrong, I appreciate their goodwill, but no one seems to understand the work it takes to coordinate all these extra visitors so no one's feelings get hurt.

I promised myself I'd finish the task in the morning and shut off my computer. The phone rang again. I glanced at the lights on the multi-lined console. It was my direct line. I lifted the receiver. "This is Ginny. How can I help you?"

"Virginia, it's your father."

I closed my eyes and pinched the bridge of my nose. "Hi, Dad. You're back from Mexico already?"

"We got back a week ago." I made a mental note that he hadn't bothered to call on Thanksgiving as he continued, "I wonder if you could do lunch on Wednesday with Brittany and me? A sort of belated birthday celebration."

Only a month late. Not too bad. I opened my date book and swore to myself. I was free. "Sure. Could we make it for 12:30?"

"Noon works better for me. I'll see you at DelRico's."

I sighed. "I'll get there when I can."

"See you at noon."

He hung up before I had the chance to say goodbye. Typical. I puffed out my cheeks and let the air out slowly, like a deflating balloon. I grabbed my coat, locked my office door, and set off down the hallway to the dining room to have dinner with my grandmother.

Edith had moved to Omaha after Grandpa Lloyd died when I was eighteen. She'd sold the farm and used the money to buy a cute two-bedroom house in Bellevue. Two bad falls and a broken hip had forced her to consider assisted living. My mother had wanted to build a guest house on her property and get Edith residential care, but my grandma had wisely refused. She still had money from the sale of her and Grandpa's farm, so she had gotten herself a room at the top-of-the-line residential home then told me to move into her house, rent-free: a dream come true for a struggling college student. I visited during the week when I could and made sure to pick her up on Sunday for church.

When Mark and I had started dating, he'd loved to visit Edith with me. We'd spent hours around her tiny kitchen table, drinking tea and eating shortbread cookies. She had a way of putting everything in perspective. She still does.

I started volunteering for the facility almost immediately, calling Bingo or helping with special events. About six months after Mark died, the Activities Coordinator offered me her job. Her husband was retiring from the military, and they planned on moving near their family in Montana. It took me two days to think about her offer. I took it— not for the money, but for the change. The work could be difficult and demanding, but it had a great many rewards as well. Not the least of which was I could visit with my Grandma Edith every night before I went home.

Frank stuffed the chocolate brownie in his mouth. Not bad. Not as good as his wife's brownies, but a close second. He looked over at Bill's plate. Bill still picked at his casserole.

"You going to eat your brownie?"

"What?"

Frank pointed at the dessert. "You going to eat that?"

Bill's eyes narrowed. "I might."

Frank sighed. "Never mind." Esther and Mary, the others who'd been at their table, had finished their meals and were probably already in bed in their apartments. Frank glanced out the window. The sun had set about an hour ago, and the street lamps burned orange in the parking lot.

"Frank, my man." Chester, the cook, sat at the table. "How are you, sir?"

"I'm good." He gestured to his empty bowl. "The soup was superb this evening."

Chester smiled broadly. "Thank you."

"He was trying to scam me out of my brownie," said Bill. "I think I'll save it for a snack tonight."

Chester raised an eyebrow at Frank. "You want another? I have a couple in back."

Frank puckered his lips together, then nodded. "If you got another handy, I could make room."

The cook squeezed Frank's shoulder. "I'll be right back."

Frank picked up his coffee cup and walked over to the machine for a refill. Nothing better than a fresh cup of coffee and a nice dessert. He watched the kitchen door swing open and Ginny walk out, carrying a bowl of soup and a roll. He noticed Chester behind her, the cook's gaze following her to the table she shared with her grandmother. He'd seen the look in Chester's eyes before. Frank grinned as he walked back to his table. Chester set a brownie on Frank's plate and offered another to Bill.

Bill shook his bald head. "No, thanks. One's enough for me."

Chester shrugged and took a bite. Frank sipped from his mug then popped his brownie into his mouth.

The cook frowned. "If you chewed your food, it would last longer."

Frank swigged a mouthful of coffee and swished it around to remove any sticky brownie leftovers from his teeth. "And if you moved to the other chair, you'd have a better view of Ginny."

Chester stopped mid-bite. "What?"

The old man leaned forward, his voice low. "Go get yourself a cup of coffee and sit down at the other chair."

"*Por que?*"

Bill looked between the two of them. "What are you talking about?"

"I don't know." Chester finished his brownie. "He's a crazy old man."

Frank chuckled. "You can't fool me. I know that look."

Bill pushed himself up from the table. "I'm done. I can't follow either of you." He grabbed his dessert and wrapped it in a napkin. "I'll see you tomorrow."

From his seat Frank watched as Ginny leaned in to say something to her grandmother. The two women laughed. The reflection of the dining room sconces sparkled in Ginny's eyes. "You're missing it."

Chester shook his head. "She doesn't think about me like that."

"How do you know?"

The cook shrugged. "She just doesn't."

"She doesn't know what she wants anymore." Frank put his pale hand on Chester's darker-skinned arm. "You need to make a move. Soon."

Chester sighed. "I have to go."

Frank tilted his head. "Don't wait too long. Someone's going to snap her up."

Chester stood and headed toward the kitchen, but not, Frank noticed, without another glance toward Ginny.

It took another fifteen minutes before Chester finished cleaning the kitchen. He groaned and took off his apron. He'd put in a double shift, and his muscles told him they'd had enough. He said goodnight to the other kitchen staff and grabbed his coat. He thought about what Frank had said. *Would Ginny ever consider going out with a guy like me?*

Chester shook his head. Too many women outside of the neighborhood thought of him only as a cook. Most people in Omaha gave him a look that read, *Oh, great, another illegal working in a kitchen.*

He shoved his hands into his pockets as the doors to the facility slid open. His breath rose in little clouds of steam. Up ahead in the parking lot, Ginny's hair glistened in the light of a street lamp. She looked up as she unlocked her car door and waved.

"Goodnight, Chester!"

"*Buenos noches,* Ginny. Be careful driving home. The roads may have iced."

"You too. *Hasta mañana.*" She disappeared into her car.

Chester paused as Ginny's car sputtered then died. She tried again. The engine turned over and purred. He waved as she passed him. She smiled and waved back. Chester shivered.

You can't risk it again. You know it won't end well.

CHAPTER TWO

Wednesday morning dawned with a brisk wind from Canada pounding down across the plains. The song says it sweeps through Oklahoma, but it's certainly made its way to Omaha often enough. The radio announcer claimed a temperature of ten degrees with the wind-chill making it feel like three below. Too cold. My warm bed with the thick down comforter beckoned to me as I grabbed my keys from the nightstand. I resisted the temptation to call in sick and burrow back under the covers. Instead, I made my way out the door.

A powerful gust blew my hair across my eyes, completely obscuring my vision. I pulled at my red tresses and fumbled for the car door handle at the same time, providing, I'm sure, some comic relief to any of my neighbors who happened to be spying out of their windows. I opened the door and flung myself into the seat. Once I managed to yank it closed again, I sat for a moment, trying to catch my breath.

I hated the cold. I hated the wind. I wished it were spring.

I sighed and headed down the narrow road. The dead grass, gray sky, and barren winter trees painted a bleak picture outside. I dreaded the upcoming day — lunch with my dad and

Bingo. If I'd only planned to have dinner with my mother tonight, I could have completed the torture.

Frank slathered his toast with butter and covered his eggs with salt and pepper. *What's the use in living this long if you can't indulge yourself?* He'd been up early this morning, as he was most mornings, a habit from the military. He enjoyed the quiet solitude before the dining room filled with residents and staff workers. Chester had come in a few minutes ago and whipped him up the omelet and toast.

Edith MacPhearson made her way into the dining room. Frank watched Ginny's grandmother with an appreciative eye. The young Activities Director had inherited her grandmother's height and regal bearing. Frank wouldn't be surprised to find royalty somewhere in their ancestry, or at least Scottish warrior blood. Maybe William Wallace had been a relative.

Edith smiled at Frank and sat down several tables away. Ana, the short, dark assistant cook came out to fill Edith's coffee cup and take her breakfast order. Frank continued to watch her as he ate his omelet.

Edith glared at him. "It's impolite to stare."

Frank blinked. "Excuse me?"

Ginny's grandmother frowned. "You're staring at me. It's rude."

"I'm sorry." Frank shook his head. "I got lost in thought. I didn't mean to stare."

Edith raised one eyebrow, giving him an imperious look. "Well, lose your thoughts in another direction, please." With that, she shifted her chair so her back faced him.

Frank grinned. If Ginny was anything like her grandmother, Chester would have his hands full. Frank's smile faded. Perhaps it would be best to get Edith on Chester's side. *No use getting the young man's hopes up if her grandmother doesn't approve.* Frank finished his omelet and coffee, careful to wipe his face with his napkin to get rid of any crumbs. Ana brought out Edith's breakfast, an English muffin and jam, and set it on the table.

Frank walked over to the chair facing Edith. "Do you mind?"

The old woman lifted her gaze to look at him. The rest of her body remained still. "Mind what?"

Frank's stomach rolled. He'd seldom been unnerved by a woman, but Ginny's grandmother was a different kind of lady. He cleared his throat. "Would you mind if I sat with you a moment? I'd like to ask you a question."

Edith inclined her head slightly. "I suppose."

Frank took a deep breath as he sat.

"Well?"

"Well, what?"

Edith let out a soft, disgruntled snort. "What did you want to ask me?

Frank tried to gather his thoughts. "It's about your granddaughter."

The old woman knit her eyebrows together. "What about her?"

He looked around. Chester was nowhere to be seen, and the dining room was empty except for the two of them and George Franklin, but he was several lures short of a tackle box. Frank leaned forward. "First off, let me say what a nice girl she is. Everyone thinks so."

Edith relaxed. "I think so, too."

Frank nodded. "It's just . . . well . . . ."

"Spit it out, man."

"The poor girl's been pining for too long. I know someone who'd be perfect for her."

Edith's eyes narrowed. "Who?"

Frank spoke in a low voice. "Chester."

Edith sat back. "Who?"

"Chester. The cook." Frank gathered his courage. "Look, I know he's not some big-shot lawyer or fancy doctor. But, he's a good man. Honest. Hardworking. He's got dreams, too. Wants to own his own restaurant someday. He'd treat Ginny well." Frank smiled. "And he's totally crazy for your granddaughter."

"Really?"

"Watch him sometime when she's around. The boy's in love."

Edith sat silent for a moment. "Chester?"

Frank nodded. "Chester."

"Let me think on it a little. See if I see the same thing you do." A slow smile crept across her face. "Maybe we can work something out."

Frank stood. "Give the guy a chance. That's all I'm asking."

Edith sipped her coffee.

Chester? She took a bite from her English muffin. *Chester?* He'd always impressed her as a considerate man. And, he could cook; that was certainly a bonus. But, could Ginny be happy with a cook? After all, she'd wanted to be a doctor.

Edith shook her head. She'd heard similar words when she'd told her mother she loved Lloyd MacPhearson.

"A farmer?" her mother had cried. "But what about Bob Tackett, the banker's son? He's been sweet on you for years."

"I don't love Bob Tackett. I love Lloyd MacPhearson."

"But Bob could take you to Europe! You'd live in one of those big houses in town with the front porch and maybe even a maid."

"And Lloyd can take me for picnics by the river on a hot summer evening or for a sleigh ride in the winter."

Her mother wrung her hands together. "Bob could do that too!"

Edith had laughed. "Bob wouldn't be caught dead without his tie on mother. And now that he's got one of them fancy new cars he won't think about driving in a sleigh."

"But...but...but...."

In the end, it had done her mother no good to argue. Edith's mind had been made up and she had been determined to marry Lloyd MacPhearson, even though he hadn't asked her. Edith smiled. In fact, he never really had proposed. She had cornered him in his barn three months later. The August heat had made his white cotton tee shirt cling to his barrel chest as sweat trickled down his forehead.

"I think we should have the wedding in early December."

Lloyd's face had reddened under his sunburn. "What?"

"December gives you time to fix up a bedroom for us and get a new stove for the kitchen. If the harvest is as good as I think it will be this year, you might even consider an ice box. I've got my trousseau ready, but in three months, I'll have enough saved up that we could take a honeymoon. Maybe St. Louis for the weekend."

He hadn't answered her but stood there, his lips moving up and down like a fish out of water.

"Lloyd MacPhearson, are you going to marry me in December or not? Bob Tackett's already asked me, and I told him I needed time to think. Do you want me to be Bob's wife or yours?"

Lloyd's mouth had snapped shut, and he'd straightened his shoulders. "Mine."

Edith had smiled. "Good. Then I'll tell Bob no."

He'd taken a step toward her. "You do that."

The sight of her granddaughter pulling into the parking lot brought Edith back to the present. Ginny struggled futilely to keep her hair out of her face as she made her way to the building. Several residents called out greetings to her as she entered the lobby. Ginny poked her head into the dining room, and Edith waved her over to the table.

"Good morning, dear." Edith pointed to the chair Frank had vacated. "Do you have time for coffee?"

Ginny shook her head. "Dad's taking me out to lunch today, so I have to get some stuff done in the office before activities start up." She gave her grandmother a kiss on the cheek. "Are you coming down for exercise and crafts today?"

"Wouldn't miss it."

"Should be fun. I've got kits for gingerbread houses, and a couple of college kids are going to help us decorate them."

Edith patted Ginny's hand. "You get going, then. I'll see you in a little while." Her granddaughter turned to leave as Chester came out of the kitchen. The enticing smell of bacon wafted out.

Ginny lifted her nose and sniffed. *"Por favor,* save me a piece of bacon, will you?"

Edith studied the cook. He was taller than most Hispanic men she knew—about Ginny's height, actually. His thick, black hair framed his face nicely. Not too long, not too short. He did have that hideous mustache, but somehow that even worked on the man. What Edith noticed most was the look in Chester's eyes as he spoke to Ginny. Frank Leno had been right. The boy was in love.

"Of course. I'll save you two today. You could use some fattening up."

Ginny laughed. "Tell my mother that!"

Her granddaughter's face lit up as she spoke to him. But, as Edith studied her, she knew that Ginny didn't even realize her attraction to Chester. Yet.

This is going to take some planning. She watched as Ginny and Chester bantered a little more before Ginny went off to clock in for work. *I'm going to have to talk to Frank. Perhaps if we team up, we can devise a plan to bring these two together.*

CHAPTER THREE

I followed a hostess through tables already occupied by the Wednesday-afternoon lunch crowd. Looking over the clientele, I knew why my dad liked this place. Up-and-coming businessmen chatted obnoxiously to the air as they finished up work on their Bluetooths. The young waiters, both male and female, wore starched white, open-collared shirts and black slacks. The women had their hair pulled back in ponytails. The men all used gel. It was youthful and trendy, just like my dad tried to be.

My dad's wife, Brittany, smiled up at me as I approached the table. "Hey, Ginny."

Dad stood and held out his hand. "Hello, Virginia."

I shook his hand, feeling as though I were one of his prospective clients. My dad wore a lavender dress shirt with the top two buttons undone. His gray suit jacket hung on the side of the booth. I sat down opposite them, admiring Brittany's baby blue cashmere twinset.

"Sorry I'm late." I shrugged off my jacket and stuffed it into the corner. The telltale tumbler of whisky and glass of Chardonnay told me how late I'd been. "It got a little crazy before I left."

A perky brunette bounced over to our table. "Can I get you something to drink?"

"Water with lemon, please."

My father put down his menu. "We're ready to order."

The brunette raised an eyebrow. "What can I get for you today?"

I scrambled for the menu while my father gave his order, complete with the litany of things to be left out or put on the side. My blood simmered at a low boil as Brittany said what she wanted. I'd only opened the five-page menu when they all turned to look at me. Great.

I knew what my dad would want me to order. Something like Brittany. Broiled fish, steamed broccoli, no rice or potato. I flipped to the entrée section.

"I'll have the bacon cheeseburger, medium well, extra onions, and no mustard."

"French fries or cole slaw?"

Dad's eyes squinted as if willing me to order something healthy. "Fries, please. And can you bring some malt vinegar with that?"

The waitress smiled. "No problem. I'll be back in a moment with the salads and bread."

My father glared up at her. "No bread."

The brunette left, and I resisted the urge to call after her, "Bring the bread, and keep it coming!"

Dad perused me with a critical eye. "You haven't cut your hair yet."

I shook my head. "Haven't had time."

"You should make time."

I turned to Brittany. "How was Mexico?"

Her movie-star-white teeth sparkled against her tan skin. She pushed a strand of blonde hair behind her ear. "Wonderful. We so needed the vacation."

"I'm sure."

The pocket of my father's suit jacket rang. He pulled out his cell phone and checked the number. "I have to take this." He gave Brittany a peck on the cheek then walked out toward the lobby, leaving me and my thirty-six-year-old stepmom to stare awkwardly at each other. We were saved for a moment by the reappearance of our waitress bearing salads and my water.

I peeled the wrapper from my straw. "So...Mexico was good?"

Brittany nibbled on the lettuce like a bunny. "Yeah. Sunny. Warm. It's too cold here."

I nodded and sipped my water. "Did you bring Emma?"

"No, our nanny stayed the week with her. Of course, we had to pay a fortune, but it was worth it."

I nodded again, feeling like a bobble-head on a dashboard, but I couldn't think of what else to say.

Brittany chattered about their trip—something about the turquoise water and the hammocks on the beach, but I only half-listened and instead played with my drink. First, I put my finger over the top of my straw and lifted it out of the glass. Then I took my finger off and watched the water spurt back down. When Brittany brought up the topic of couples massages at the spa, I stabbed my lemon and tried to sink it to the bottom of the glass. Bits of lemon pulp floated up to the top as I continued my attack.

"Oh." The sound of Brittany's fork hitting her plate made me look up. "Before I forget, Greg wanted you to have this."

She pulled out a pink envelope and handed it to me. "Happy birthday."

"Thanks." By the color of the envelope, I figured Brittany had picked out the card, not my dad. I'd wait until later to see if he'd actually signed it this year.

Brittany pulled out another envelope. "You want to see pictures?"

I shrugged. "Sure."

She handed them to me one by one, with her own running commentary. "Here's the beach at sunset. And here's Greg getting ready to parasail. Here he is in the air."

I tried not to focus too hard on the sight of my dad in his Speedo, hundreds of feet in the air. I was pretty sure I'd get nightmares. Brittany passed me another dozen pictures of Mexico before pausing.

"Here's some from Emma's Thanksgiving play at kindergarten. Do you want to see?"

"Of course." I'd never had the opportunity to know my half-sister. Brittany kept her busy in all kinds of dance and educational classes. I only saw her on holidays.

Emma had inherited every fabulous gene from both parents: her mother's sun blonde hair with my father's luxurious curls, Brittany's bright blue eyes with my dad's thick, dark lashes. The kid was gorgeous, and she knew it. She'd already done some modeling for local department stores, and Brittany had her signed with an agent. It wouldn't be long before the kid had her own sitcom.

I flipped through the pictures of Emma in her pilgrim costume and chuckled. Of course, she got to be the pilgrim, while the other, less beautiful kids had to be pumpkins, cornstalks, and turkeys.

"Where did you get the costume?" I asked.

"The nanny made it." Brittany passed me another photo. This one showed Emma with my father. He was kneeling beside her and giving her a hug. My heart froze.

Brittany tried to pass me another picture, not noticing that I still held one in my hand. This new one showed my father giving Emma a kiss on the cheek. I didn't take it. "Dad went to the play?"

Brittany looked up. "Of course."

"What do you mean, 'Of course'?"

"He comes to all of Emma's performances."

I struggled with the urge to crumple the photo in my hand. "Performances?"

Brittany shrugged. "Ballet recitals, school concerts. You know."

No, I didn't know. My dad had never come to any of my school functions, not even when I'd had the lead in the senior play. He hadn't even come to Mark's funeral. I chewed on my lower lip and placed the photo down on the table.

Brittany's eyebrows furrowed. "You okay?"

No! My mind screamed, but I didn't. I wrestled with the wave of negativity pounding through my body. I couldn't keep my eyes from the picture of my father giving Emma a kiss. I looked around the restaurant. My father was nowhere to be seen. Here he was, supposed to be taking me out for a belated birthday lunch, and he couldn't even bother to sit at the table with me.

I grabbed my coat and purse. "I gotta go."

"What's the matter?" Brittany glanced at the pictures. "Is it Emma?"

I shook my head and swallowed the huge rock in my throat. "Emma's great. She's beautiful. She's perfect."

"Then what's wrong?"

"Me. I must be wrong." I pushed myself up off the bench.

Brittany looked at me, her eyes filled with utter confusion. "What about your burger?"

I snorted a laugh. "I'm not hungry."

"What should I tell Greg?"

I pursed my lips together and willed myself not to cry. "I doubt he'll even notice I'm gone."

She glanced at the photos and then at my face. "Oh. I get it."

I had to hand it to her; she was a lot smarter than most people gave her credit for, as long as you gave her a minute to get her brain up to speed. She picked up the pink envelope. "Here."

I stared at it, tempted not to take it. I didn't want to give him the satisfaction of thinking he'd given me anything.

Brittany sighed. "Take it. You need the money, and you know it won't make a difference to him one way or another." She smiled sadly and thrust the envelope toward me.

"Thanks." I took it and headed toward the exit.

I found myself in Marigold's parking lot without the faintest idea of how I'd gotten there. A stream of tears flowed down my face, and there was nothing I could do to stop it. I wouldn't let myself give in to sobs, though. That would have been too much. Besides, my father wasn't worth the effort.

Someone rapped on my window, and I stifled a scream.

Father Dan.

I wiped my cheeks and sniffed my drippy nose before lowering the glass.

The wind spiked up his light-brown hair. His nose was red from the cold. "You okay?"

"I'll be fine." My swollen eyes must have betrayed me.

"You shouldn't lie to a priest." He smiled. He had a beautiful smile.

"You here for mass?" I asked.

He nodded. "Don't try and change the subject. What's up?"

"It's nothing." I glanced at the clock on my dash. "You'd better get up there. Agnes will eat you alive if you don't start at one. She naps at two so she can come down for Wii Bowling at four."

He straightened up and stepped away from my car. I rolled up my window, tempted to stay there until he left, but he gave me a look that said he wasn't going anywhere until I did. When I got out of the car, he took my arm as if he were escorting me to the prom.

"Virginia Elizabeth Stafford, whatever is wrong?"

"It's nothing that a pint of Haagen-Dazs won't fix later." I smiled, I'm sure pathetically, and patted his arm. "And maybe a bag of Doritos."

He held the outer door to the facility open for me while I punched in the code for the lobby door. I turned toward my office but stopped when he touched my shoulder. "I'll pray for you today."

"Thanks."

∾

Forty-five minutes later, I stared at my computer, trying to think of clever things to put in the monthly newsletter. The door to my office swung open, and Father Dan strode in, carrying two dishes of soft serve ice cream from the machine in the game room.

He sat on the corner of my desk and passed me one. "It's not Haagen-Dazs, but I did put lots of chocolate sauce and sprinkles on it."

I laughed in spite of myself. The Styrofoam dish overflowed with sugar. Dan pulled two plastic spoons from his pocket before taking off his jacket and throwing it on an empty chair. I still found it odd to see him in the black suit and clerical collar. Dan's sister Marge had been my best friend, and I'd spent far too many years in and out of their house to think of him as anything more than another brother. We'd lost contact after my parents had moved us from Missouri when I was twelve. I'd been shocked when Dan had shown up a year ago to lead the Catholic mass.

"So." He took a spoonful of ice cream, careful to lick the chocolate sauce that dripped off the bottom. "What's bugging you?"

The tears threatened to appear again, but I swallowed them down.

"Is it Mark?"

I stabbed the spoon into my ice cream and swirled it around, turning the contents of the cup into a brown mess.

He took another bite from his treat. "Talk to me, kiddo."

I shrugged. What was I upset about? It wasn't just my father. I knew that. I took a huge spoonful and swallowed. "It's everything."

He put his cup down. "A little more specific, please." He leaned forward, his eyes prying out the pain I was trying to keep inside.

The words started to flow, as if Dan were the little boy with his finger in the dam and he'd decided to pull it out. "You know . . . when my parents divorced, I accepted it. I knew they weren't happy. My dad was never around, anyway, so nothing really changed." I swirled my spoon around in the ice cream. "And I had hope. I believed that God would work all things for good. That's what Edith told me. That's what the church told me."

I glanced up at him, not liking the compassion I read on his face. I didn't want his pity. I wanted some answers. "I could accept being left by my father. I could accept being ignored by my mother, because I had hope. I knew that one day God would bring someone to me. Someone who would love me and care for me, just the way I am."

I found myself biting on my lower lip again, trying not to cry. Father Dan didn't say anything, but he didn't take his eyes off me. I put the ice cream on my desk. "Mark loved me that way. I told him everything — every fear, every dream." A tear dripped from my eye. "We were going to have four kids. We didn't care what they were — four boys, four girls, a couple of each, it didn't matter." I cried freely now. What was the point in hurting myself further trying to keep the tears in? I glared up at Dan. "I could have even handled if there'd been a problem, you know, like Down's syndrome or cerebral palsy. I could have dealt with that, because I would have had Mark there with me. That was the plan. He was supposed to be with me."

I hated the way my voice sounded whiny and bitter. I pointed at Dan. "You chose this life. You chose not to spend it with someone, but I didn't." I hoped the little Dutch boy had moved out of the way, because the dam totally broke. "I never chose this. I wasn't supposed to be alone."

Dan came around behind the desk and knelt by my side. He enveloped me in his arms and let me sob on his shoulder. He smelt of incense and aftershave. It wasn't an unpleasant mixture, but weird. I reached out and grabbed a tissue from my desk trying not to let my nose drip on his suit.

I blew my nose. "Sorry."

He sat on his heels and lifted his shoulders in a "no problem" kind of gesture.

"I don't know what came over me."

His ice-blue eyes stared into mine. "It's been almost two years, hasn't it?"

"It was two years on Thanksgiving."

Dan nodded. "You dating?"

"Mr. Simmons asked me out the other night, but he thought I was his wife at the time, so I don't think that counts."

His lips formed a hard line. "I don't like to tell people how to grieve, but . . . ."

My heart turned to stone. "Don't say it."

Dan tilted his head, his blue eyes riveting me to my chair. "You're young. Only twenty-seven, right?"

Twenty-eight, but why let him know I was even more pathetic?

"All I'm saying is, don't close yourself off, Ginny. Don't turn your back on everything that God has to offer you because you're too stubborn to let go of your anger. Have you been going to church?"

I broke his stare and grabbed another tissue.

"Ginny?"

I shrugged. "No."

"Why not?"

I shredded the tissue into soggy strips. "I tried for a while."

"But?"

I put the pile of shredded fuzz on my desk. "We were going to get married in that church. Every time I went, I'd just sit there and ask, 'Why?'"

Father Dan groaned as he pulled himself up off the floor. His knees made a popping sound as he stood. "There are other churches."

"I know." I swiped the tissue mound into my trash can.

Dan pulled a chair up and sat next to my desk.

I picked up my bowl of ice cream. It had turned to soup. I drank it like a milkshake, wiping the mustache from my lip with another tissue.

"You going to ignore me now?" Dan asked. "After I bought you ice cream?"

"You didn't buy it. It's free."

"I expended energy walking to the machine to get it. I labored over the sprinkles and the chocolate sauce. Then I had to carry my burden all the way down to your office." He sighed as if he'd climbed Mt. Everest.

"You could have taken the elevator. Saved yourself some of that effort."

He chuckled softly. "Come to lunch with me? Sometime this week?"

The shocked look that must have crossed my face made him laugh louder. "Not a date! I'm a priest, or haven't you noticed? Just friends." His demeanor turned serious. "You look like you could use one."

"Are you allowed?"

"Friends? Yeah. The pope said we had to give up sex, not acquaintances."

I gave him my "oh, be serious" look. "Aren't there rules or something?"

"I'm not stupid. We'll go somewhere public. I'll tell Father Asner where I'll be and why. I'll even give him a time to call me if I'm not back at the rectory. That way, if you try and seduce me, he can remind me of my vows."

"I won't try and seduce you, you jerk. I'm in mourning, remember?"

Dan's smile turned sad. "I remember." He stood and put on his jacket. "I'll call you later this week and set up something. You free Saturday?"

I nodded. "Thanks for the ice cream."

"Anytime." With that, he swept out of my office and shut the door. I looked at the mess on my desk and wished for a genie to make the paperwork disappear. I swiveled my chair and stared at the computer screen. If my first wish was for disappearing paperwork, my second would be for someone to finish the December newsletter. My third wish? A new heart to replace the one shattered inside of me.

🙚🙚

Edith sat in the dining room, her eyes focused on the hallway beyond the lobby. A knobby finger poked her shoulder.

"I said, would you pass the salt?"

Edith rubbed her arm. "You didn't have to hit me."

Agnes Pendleton frowned. "Can you pass the salt?"

Edith pushed the salt shaker over to Agnes, then caught sight of Ginny and waved. Her granddaughter walked in and gave Edith a kiss on the cheek before sitting next to her.

Ginny smiled at Agnes and Sam, who also sat at the table. "Hello, everyone."

Sam's pink jacket hung on the walker next to the table. She sported a rhinestone-studded T-shirt with bright purple and pink flowers. "Hello, yourself." She glanced at the plate of noodles before her. "If you have a choice, I'd go with the stew tonight. The tuna casserole looks a little iffy."

"I'll take what I can get." Ginny peered at the service cart as the kitchen aide came by. She leaned on her elbows. "You missed manicures on Tuesday, Grandma. You want me to stop by tonight to do them?"

"I had them done last week." Edith held up her hand. "They still look good."

"You sure?"

Edith smiled. "You worry too much." She took a sip from her bowl. "How did your day go?"

Ginny shrugged. "Fine."

Edith studied her. She was obviously hiding something. "What's wrong?"

The girl's hazel eyes grew moist. "Lunch with Dad." She bit her lip. "Same old stuff. I'll be okay."

"Are you sure?"

Ginny grinned. "Yeah. A hot fudge sundae and a lunch date with a priest does wonders."

"What?"

"Father Dan." Ginny laughed. "He stopped by to see me after mass. He wants to get together and talk on Saturday."

"That's your mother's party, isn't it?"

Her granddaughter frowned. "Don't remind me. It doesn't start until seven anyway should I pick you up at say . . . nine?"

Edith laughed lightly. "I think I'll claim the sniffles and bow out of this year's affair. I survived Thanksgiving. Two visits with Joyce in as many weeks is asking a little much."

"But, I was going to be sick and duck out early," Ginny whined.

"I called it first." Edith reached over and patted Ginny's hand. "Besides, you're younger. You can put up a better front. I'm old and crotchety."

"You're not crotchety. You're honest."

"I see you didn't contradict the 'old' part."

"You're only as old as you feel," chimed in Sam. "Ain't that right, Agnes?"

Agnes looked perplexed. "What?"

Sam leaned toward her and yelled, "You're only as old as you feel!"

The confused look stayed in Agnes's eyes as she appeared to decipher what Sam had said. Then her face lit up. "How old am I? I'll be ninety come April. They're going to give me a big party!"

Ginny glanced at her grandmother. "I'm going to see what's left. I'll be back in a minute." She pushed herself up and headed toward the kitchen.

Sam touched Edith's arm as she watched Ginny disappear behind the double doors. "She's a good girl. You should be proud of her."

Edith smiled. "I am."

Sam's eyebrows knitted together. "But, we need to find her a man."

"That we do." Edith nodded. "That we do." She took a quick glance at the table where Frank sat. He seemed to be in a heated debate with one of his table mates. Edith thought the other man's name was Bill.

Frank waved his arms in a frustrated gesture. "The Cubs? C-U-B-S, Cubs? Doesn't that stand for 'Completely Useless By September'?"

Bill groaned loudly. "The Cubs are the best baseball team in the country, bar none!"

Frank's fist pounded the table. "They haven't been to a series in how long?"

"It don't matter. Fate is against them." Bill's bald head sweated under the hot dining room lights. "If it weren't for the curse—"

"Curse?" Frank let out a short, loud laugh. "They can't hold a candle to St. Louis."

At the mention of the opposing team Bill's face reddened. He stood up and spoke loudly enough for the whole dining room to hear him. "Better my son a thief than my best friend a Cardinals fan."

Ginny hurried out of the kitchen carrying a bowl of stew, as well as a plate with a cookie, and holding a roll between her chin and her chest. She made her way over to Frank's table as Frank laughed again.

"Settle down, you old coot. I don't even like baseball! I'm just trying to get a rise out of you!"

Ginny put her plates down, let the roll fall to the table, then placed a hand on Bill's shoulder. "What's the matter?"

"Did you hear what he said about the Cubs?"

"Have a seat, Bill. He said he didn't mean it."

Bill sat back down, but his body shook from the stress of the argument. "I want an apology. That's what I want."

Ginny raised her eyebrows to Frank. It was a look that could only mean "humor him, all right?"

Frank sighed. "I'm sorry. The Cubs are a fine team."

"The best," Bill muttered.

"Everyone's entitled to their opinion." Ginny patted the bald man on his back. "Did you get a cookie yet?"

Bill shook his head.

"Here, have mine." Ginny slid her plate over to Bill, then picked up her stew and roll. "Enjoy." She gave a stern look to Frank. "Now, behave yourselves, or I'll have to separate you two for good."

Frank smiled. "Yes, ma'am."

Bill grunted and stuffed the cookie in his mouth. Ginny walked back to her grandmother's table.

Edith maneuvered so Ginny had room to put her bowl down. "You handled that well, dear."

"Frank's just bored. I don't know why he stays here." She took a spoonful of stew and blew on it.

"What do you mean?"

"He only came in because his wife needed to be here. She's been gone a year now. He's well enough he could live on his own."

Edith stole another glance at the gray-haired man. "Is that so?"

Ginny sipped her stew. "Yeah. Maybe he doesn't like to cook or clean. Maybe that's why he stays."

"I wouldn't know." Edith shrugged. "I don't think I've spoken more than ten words to him since he's been here."

"Who? Who aren't you speaking to?" interrupted Agnes.

Edith frowned. "I didn't say I wasn't speaking to him, only that I haven't spoken much to him."

"Who?" Agnes asked again.

"Frank Leno."

"Who?"

Ginny put her hand on Agnes's and spoke loudly. "We were talking of a friend she hasn't spoken to in a while."

"Oh." Agnes went back to eating her casserole.

Ginny leaned over to her grandmother. "You know, I'll bet he'd like to play Scrabble or Rumikub."

Edith peeked at Frank again. "You really think so?"

"Uh-huh. If he's still around when we're done with dinner, I'll introduce you."

"Oh, pishaw." Edith snorted. "We've met before. We've lived in the same building for over a year."

Ginny took another spoonful of stew. "It's not the same thing, and you know it. I think it would be good to have a friend who could challenge you a little."

"I get challenged enough."

"By your books, yes. But, there's no one here who can keep up with you mentally, except maybe Frank. It would help him, too."

"You think so?"

Her granddaughter finished her dinner and ran her remaining roll around the bowl to suck up any leftovers. "I know so." She popped the roll into her mouth and looked around the room. Frank sat alone at his table, sipping from his coffee cup.

"Come on, Grandma. Let's go."

Frank looked up as Ginny and her grandmother walked toward him. Ginny's eyes shone with a hint of mischief. Edith walked a few steps behind her with her own look of conspiracy flashing across her face as she caught his glance. He stood.

"Frank, I'd like to introduce you to my grandmother, Edith MacPhearson."

He couldn't help but frown. "We've met before."

"Yes, but not officially." Ginny pulled a chair out for Edith and then sat down herself. "Grandma's been looking for someone who still likes to play something other than cards. Do you like games?"

"I've been known to play a few in my day." Frank took a seat. "What games are you thinking about?"

"Grandma?"

"Parcheesi or Scrabble? Or maybe checkers? Backgammon?"

Frank lifted his eyebrows. "Backgammon? I used to play a lot of backgammon."

Ginny smiled. "I'll pick you up a board on my way home from work tonight and bring it in tomorrow. What do you say?"

Frank waited for Edith to give a positive response before he answered, "Sounds good."

The younger woman stood from the table and gave her grandmother a kiss. "I should get going. I'll see you tomorrow."

Frank remained quiet until he could see by Edith's eyes that Ginny was out of earshot. "What's this all about?"

Edith chuckled. "She came up with this on her own. But, it's the perfect ruse."

"Ruse?"

Edith pursed her lips together. "Don't be dense, man. You told me today you wanted my help getting Ginny and Chester together. Well, this forced setup will give us the opportunity to plan." Her elegant fingers tapped the table lightly. "It'll have to be subtle, or she'll smell a rat."

"Chester can't know about it, either, or he'll get too scared and chicken out."

"Between the two of us, we should be able to think of something. Put your thinking cap on, and we'll trade ideas tomorrow over a game of backgammon. All right?"

Frank nodded. "It's a plan."

Ginny's grandmother rose and strode out of the dining room.

CHAPTER FOUR

I struggled to get my keys out of my purse as I headed into the facility the following morning and ended up plowing into a woman on her way out. My purse and the backgammon board I'd bought crashed to the floor. Thank goodness I hadn't given in to curiosity the night before and cut open the plastic wrap protecting the game. I glanced over, caught the woman's eyes, and tried to place her. She was a resident's daughter. My brain finally made the connection: Rachel Johnson's daughter, Paula.

"Sorry," Paula mumbled.

"My fault." We bumped arms again as we tried to recover our handbags. She swore under her breath. I could tell it wasn't at me, but at life in general. She had that telltale look of someone trying hard not to cry. As I'd been in that predicament yesterday, I found it easy to recognize.

"You okay?" I jammed the game up under one arm and slung my purse over my shoulder.

She nodded but turned her head away.

"No, you're not." I took hold of her elbow with one hand and grabbed my keys out of my purse with the other. "Come in."

Paula shook her head. I marveled at how her short brown hair didn't move. Maybe my parents were right and if I cut my hair, mine could look that good.

Paula pulled away. "I need to go."

I got my door unlocked. "Believe me, it's no use driving when you're upset. I know."

The petite woman sighed and stepped into my office.

I closed the door behind us. "What did Rachel do?"

She let out a sound that was part chuckle, part sob. "Why can't I do anything right? No matter what I do, I don't do it right. It's all Patrick, Patrick, Patrick."

"Your brother?"

Paula nodded.

I dropped my stuff onto a chair and put a hand on her shoulder. "A lot of it has to do with the dementia. You know that."

Paula stepped away, her arms folding across her chest. "You all keep saying that, but she's always been like this. I was sixteen when Patrick was born, and since that time it's like I don't exist. He can do no wrong, and I do nothing right."

"She's frustrated at being here, and she'll take it out on the person closest to her because deep down, she knows you'll stay with her."

"I don't know." Paula wiped a tear on her cheek. "I don't know how much more I can take. She's always so critical."

"Her new meds are helping some," I offered. "She's been a lot nicer to the staff lately. Well, except for the sausage incident on Monday."

Paula's mouth rose in a quick smile. "Don't mess with the woman's breakfast. You should know that by now." She ran a hand through her hair. "I don't know what it's going to be like once Patrick gets here."

I pointed to the empty chair in front of my desk. "Is he coming for the holidays?"

She flopped down into the seat. "I wish. He's moving out here."

"Maybe that will help things. He could relieve some of the pressure of visiting your mom."

"I don't think so. It'll only get worse. Everything I say and do will get compared to him." She shook her head. "Besides, I doubt he'll visit her much. No offense, but he keeps saying how he hates these kind of homes."

I slipped my coat off, then threw it into my chair. "No offense taken." I sat down on the corner of my desk. "I don't know what I can do to help, besides trying to keep her busy."

Paula let out a long sigh. "Thanks for listening to me vent. That helps a lot."

"Anytime." I gave her arm a pat. "Believe me, I know what it's like to deal with critical parents."

I walked her to the lobby door and turned to see George Franklin wandering down the hallway, mumbling under his breath. I approached him with caution.

"George? Are you looking for something?"

He jerked his head up. "My briefcase. I can't find my briefcase, and I'm late for work." His hair stood in a wild mane, and he hadn't shaved this morning. I looked around for a med aide, but the only people in the lobby were Frank and Bill, reading the morning paper.

"Come with me, Mr. Franklin," I encouraged. "I think you left it in your room."

He followed me down the hallway and back to his apartment, muttering incoherently the whole way.

I didn't want to startle his wife, so I knocked on the door before I opened it. "Here you go, sir."

His white hair flopped about his face as he shook his head. "This isn't my house. And there's a strange woman in there." He backed away. "That isn't my house."

I hated to lie, but I had to get him into his room. "It's your hotel room, sir. The woman is probably the maid. Let's go in and look for your briefcase. I'll call the office and tell them you're running a little late today, all right?"

My story seemed to ease his agitation. I opened the door, and George stepped inside. "That would be wonderful, Gladys. And please, call my wife. I don't think I told her I was going out of town. She'll be worried."

Helen came out of their bedroom, wearing a pale blue robe. "Oh dear, not again. I guess he's figured out the locks on the door."

George glared at me. "Are you sure she's the maid?"

His wife sighed. "Actually, I'm room service. Why don't you have a seat, and I'll fix you a cup of coffee."

I helped George sit at the dinette table and gave Helen what I hoped was a sympathetic look. "Do you want me to send the nurse down?" I whispered.

"I'm not sure it'll help," Helen whispered back. "I don't know what she can do for him." Helen took down a can of coffee and scooped the grounds into the pot on the counter. "I'll call Dr. Preston this morning, see what he says." She grabbed a piece of newspaper from the table and gave it to her husband. "Here you go, sir. Why don't you read the paper while I make you breakfast?"

George nodded distractedly and began to scan the paper. Both Helen and I knew he couldn't understand a word he read anymore, but somehow the familiar action calmed him further.

Helen smiled. "I think I can handle it from here. Thanks, Ginny."

"Don't mention it." I left her to take care of her husband and headed back down the hallway. If George could figure out the locks on his apartment, it might not be long before he figured out the code on the lobby door. Once that happened, he'd be considered a flight risk, and he'd have to be moved to a more secure facility. The Franklins had been residents since before my grandmother had started living at Marigold. I would miss them if they had to leave.

Much to Frank's amusement, Edith insisted they play backgammon on one of the tables in the lobby.

"A lady doesn't spend time alone in a man's apartment, even if it's to play backgammon."

He chuckled at her propriety.

Edith plopped the game down on the table. "What are you smirking at?"

Frank stopped smiling. "Nothing, Ma'am." *Why do I feel like I'm twelve around this woman?*

She eyed him suspiciously as she opened the box and set up the board. Frank couldn't help but notice the faint scent of perfume that wafted his way as she worked. Nice. Not too floral. Not overdone. The sun shone in from the windows and reflected off the highlights in her well-coiffed white hair. He liked when a woman didn't dye her hair at this age. Some of them visited the facility's beauty shop monthly to try and fool themselves that they were still young. No amount of red, black, or blue dye could hide the fact that they were past their prime. Not Edith. She had her hair cut short; it barely touched the base of her neck. He'd seen his wife in curlers enough to know that Ginny's grandmother probably slept with her head bound up in foam and plastic. *Maybe it's natural.* He frowned at that. Ginny's hair was straight, but maybe Edith came about her curls . . . .

"Are you just going to sit there?"

Frank looked up in surprise. "Sorry. Lost in thought."

Edith scowled. "You seem to lose your thoughts a lot. I thought Ginny said you were still with it."

Frank straightened up. "I am. I have a lot on my mind lately."

Edith huffed and pointed to the board. "Do you want to begin, or shall I?"

He bowed slightly. "Ladies first."

She rolled the dice and moved one of her pieces across the triangle shapes on the board. "Did you come up with any plans for this matchmaking venture?"

Frank took his turn. "There's going to be a lot of opportunities this month with the holidays. It's a very romantic time of year."

"Not for Ginny. This is when she lost Mark." Edith made another move on the board.

"Hadn't thought about that. But, still, it's been long enough that we could at least plant the seed for something. Don't you think?"

"As I said last night, it has to be subtle. She's always had a strong will, and if she thinks she's being manipulated into something, she'll balk so fast it'll make your head spin."

Frank smiled. *I'll bet I know whose side of the family that comes from.*

Edith raised an eyebrow. "Lose your thoughts again?"

He kept his grin. "No. Just making plans."

"Well, take your turn, and tell me what they are."

CHAPTER FIVE

Saturday morning, I sat in my office finishing the new bulletin board then sending out calendars and newsletters to the residents' families. The mailers included invitations to the December open house on the seventeenth — a little late this year, but we were lucky to get Johnny Miles and his swing band to come in and play. I had an additional five hundred postcards to mail out to the community. We hoped to draw in some outside interest with the offer of Johnny's band, a dance floor, and free food. With eight rooms empty, the marketing director was desperate for new blood.

Once my paperwork was done, I pulled out the Christmas decorations from storage, then shoved the boxes into my office. I found the tree for the lobby and set that up. The plastic pine needles left red scratches all over my hands and arms. I looked as if I'd been attacked by a frenzied kitten. The residents who wandered down into the lobby all "oohed" and "ahhed" appropriately as I strung the colored lights and hung the ornaments.

I finished decorating the tree by ten-thirty, then headed home to shower and get ready for lunch with Father Dan. What did one wear to have lunch with a priest? I opted to forget he was a "man of the cloth" and instead thought of him as my friend Marge's big brother, the one with the long hair and goofy grin. He must have gotten braces after I moved, because his teeth now were perfectly straight. I decided to wear my good jeans (no holes or fraying hem) and a light brown sweater. I pulled my hair up into a clip and went with basic makeup.

Dan met me outside one of the chain restaurants near the mall. "Hope you don't mind eating here. I have some errands to run."

I chuckled under my breath.

"What's so funny?"

"I can't picture a priest needing to run errands. It's like seeing your second grade teacher at the grocery store. Somehow you always think of them as living in the coat closet at school."

Dan held the door open for me. "Well, contrary to popular belief, we priests do not live on communion bread alone. I, for one, am in desperate need of some Pop Tarts and Mini-Wheats. And, I'm sure the entire congregation will be grateful for some new deodorant. Especially in the confessional."

The hostess sat us at a booth near the front of the restaurant. We'd received our drinks and ordered our meals when Dan waved to a couple coming through the door. "Luke! Nancy!"

One of the tallest men I'd seen in a long time strode over to the booth. He must have been at least six foot three. His much shorter companion stood only up to his shoulder. Luke shook Dan's hand. "How've you been?"

Dan smiled. "Great, great!" He gestured to me. "Luke, Nancy, this is my friend Ginny. Can you guys join us?"

The couple exchanged glances, and I knew right away I'd been set up. Luke took off his coat and helped Nancy with hers. He hung them over the back of the booth and slid in next to Dan. I moved in closer to the wall to give Nancy room on my bench. The sheepish grin she gave me as she sat down confirmed my suspicions.

I cast a sidelong glance at Dan. "I smell a rat."

Dan gave me a look that attempted to make him appear innocent. It only cemented his guilt. He shrugged. "I confess. Luke is a good friend of mine who happens to be a pastor at a church in the area."

I shook my head. "Not fair."

Nancy glared at the two men across the table. "You told me she knew we were coming!"

At least they had the grace to look ashamed.

"Sorry," Dan mumbled.

Luke pushed his shoulder against Dan's. "He made me do it."

I laughed in spite of my feelings of dread. "Can you not get too preachy? I really want to enjoy my cheeseburger." I'd been craving one since I'd abandoned lunch with my father.

Dan smiled. "I promise. We'll be good."

It surprised Edith how much she wanted to get back home and play some backgammon that afternoon. Usually, she had such a good time out with her friend Donna she dreaded returning to her apartment. The weekends were the hardest at Marigold. They seemed to drag on forever without any activities and little on the television worth watching. Donna's Saturday luncheons and Sunday morning at church were the only things Edith had to look forward to those two days. She glanced up from the chicken sandwich she was eating.

"What time is it?"

"About one. Why?" Donna patted her lips with her napkin.

"No reason." Edith smiled at her friend. "Where did you get that top? That turquoise looks lovely on you."

"My daughter gave it to me for my birthday." Her friend's eyebrows furrowed. "What's up with you today? You're awfully edgy."

Edith feigned surprise. "Am I? I don't mean to be."

Donna pursed her brightly colored lips together. "Fess up. What's going on?"

Edith leaned in close to her friend. "I'm trying to fix Ginny up with someone."

Donna shook her head, her ash-blonde hair swaying with the movement. "You shouldn't be doing that."

"Somebody has to do something. The girl's becoming a hermit." Edith took the top off of her roll and scraped off the excess mayonnaise. "We're not trying to force anything. We're just trying to open her eyes up to an opportunity."

"It's still danger — wait a minute." Donna's head tilted to the side. "Who's 'we'?"

"What?"

Her friend gestured at her with a fork, a tomato dangling precariously from its tines. "You said, 'We're trying to open her eyes.' Who's 'we'?"

Edith's stomach fluttered. "Frank and me."

Donna put down the tomato, placed her elbows on the table, and rested her chin on her hands. "Do tell."

"Oh, please. Don't make more out of this than necessary." She replaced the top of her roll and took a bite of her sandwich. Donna continued to stare at her. "Frank's a resident at Marigold as well. He happens to be friendly with Chester." The other woman gave her a quizzical look. "Chester's the cook, and he seems to have quite an attraction for Ginny."

"Then why don't you let Chester work things out for himself?"

"Because he's too shy. Thinks Ginny might be too good for him."

Donna nodded. "Ginny's too good for almost any man."

"That's true. But, Chester's got a kind heart. I think he may be just what she needs."

Her friend ate a mouthful of salad before speaking again. "Tell me more about this Frank."

Edith's cheeks grew hot. "He's only a friend." Her lips betrayed her and curved upward in a smile.

"Look at you blush!" Donna laughed.

Edith raised her hands to her cheeks. "Oh, dear, I can't believe this."

"Edith MacPhearson, do you have a crush on someone?"

"No!" Edith shook her head.

"I think you do." Donna sipped her water. "I'm going to have to meet this gentleman."

"No, you don't." Edith shook her finger at her friend. "Now, look. I know you've been one of my best friends since I moved here, but I'm not going to let you scare him away."

"How would I do that?"

"I don't know, but you'd find a way. Besides, we're friends is all. It's nothing serious."

Donna took another bite of salad. "If you say so. But, when you do decide it's serious, we'll invite him out to dinner with Harvey and me."

∽

I had to admit I enjoyed Dan's friends, Luke and Nancy. I told tales about Father Dan as a kid, and they shared stories of his mishaps with Habitat for Humanity.

"You should have seen him." Luke ran a hand across his eyes to wipe away the tears of laughter. "He must have stood there for five minutes, trying to drill in that screw before the foreman pointed out the thing was in reverse."

Dan shrugged. "So I'm not a carpenter. There are many other ways I fail to be like Jesus, but I don't think my lack of hand tool skills is the worst."

The waiter came over and cleared our table. We opted not to get dessert but did order a round of coffee.

"So, what's your pitch?" I finally asked as we put sugar and cream in our mugs.

The others went quiet.

"You're all really nice, but I know there's a reason why Dan wanted you to meet me. You might as well get it over with."

Dan rested his elbows on the table. "Look, I know you're not Catholic, so trying to get you to come to my church would have been awkward." He smirked. "Even though I happen to be a truly dynamic teacher."

I wadded up a sugar packet and threw it at him. He dodged it easily. "Luke's been a youth pastor in the area for about seven years and was just given the pastor position at a church in Ralston. It's young, it's growing, and they have a grief ministry."

I frowned. "Grief ministry?"

Luke nodded, then gestured to his wife. "It's really Nancy's ministry."

"We lost our daughter to leukemia three years ago." Nancy looked down at her hands. "I never thought I'd get over it."

The burger in my stomach turned to lead. "I'm sorry."

She took a deep breath. "We're never the same after a loss like that. But, the more I held onto the grief, the more I felt myself dying inside." She lifted her gaze to meet mine. "Dan's told us a little about your situation. If you don't think you'd feel comfortable coming to church right now, at least come to one of our grief share meetings." She passed me a lavender business card imprinted with a silver tear drop. *Silent Tears Ministry; Nancy Donaldson, leader,* was printed below, along with her phone number. "We meet Thursday evenings from seven to eight-thirty in one of the church classrooms."

Luke chimed in, "That would be Abundant Grace Church off of Q Street, by the way."

I fingered the card before slipping it into my wallet for safekeeping. "I'll think about it."

Nancy leaned toward me. "Please do. It's not all weeping and wailing, I promise. We laugh a lot. We support each other. That's what it's all about. Having a group of people who understand what you're going through."

I nodded. "Thanks."

By that time, we'd finished our coffees, and Father Dan took the check up to the register to pay as the rest of us put on our coats. I shook Luke's hand, but Nancy refused to let me off that easy.

"Give me a hug." She pulled me against her chest. The woman was small but strong. "Please come," she whispered in my ear. "I'd love to get to know you better."

"I'll try." I said, not wanting to commit to more today.

Dan walked me out to my car. "Sorry if that made you uncomfortable. I only want to help."

"It's okay. They seem like nice people."

He smiled. "The best."

The clouds had turned a dark gray while we'd been inside, and the air smelled like snow. Dan leaned against the hood of my car as I fished out my keys.

"Can I say one more thing?"

I shrugged. "I guess so."

"I was reading this week about a monk in medieval Europe. France, I think it was. Brother Lawrence. He hadn't always wanted to be a monk, but he had a kind of revelation one day." Dan shifted to face me. "It was winter time, and he stood outside his family's house and watched the winter trees struggling in the wind. It occurred to him that we're all like those trees: barren, lifeless, until something gives us new life. Hope. For him, for me . . . God gave us that life." He laid his hand on my arm. "When I saw you on Wednesday, that's the image that kept popping into my head — you as one of those winter trees. But, there will be a spring, Ginny. If you open yourself up and allow hope in."

What could I say to that? "Thanks."

"Tell me you'll try Nancy's group? At least once?"

I folded my arms across my chest.

He waited.

I groaned. "All right."

He flashed me his fabulous smile. "Great. I'll tell Nancy."

I started to protest, but he waved his hand in front of my face. "You said! I heard you. If I tell Nancy you're coming, then I know you'll go. You're much too nice to disappointment someone like that."

I frowned. "Fine. I'll go. If not this week, then the next."

"If you don't go in two weeks, I'm tracking you down and taking you myself."

I unlocked my car and growled as I got in.

"You can't scare me away with your animal impression." Dan held onto the top of the door. "I've seen you with green goo on your face. Nothing was as frightening as that."

I giggled, remembering the spa sleepover his sister had hosted one of the last times we were together. Dan and his brother Todd had sneaked into Marge's bedroom, only to be set upon by five screaming girls covered in mud masks and body glitter.

"Thanks," I said as I closed the door. "For everything."

Father Dan smiled and waved as I pulled away.

"Again!" yelled the pig-tailed six-year-old. "Do it again!"

Chester sighed at his niece, then thrust his lower jaw out and slung his arms over his head. He beat his chest and proceeded to chase the youngster around the living room while screeching out a wild gorilla call. Katy giggled then screamed and ducked behind the couch. Chester stood up.

"The gorilla has to go think about what to make for dinner."

"No!" cried Katy from her hiding place. "He has to try and find me!"

"Oh, please," grumbled eleven-year-old Maria from her seat on the couch. She peered over the book she read. "He knows where you are."

Chester scowled at her. "Don't ruin her fun."

Maria gave him a classic annoyed tween look. "You call that fun?"

"I don't, but your sister does." He pointed a finger at her. "Cool it."

"Again!" pleaded a muted voice.

Chester leaned over the back of the couch. "Maybe after dinner. But, your mama will be home soon, and she's had a long day at work." He pulled on one of Katy's long, brown pigtails. "You want to help with dinner?"

Katy chewed on her lower lip while she thought about his offer. "Okay."

He reached down and pulled her up and over his head. She squealed as he spun her a few times, then set her on the floor. "Let's go."

Uncle and niece made their way from the cramped but comfortable living room into the kitchen. It, too, was cramped but comfortable. When Chester had moved in with his sister four years ago he'd ripped up the old linoleum floor and replaced it with hard wood. The plywood cabinets had been exchanged for light oak and the old appliances replaced with the best he could afford. He wished he could have done more after his brother-in-law had abandoned the family, but Chester did what he could. Each year he and his sister picked a new room to renovate. The kitchen was first, and then the bathroom the four of them shared. The following year, they did the girls' bedroom and then his sister's room. This past summer, Chester had skipped doing his room in favor of building a deck on the back of the house.

He opened up the refrigerator and pulled out the chicken he'd left to marinate. Katy wrinkled up her nose.

"It looks gross."

"But, it will taste delicious. Get me out the big frying pan."

They spent the next half-hour sautéing the chicken in olive oil and making up a large pot of Spanish rice. The aroma of garlic and cumin filled the kitchen when his sister walked through the door at six-thirty.

"*Hola, mi familia!*"

Katy rushed into her mother's arms. "*Hola*, Mama!"

Louisa kissed the top of her daughter's head. "How was your day?"

Katy pulled her mother into the kitchen and pushed her down on one of the hard-backed chairs. "*Tio* Chester helped me make a fort in the bedroom, and then we played jungle safari."

Louisa smiled. "Sounds like fun." She plopped her purse on the floor and used her foot to push it toward her daughter. "Take this into my bedroom, will you, baby?"

Katy trotted off down the hall while Louisa slipped off her shoes and coat.

Chester took the lid off the chicken and stirred it. "You look tired."

His sister sighed. "It was back-to-back at the salon today. Everyone wanting to look beautiful for the holiday *fiestas*. It'll be like this through New Year's." She glanced up at her brother. "Speaking of which, what do you think about us having a party?"

He frowned. "*Por que?*"

"Because that's what normal people do over the holidays. We could have a New Year's Eve *fiesta*. You wouldn't have to do anything."

Chester raised his eyebrows.

"No, really. I'd do the cooking and cleaning. The girls can help me."

"Who would come?"

"The girls from the salon. Rita and Barbara. Maria, Julie and her boyfriend." She stole a quick glance at Chester. "Maybe Tina."

Chester shook his head. "You won't give up, will you?"

Louisa picked up her coat and shoes and walked out to the living room to hang them up in the closet. She leaned against the kitchen counter when she returned. "What's wrong with Tina? She asks about you all the time. She's a nice girl."

Chester handed his sister plates and silverware. "She's not my type."

Louisa set the table. "And what is your type? You never go out with anyone."

He filled two glasses with ice and water. "I've been out plenty of times."

His sister filled two more glasses with milk. "Not in over a year. What's the matter with you?"

"Drop it, okay?" He put a piece of chicken on each plate.

"No. The girls are older now. I don't need as much help at night. You need to get out and start having a life of your own."

Chester put the pan back on the stove and served up the rice and broccoli he'd made. Katy traipsed back into the kitchen. He looked at his sister. "Don't worry about me. I have a life."

"Taking care of everyone else but yourself." Louisa walked over to the dining room threshold. "Maria, come to the table."

The four sat down and bowed their heads. As a habit, Chester began with the prayer he and his sister were taught when they were children. "In the name of the Father, Son, and

Holy Spirit, bless us, O Lord, and these thy gifts which we are about to receive from thy bounty through Christ our Lord. Amen. And Lord," he added, "please bless Louisa with energy during this busy time. Keep her healthy and strong during the holidays."

"And please, Lord," interrupted his sister. "Bless my brother. He has given up so much to help my family. Give him the desires of his heart and reward him for all he has done for us."

Chester sighed and said, "Amen."

CHAPTER SIX

In the big scheme of things -- wars, famines, tsunamis --
my mother's Holiday party wouldn't be considered a disaster.
Unless you're me. This annual tradition began the year she
married my stepfather, Roger. I'd been sixteen and forced to
move to Omaha from my grandparents' farm in Iowa, where
I'd lived since I was twelve. My mother had insisted we could
be a family again. She'd forgotten we'd never been much of a
family in the first place.

Friends had introduced my mother to Roger, a retired
Marine officer. He'd inherited an obscene amount of money,
and I think their friends thought that his wealth and her social
connections would make a good match. They dated for six
months before getting married. Roger told me once that he fell
in love with my mother's vulnerability. I guess that's a side
she only shows to him.

I like Roger. His years as a Marine made him tough as
nails and disciplined, which is what my mom needs. He also
has a wild side that I admire. He's not afraid to do anything. I
wish some of that had rubbed off on me.

The holiday party always falls on the first Saturday of
December. It gives my mother the opportunity each year to
humiliate me in public. From the first party, when she

exclaimed to her guests that I looked like a beefsteak tomato in my red velvet dress, to last year, when she lamented to everyone that I'd quit medical school and was destined to be a welfare case, she could always be counted on to find something wrong with me.

What would it be this year? I'd lost forty pounds after Mark died, so she couldn't compare me to tomatoes anymore. Maybe she'd think I was too thin. At five foot eight and a hundred and thirty pounds I could stand to put a few more back on, but what was the point? I wasn't trying to diet, and I certainly wasn't trying to impress anyone. I ate when I was hungry now. Better than after Mark had died and I only ate Capt. Crunch cereal for two months. Usually dry. Right out of the box.

I slipped on a pair of cream-colored slacks and a pine-green cashmere sweater I'd bought last year during the after-Christmas sales. Regularly $250, I'd paid $45 and hid it away especially for this day. I put on the pearl necklace and earrings my father had given me for my twenty-first birthday and French braided my red hair. A little bit of makeup, my gold flats, and I was ready to face the firing squad that was my mother.

❧

"Hey there." My stepfather opened the door, his blue eyes twinkling. He had rugged good looks and still wore his salt-and-pepper hair in a Marine buzz cut. "Nice to see you."

I gave him a kiss on the cheek. "Hi. I'm not late, am I?"

"You're not the first, but you're not last, either."

"Thanks."

Roger knew how tough my mom could be, and I appreciated the way he always made me know it wasn't all my fault. He took my coat and pointed me to the dining room. "Get yourself some punch and food. Your mom's already in the living room with the Schmidts and Hugheses."

I declined his offer of food and opted instead to head straight for my mom. She lounged across a French-style loveseat, wearing a long, black taffeta skirt with a cream silk blouse. She'd swept her blonde hair up in a sleek chignon. Elegant, but understated. She raised her hand in a kind of queenly wave when she caught sight of me in the doorway.

"Ginny, darling, don't stand there like a wilted fichu. Come in."

I crossed the room to where she held court. She didn't stand. I bent down and gave her a kiss on the cheek. She turned and offered me her other one. *When had this little affectation become a habit?* "Hello, Mother."

She patted my lower back as a signal for me to turn around and face the room. "Everyone, this is my daughter, Ginny."

I greeted Bunny and Alex Schmidt, whom I'd met at a previous Christmas party, then shook hands with Trish and Wallace Hughes. The husbands hovered behind the couch on which their wives sat.

Bunny, who had to be pushing sixty, whispered something to the younger Trish before turning her focus to me. "How are you, dear?"

I sat in one of the overstuffed wingback chairs next to the sofa. "I'm doing well, thank you. How was your trip to Venice?"

The older woman gave me a wide smile, causing her red lipstick to bleed slightly. "I can't believe you remembered we were going!"

I ran my hands down my legs, hoping to work out any creases that had occurred on the ride over here. "I've always wanted to go to Venice. I guess that's why."

Bunny sipped her amber-colored drink. "The weather was dreadful. Don't go in March, that's all I can say."

My mother crossed her legs. "I could have told you that. Italy is too unpredictable in the winter. Summer's the time to go." She waved a dismissive hand. "Then, of course, you have to deal with the tourists, unless you rent a villa."

I squirmed at the word "tourist." She said it in the same way she says "bed bug" or "hired help." I bit my tongue and refrained from reminding her that even though she rented a villa, she was still a tourist.

My mother gave me a reproachful look. "What's the matter, darling?"

I shook my head. "Nothing."

"You look as if you want to say something."

"Nope."

Bunny leaned forward and placed a hand on my knee. Didn't this woman respect a person's privacy bubble? I willed myself not to jerk my leg away from her.

She gave me a little pat. "Are you seeing anyone yet?"

My mother answered before I could. "Of course not. She's still working with the senile people. How is she supposed to meet anyone there?"

I flashed her a grin. "Wait until I tell Grandma that you called her senile."

Joyce pursed her lips. "You will do no such thing. You know what I meant."

I raised my eyebrows. "You were the one who said the people who lived there were senile, not me."

She waved a finger at me. "Don't get fresh, young lady."

Bunny had removed her hand, but she interrupted our little argument, I think as a way to ease the tension. "A pretty girl like you. It's a shame you aren't dating anyone." She turned to Trish. "Don't you have a son about her age?"

The brunette beside her nodded. "But he's in Houston." She gave me the once-over, as if I were a piece of artwork she considered buying. She must have liked what she saw. "Would you think about relocating?"

I tried to keep my sense of humor. "No, Ma'am. I don't look good in cowboy hats." I stood. "I think I'll check out the buffet."

My mother frowned. "Stay away from the cream puffs and the dips. You're finally looking good." She turned to her friends. "They say a woman can gain five to ten pounds in December. Can you believe it?"

I meandered through the various couples engaging in idle chit-chat, amazed, as always, at the amount of makeup, sequins, and velvet the holiday season brought out. I stopped to greet several people I'd known since my teenage years, careful not to get too comfortable in one position in case I wanted to make a quick getaway to the dining room.

It took me about fifteen minutes to make it to the feast my mother — or should I say the caterers — had prepared. The leaves had been placed in the cherry wood dining table, extending it to twelve feet. Around the candle centerpiece and pine garland sat every savory dish imaginable. A turkey the size of a cocker spaniel had been roasted and carved at one end, and a white-jacketed chef sliced prime rib at the other. Bowls of cold shrimp, plates of salmon, vegetables — roasted and raw with dip, and of course Russian caviar were squeezed in where space could be found. The desserts sat on the buffet table along one side of the room. A bartender in Roger's lounge dispensed various holiday cocktails.

The hamburger I'd had for lunch still sat in my stomach like a rock. It had been a good plan. This way, I wouldn't be hungry tonight and wouldn't incur my mother's wrath regarding my appetite. I shuffled into the queue around the buffet and took a china plate. I selected a slice of turkey, a spoonful of squash, and a couple of garlic-roasted potatoes.

Elegantly decorated tables had been set up in the library and informal sitting room. Each area had a differently themed Christmas tree to add ambience to the affair. The formal living room had been decorated in gold with white lights. The sitting room had blue lights with silver decorations, and the library, red lights with tartan ribbons. Servers lurked in every corner, waiting to pounce and clear away used silverware and plates. Another would whip down a fresh linen napkin and place setting as soon as crumbs were wiped away. I wondered how much laundry the company would have to do tomorrow, with all the soiled napkins and tablecloths.

Fortunately for me, most people chose to dine in the sitting room. I opted for the smaller library. Only one other couple occupied the room. I sat as far away from them as I could, hoping to blend in with the Christmas tree, which blinked behind me. I'd only started to eat when Roger's son Tony and another man walked into the room. Tony spotted me right away.

He sat down next to me. "Hey, Sis. Long time no see."

Tony was three years younger and ten years less mature than me. Roger had set him up in an apartment and a job while he went to college, hoping the boy would graduate and become a productive member of society. No such luck so far.

As my mouth was full, I muttered out a "Hey," and finished chewing.

He took a swig of beer and winked at me. "You change your mind yet about going out with me?"

I cringed. Tony had this fantasy about dating his stepsister that bordered on obscene. I take that back; it was obscene. "Nope."

"You don't know what you're missing."

His friend sat down across from us. "I think she does. That's why she's saying no."

I chuckled as I looked up. Tony's friend had light brown eyes and slightly shaggy blond hair. He smiled as he reached his hand across the table. "I'm Brad."

He had a firm handshake, but not like he was trying too hard. It's a delicate balance between that slimy fish feeling and someone trying to break the bones in your fingers. Brad's was perfect.

"I'm Ginny."

"Vir-GIN-ya," enunciated Tony with a wink.

I shook my head. I was an anomaly to my stepbrother. He couldn't fathom any woman not jumping into bed with him or any other male at a moment's notice. Thankfully, Brad ignored the comment.

"Ginny. Do you live in Omaha?"

I swallowed my mouthful of potato before speaking. "Out in Bellevue."

"Old Towne or new?"

Tony interrupted before I could answer. "Old. Her grandmother gave her a house." I could tell he wanted to let his friend know I didn't live the same lifestyle as they did. Brad didn't seem to care.

"I've always liked that area. Nostalgic. Like an old movie. I take my boat out on the Missouri sometimes and ride by."

I took a drink of my diet soda. "I walk down there when the weather's warmer."

"You lived there long?"

I shrugged. "About four years. After college, I came back to Omaha to go to Creighton Medical School."

Brad looked impressed. "You going to be a doctor?"

I smiled. Most people asked if I was going to be a nurse first. "I was."

He frowned. "But?"

"It's a long story."

"I'll tell him," offered Tony.

"Don't bother," said Brad.

Tony shot his friend a bewildered look. "What?"

"I don't think the lady wants to talk about it right now. Let's not ruin her night."

My stepbrother made a raspberry noise with his lips. "Fine."

I gave Brad a grateful smile. "How about you? Where do you live?"

"I have a condo in Old Market."

"Nice." The Old Market side of Omaha was urban, trendy, and expensive.

"I like it." He washed down a mouthful of food with a sip from his beer. "I work part-time at a bar downtown while I'm taking classes."

I raised my eyebrows and looked over at Tony. "You have a friend who actually works? Amazing."

Brad laughed. "My folks think that if I have to earn my college degree, I'll actually appreciate it."

"And do you?"

"You bet. When you're shelling out the money for it, you make sure you get to class."

Tony waved his hands defensively. "Hey, I get to class." He slouched a bit in his chair. "I may be hung-over, but I get to class."

I glared at my stepbrother. "Such a work ethic you have." I glanced over at Brad. "How did you meet this wonder of humanity?"

A slow blush crept up his face.

"What's so embarrassing?"

Tony sat up. "Go ahead. Tell her."

Brad looked away guiltily. "A course in women's literature."

"Don't judge." Tony swatted me on the arm. "Maybe we're trying to be enlightened men of the new millennium."

I snorted out a laugh. "Or maybe you're trying to pick up some girls."

Brad nodded. "I thought it would be a good place. But, it turns out most of the girls who take the class are lesbian." He leaned forward. "Not that I'm against that, but it does limit my chances of getting a date."

"I guess so." I finished the last bite of food from my plate and stood up. "It was nice meeting you, Brad." I placed my hand on my stepbrother's shoulder. "Tony, let's do this again next year." He groaned, and Brad chuckled as I walked away.

Instead of going directly back to find my mother and make small talk with the rest of the guests, I took a detour up the stairs to use the restroom. I checked out my reflection in the mirror, happy to see my makeup and hair still looking good. I paused for a moment outside of my old bedroom. My mother had kept my canopy bed and furniture, but my photos and stuffed animals had long since been packed away. The room appeared spotless, like a picture from a magazine, a far cry from how it looked when I'd lived in it. I closed the door and headed back to the party.

I followed the sound of my mother's voice into the study. She had a fresh drink in her hand and was speaking to a middle-aged woman I didn't know.

"I know how you feel, Laura." She put her manicured hand on the other woman's arm. "You try your best to raise them right, but there's nothing you can do. I treated them all the same, gave them everything they ever wanted, and only my son James turned out well."

James. *James turned out well because he went to Princeton and became a lawyer. Simon and I are garbage because we don't make a six-figure salary. How nice.*

Laura murmured something to my mother, who responded with an exaggerated wag of her head. "It's not your fault. You can't keep bailing him out. I finally gave up with my two. You're on your own, I told them. Wiped my hands of them."

I wish it were that easy. My mother had her claws in me so deep I was surprised I didn't have visible scars.

"It's Ginny I worry about the most. She has so much potential. I hate to see her squander her life in that home she works at. She could be so much more."

It'd been ages since my mother had complimented me about anything. I figured I'd leave the party on a positive note this year. I stepped farther into the room and into my mother's line of sight. "Sorry to eat and run, but I need to get going."

She actually looked concerned. "You've barely been here an hour. You have to stay longer."

I gave her a kiss on the cheek. "No, I really have to go."

Her eyes brightened. "Is it a date? Are you going out with someone?" She kept rattling on without giving me a chance to answer. "Why didn't you bring him here? I would love to meet your new boyfriend."

I backed away. "No, Mom. It's not a date."

Her countenance fell. "Of course not."

"What's that supposed to mean?"

She shook her head. "I don't understand you. You're wasting all the talent you have. If you'd only get a better job. Or go back to school. Meet a nice doctor."

I should have left then. I should have found my coat under the pile in the guest bedroom and said goodbye to Roger. I should have. But, I didn't. "I didn't go to school to meet a nice doctor. I went to school to become a doctor."

She spread her arms out to her sides, causing her drink to trickle over the top of her glass. "Whatever." She took a sip. "At least you were doing something with your life."

"I am doing something. I'm helping people."

"It's so noble of you. But, you're never going to make a life for yourself if you don't get a real job. Playing Bingo isn't a career."

"Neither is going to the gym and throwing parties for your friends."

She always brought out the worst in me. I wished I could take back the words I'd spoken when I saw her lower lip tremble and the tears well in her eyes. She struggled to take a deep breath.

Roger entered the room. I'd always admired his ability to sense when he was needed. "Joyce, darling, the Cummings are asking about the painting in the living room." He placed an arm around her. "I can't remember the name of the art dealer you got it from." He led her out of the room, whispering to me as he passed, "See you later."

I stood in the middle of the room, wondering if I'd ever learn to keep my mouth shut. My mother's friend Laura exited without saying a word. I steadied my breath before turning around to find Brad standing behind me.

"You're not leaving, are you?"

I nodded.

"Can I call you sometime?"

I shut my eyes. This was too surreal.

"I know you don't think much of your brother, but it's not like we're best friends or anything. He felt sorry for me because I don't know many people around here. My family lives in Missouri." He stuck his hands into his jacket pockets. "Please? I won't beg or anything, but I'd like to give you a call sometime. Maybe do lunch?"

What is it about lunch lately? Do I look like I'm starving, and men have a sudden desire to feed me? I could hear Father Dan's voice in my head. "You have to take a chance. You have to start living again."

"Okay."

He looked surprised. "Really?"

"Yeah. Follow me, and I'll give you my card. It has my cell phone number on it."

Brad trailed me like an eager puppy hoping for a treat. I found my coat and purse in the pile and fished out a card. "Here. I'm usually home by seven."

"All right." He tapped the card against his fingers. "I'll call you this week."

I stood there for a moment, feeling awkward. "Okay, then." I had to step around him to get out of the guest room. "See ya."

"Goodnight."

I didn't turn around but I raised my hand in a kind of wave and walked quickly to the front door. What had I done? I didn't want to go out with Brad. I didn't want to go out with anyone. I just wanted to be left alone.

CHAPTER SEVEN

I swallowed two ibuprofen with the cold remains of my coffee before getting ready for Sittercise. I'd woken up with a pit in my stomach and a bad headache from lack of sleep. Brad had been true to his word and given me a call on Tuesday night. He'd been charming on the phone. Casual and funny. That's what had suckered me in. I hadn't laughed in a long time. We'd made plans to meet for dinner at a restaurant in the Old Market on Friday night. And here it was. Friday.

My mind wandered during Sittercise. *What am I going to wear? What are we going to talk about?*

"We did that one already!" complained Sam.

I stopped in mid-count. "What?"

"We already did the leg circles."

"Sorry. What are we on?"

My grandmother squinted at me. "Is something wrong, dear?"

"We're on the arm crosses," Sam interrupted.

We stretched our arms out to the sides and crossed them in front of our chests as I counted up to ten. I made it through the rest of the session without another major flub, the residents all too eager to yell out what exercise came next. I collected the bands and dumbbells as they left, putting them away in the storage cupboard. My grandmother stayed behind.

"Are you feeling all right?"

"I'm fine. Just a lot on my mind today, and I didn't sleep well last night." Well? I hadn't slept at all.

"You want to talk about it?"

I put the last dumbbell in the bin and shut the cupboard door. "I want to keep it quiet. Don't tell Mom or the residents, okay?"

Edith frowned. "You know I can be discreet."

I sat down. "I'm going out on a date tonight." My grandmother didn't smile as she sat down opposite me. "I thought you'd be happy for me."

"I am! It's a surprise is all. Who is he? Where'd you meet him?"

"I met him at Mom's party. He's a friend of Tony's."

Edith's eyes grew round. "Roger's boy?"

"He seems okay. He's funny and polite."

My grandmother raised an eyebrow. "Really?"

I nodded.

"How much do you know about him?"

"Not much." I shrugged. "It all came about rather suddenly. I'm not sure I'm ready."

Edith patted my leg. "You're ready, dear. It's time you start dating again." She paused for a moment and squeezed my knee. "But, I've never liked Tony. He's too . . . too . . . ."

"Immature?" I offered.

"Immature, yes. But, there's something else." She sat back in her chair. "He acts as if he owns the world. Like everyone and everything is here to serve him. I'm not sure I'd trust a friend of his."

Grandma was perceptive. She'd nailed Tony to a T. "Well, I'm not planning on marrying the first guy I go out with. I figured this would be a pretty low-stress way to ...." I waved my hand. "Get out there again."

Edith nodded. "Be careful. There are a lot of good men out there and you deserve the best."

"Thanks." I leaned over and gave her a kiss on the cheek. "I'll call you tomorrow and let you know how it went."

Edith made her way to the lobby, where Frank already had the backgammon board set up. She hurried over to the table. "Houston, we have a problem."

Deep lines creased Frank's forehead. "What do you mean? You haven't heard my news yet."

Edith sat down. "And you haven't heard mine. Ginny has a date tonight."

"With who?"

"Some friend of my daughter's stepson." Edith's fingers tapped against the table. "I don't know the boy, but I wouldn't trust him as far as I can spit. Tony's trouble. Any friend of his is bound to be trouble, too."

"But, why now?" Frank asked.

"I suppose it was bound to happen naturally, anyway. And she told me about her lunch with Father Dan last weekend. He pushed her to get out there and start living again."

Frank swore under his breath. "Rotten timing."

Edith nodded. Her fingers slowed their drumming. "Tell me your news."

Frank shrugged. "It's Chester. We had a little talk over breakfast. He told me he wouldn't be able to go to the office party tomorrow because his sister will have his car."

"Why is that a good thing? I thought we wanted them to get together at the party."

"I know," he nodded. "That's the thing. I thought you could drop a hint to Ginny that Chester needed a ride tomorrow night. You know her. She's bound to offer to pick him up."

Edith smiled. "Now, that's a good idea. It wouldn't be like a date, since they'd be going to an office function—"

"But, they'd have to talk to each other in the car while she drove. It'd be perfect!"

Ginny's grandmother picked up the cup of dice and shook them. "I think it could still work. I have a bad feeling about this character she's seeing tonight. I want her to realize quickly that she has other options." She moved one of her backgammon pieces across the board.

Frank took his turn. "Do you think you can let Ginny know about Chester without her figuring out we're trying to fix them up, or do you want me to do it?"

Edith lifted an eyebrow. "Don't worry about me, Frank Leno. She'll never know."

❧

Chester pulled his coat on and headed out through the dining room. He smiled at Ginny who stood at one end calling Bingo. Rachel Johnson waved him over to her table.

"Can you get me a glass of water, sweetie? With ice?"

"Sure thing." He glanced at her tablemates. "Anyone else want something?"

Sam chimed in, "A cup of coffee would be lovely."

He nodded. "Be right back."

Ginny called out "B-fourteen. B, one-four, fourteen."

Chester delivered the drinks, then tried to make his way out without disturbing the game further.

"N-fifty-two. N, five-two. Excuse me a minute, everyone." Ginny ran over to him. "Can I talk to you?"

"Sure." He walked with her out to the lobby. "What's up?" She stood so close he could smell the scent from her shampoo. Light and fruity. Maybe grapefruit? He shook his head and concentrated on what she was saying.

"A little bird told me you weren't going to be able to go to the dinner tomorrow night because you didn't have a ride. Is that true?"

"Who told you?"

Ginny chuckled. "There are no secrets here. You know that."

Chester shrugged. "My sister's car broke down. She'll need mine tomorrow."

Ginny smacked his arm good-naturedly. "I'll come get you."

His chest tightened. "You will?"

"Sure." Ginny leaned in close to him. "It'll be the first time I go to one of these holiday parties, and I don't really hang with a lot of the staff. I'd like someone I know there."

Chester tried hard to swallow, but his mouth had gone dry. "You sure you won't mind?"

"Not at all." She glanced back into the dining room. "The natives are getting restless. You leave your number on my desk, and I'll call you tomorrow for directions, okay?" She turned and hurried back to the Bingo game. "Sorry about that! The next number is O-seventy-two. That's O, seven-two."

"Seventy-nine?" asked one of the residents.

"No," Ginny answered. "Seventy-two!"

Chester watched her, his heart finally slowing down to a normal rhythm. He made his way to her office. He'd only stopped in her corner of the building a few times, usually to see if he could borrow napkins or peanuts or something else from her storage closet. He chuckled as he looked around the room. She probably had some kind of system to make order out of the chaos on her desk, but he'd never figure it out. Stacks of paper lay strewn about. Bookshelves behind it were lined with brightly colored binders and magazines. The screensaver on her computer was of sunset over a mountain lake. He wondered whether she'd taken the shot or if it was something she'd found on the Internet.

Chester found a pen and a green Post-it note and wrote out his name and phone number. He looked around the desk for a suitable place to put it and realized she'd never see it if he laid it down. He opted for sticking it to her computer screen. It was then he saw the picture — Ginny standing next to a dark-haired man. It had been taken in the fall. The trees behind them boasted bright yellow and orange leaves. They stood side by side. The man looked at the camera, his smile bright and his eyes shining. She had her head on his shoulder and gazed up at him. Chester tried to swallow the lump in his throat. Ginny looked happy. It radiated out of the photo. She loved him very much. Chester picked up the frame and stared even closer at the picture. *Who am I, to think I can compare to a love like that? She'll probably never be over him.* He put the photo back where he'd found it and closed the door behind him.

The flickering candle in the middle of the table did little to brighten the dim lighting in the restaurant. I hoped the clinking of silverware and muffled conversations of the strangers at nearby booths would drown out the nervous pounding of my heart. I hadn't been out with anyone in so long that I prayed I could think of something to talk about. I sat across from Brad and wondered why on earth I was putting myself through this torture. I take that back. I knew why. It was all Father Dan's fault. "*Mark wouldn't want you to wallow in self-pity. Mark helped you to live life. Don't let all that he gave you get buried with him.*"

Ugh. Why did Dan have to be so smart? And where was he when I needed him the most? I hadn't made small talk with a guy in years.

"Am I boring you already?" Brad turned on the cute. He reminded me a little of Keith Urban. Too bad I didn't look like Nicole Kidman.

"I'm sorry. I haven't been out in a while."

"Tony told me a little about you." He paused for a moment. "Do you want to tell me about Mark?"

I caught my breath. "What did Tony say?"

"Not much." Brad took a sip from his beer. "Just that you'd been engaged for a couple of years and that Mark died in a car accident on Thanksgiving."

"That about sums it up."

Brad watched me. "What was he like?"

I played with my water and wished the waitress would hurry up and bring our salads.

"I'm sorry. I don't mean to pry." He took another drink. "I thought it might help to get things out in the open."

I stirred the ice in my glass with the straw. "We met in med school. He was in his last year. He went home for

Thanksgiving break but wanted to surprise me at my mom's house. He fell asleep at the wheel."

"That stinks."

I let out a snort of air. "Yeah." The waitress arrived with our salads and some fresh-baked rolls – always a weakness of mine, and I wasn't in the mood to act coy around Brad. I went ahead and grabbed a roll and two pats of butter. He laughed.

"Finally! A girl who's not watching her carbs!"

I slathered the roll with butter. "This is the first time I've been out in two years. I'm not going to let baked goods go to waste."

"Does this mean you might save room for dessert?"

I sucked on my lips, making a squeaking sound. "I don't know. I haven't been here before. Is it worth it?"

Brad's eyes grew wide. "Oh, yeah. They have a triple berry pie that's phenomenal."

I wrinkled my nose. "I'm more of an ice cream, chocolate cake girl myself."

"I'm sure they can hook you up. Everything here is good."

I relaxed a little after the food banter. Brad told me about his family in Missouri. His dad owned a tool company. A sister and brother worked there while another sister taught school in Michigan.

I pierced a crouton. "What are you studying?"

"Business."

"You going to join your dad when you've graduated?"

Brad shook his head. "Nah. I want to move to New York or Chicago. A big city."

"Why didn't you go to school there?"

"I did, at first." He smiled mischievously. "I was asked to leave Columbia after I flunked all my classes the first semester."

"I see." Maybe he was more like my stepbrother than I'd thought.

He brought his hand up. "Now, wait a minute. I've gotten my act together since then."

I lifted one eyebrow.

"No, really. I took a year off and worked for my dad. Then I applied up here at UNO and got accepted."

"Why Omaha?"

"My mom's parents live nearby. Dad liked the idea of me going somewhere a little less populated."

"But, you liked the city, huh?"

He nodded. "Loved it. The nightclubs, the theater. So much going on all the time. " He crunched on his salad. "Have you ever been to New York?"

"Once with my mom to see a show." I didn't volunteer any more information.

"You weren't impressed?"

I shrugged. "It was fun to visit, but I wouldn't want to live there."

"Where would you like to live?" He watched me over the top of his glass. "If you could live anywhere in the world?"

"I don't know." I fiddled with my fork. "I guess by water somewhere." My grandparents' farm had been near a creek. I'd loved sitting on its banks and watching the current flow. I'd missed it when I'd moved in with my mother and Roger.

We talked more about places we'd been to and places we wanted to visit as we waited for our entrees. The chicken parmesan I'd ordered kept me too busy to converse much during dinner. By the time the waitress cleared away the plates, I was stuffed.

Brad brushed a blond hair from his eyes. "So, what do you think? You got room for dessert?"

I groaned. "Not even a wafer-thin mint."

Brad laughed. "*Meaning of Life*, right? Monty Python?"

I nodded and added a few more points to his acceptability meter. "You a fan?"

"Don't get me started, or I'll quote all of the parrot sketch for you!"

"Cool." I smiled and shifted back against the bench. My stomach ached. I hadn't indulged in such a big meal in a long time.

Brad leaned forward. "You okay?"

"I'm stuffed." I rubbed my midsection. "I see Tums in my future."

He caught our waitress's attention, and she hurried over with our bill. I offered to split it with him, but he refused. Once his credit card had been returned and the receipt signed, we slipped out of the booth. Brad helped me with my coat and held the door open as we exited. A stiff, cold wind slapped me as soon as I walked outside, and I was thankful I'd pulled my hair back with a clip so it wasn't blowing in my face. Brad walked me to my car and waited while I fished out my keys. He stuffed his hands in his coat pockets.

"I had fun tonight."

My hands shook as I tried to unlock the car door. "Thanks . . . uh . . . me, too."

"Can I call you again?"

I finally got the key in the lock and opened the door. The way my heart was beating, you'd have thought I'd run a marathon. "Sure." *Please don't try and kiss me. Please don't try and kiss me.*

Brad moved toward me, but I took a step behind the door, using it as a wall between us. "I'm busy the next two Saturdays, but other than that, I'm free."

Brad nodded as he took in my defensive posture. "I'll give you a call this week. Maybe we can do something Friday?"

"Yeah. Thanks for tonight." I slipped behind the wheel. Brad placed his hands along the top edge of the door.

"Good night, Ginny."

"Good night."

He shut the door and stepped away from the car. He waited while I backed up and waved as I pulled away.

Well, you jerk, you totally screwed that up. He's never going to call you again. I clutched the steering wheel as I made my way through the brightly lit Omaha streets. *I don't care. He doesn't have to call again. It doesn't matter.* I opted against taking the highway home and instead took 13th Street south through downtown. *He seems decent. He's cute. And you've ruined everything.*

I passed the illuminated Desert Dome of the zoo and tried to concentrate on the road, not the voices in my head. *He's not Mark.* No, he wasn't Mark. There'd never be another Mark. But could someone fill the aching hole that he'd left behind? By the time I pulled into my driveway and got into my house, my stomach was in such knots I had to run into the bathroom and throw up. So much for the fabulous parmesan.

CHAPTER EIGHT

Edith's knee bounced as she waited at the back table for Frank to come with the backgammon board. Her friend Donna would pick her up at eleven-thirty for their Saturday lunch date, and Edith didn't want to subject Frank to her friend's scrutiny. *After all, Frank and I are just friends. I don't want him to feel uncomfortable around me thinking I'd like more of a relationship.* She let out a soft chuckle. *A relationship, at my age?* Donna was foolish to even think like that.

Frank arrived a few minutes later, board in tow. "Can I get you a cup of coffee?"

"I'd love a cup of tea, if you wouldn't mind."

"With cream and sugar, right?"

Edith nodded, and Frank went into the dining room while she busied herself with setting up the game. She'd gotten all the pieces on their proper spaces by the time he returned.

"Here you go." Frank put the cup of tea next to her and sat down. He pushed his chair closer to her so he could speak softly. "So? Did you talk to Ginny this morning?"

Edith removed the tea bag. "The good news is there were no fireworks. She doesn't seem smitten at all."

Frank smiled. "That's a word I haven't heard in a while."

"I only meant that I don't think she's serious about this boy."

"Details." Frank took a sip of his coffee. "Give me the details."

"She said they met at the restaurant, which I thought was strange."

"Why?"

"My father would never have let me 'meet' a man. He should come to the door and pick his date up."

Frank smiled. "It's the new millennium, my dear. She probably split the check with him."

"No, she didn't, although she did offer." Edith shook her head. "It's a different time, I guess."

"And what were your dates like? Back in the day?"

Edith scrutinized him with a cautious eye. "Why?"

"Just curious. I grew up in Chicago. I'm guessing our social lives were different. I'd like to know what you country folks did for fun."

"You make me sound like a hick." Edith pursed her lips. "I'll have you know the young men who called on me were all gentlemen. We did more than hay rides and the soda fountain store."

Frank's eyes twinkled when he laughed. "Don't get mad. I'd like to know more about you. Is that so horrible?"

"My family worked a farm out east of Des Moines. I had one young man who would drive his new car out on our dirt roads to pick me up for concerts downtown." She stared into the flames in the fireplace. "He was quite taken with me. We spent almost every Friday night at the dance hall."

"I'll bet you cut quite a rug."

Edith returned her attention to Frank. "I certainly wasn't the best dancer, but I wasn't half bad."

"Was this your husband?"

"No, Lloyd wasn't much for dancing in public." Her mind wandered into the past before Frank interrupted her.

"I'm sorry if I upset you."

"You didn't." She sipped her tea. "It's nice to think back on things sometimes. Remember when I was young and beautiful."

Frank stared at her for a moment before saying softly, "You're still beautiful."

She let out a nervous giggle. "Oh, pishaw. I'm old and wrinkly. Sometimes I look in the mirror and think, *Who is that old prune?*"

"I know what you mean. I don't feel like I'm in my seventies. I still think I'm a young man. I did a double-take the other day when I passed a window. I wondered who the geezer staring at me was." Frank shrugged. "It was my reflection."

They sat in companionable silence for several minutes, watching the flames pop and crackle in the fireplace.

Frank finally spoke again. "So, Ginny . . . has she got another date with this fellow?"

Edith put her cup down. "She's not sure. He said he'd call her again this week, but you know what they say."

"No, what?"

She threw her hands up in mock exasperation. "If he doesn't call, he's just not that into you."

"Did Ginny get the feeling this was a one-time deal?"

Edith shrugged. "She wasn't sure."

Frank finished his coffee. "Did they kiss?"

"Frank Leno, what a question to ask! Ginny's not the kind to kiss and tell!"

"She'd tell you. I know she would. If she didn't, it means they didn't."

"That's what I thought, too."

"And how about Chester? She still planning on picking him up for the party tonight?"

Edith nodded.

"That's a start for our cause, anyway. When do you think she'll call you again?"

She shook her head. "No telling. We don't usually talk on Sundays, but I could call her and ask her how it went."

"What time?"

She surprised herself by swatting his knee. "You're worse than the town busybody!"

Frank lifted his arms in surrender. "I'm worried for Chester. I'm not being a *voyeur*!"

"Yes, you are, and you know it." She picked up her teacup, sorry to see it empty. She put it back down. "Why don't we meet here tomorrow afternoon before dinner? Say four o'clock? I should have more news by then."

Her heart fluttered as Frank looked at her and smiled. "I'll look forward to it."

ᗯᑎᗢ

Katy sat on the edge of the bathtub, staring at her uncle's reflection in the mirror. "Why are you shaving?"

Chester concentrated on the task at hand. "Because I'm going to a special dinner tonight."

She giggled as he pulled his chin in an awkward position to get a better angle at the last of his whiskers. He stuck his tongue out at her, and she returned the gesture.

"Why is it special?" Katy asked.

Chester rinsed the razor blade and splashed off the excess shaving cream. "Because it's for my job."

Katy's eyebrows furrowed. "They make you eat dinner for your job? But, I thought you made the food?"

He patted his face dry. "Tonight, they're treating us to dinner as a thank-you for our hard work this year."

His niece nodded, then looked puzzled again. "I still don't see why you have to dress up. We don't dress up for dinner here."

Chester opened the medicine cabinet and pulled out a bottle. Before he could answer Katy's first question, she asked another.

"What's that?"

"It's aftershave."

"What's that?"

He laughed in exasperation. "It's something men put on their faces after they shave."

"Why?"

"I'm not really sure. We just do." Chester splashed a small amount into his palm, rubbed it into his other hand, then slapped his cheeks lightly.

Katy's face lit up. "It smells nice!"

He replaced the bottle. "Thank you." He rinsed his hands and dried them off. "Now, if you'll excuse me, I have to change." Before Katy could ask another question, he added, "And you can't follow me into my room."

The little girl jumped off the side of the tub. "Will you come show me what you look like when you're done?"

"Sure."

She smiled. "I'll wait for you in the living room."

He kissed the top of her head, and she ran off. He took another look in the mirror before leaving the bathroom to make sure he hadn't missed a spot shaving. He'd even taken a stab at trimming his mustache. He turned his face from side to side. Not bad.

In his room he pulled a set of freshly ironed clothes from his closet. The button- down shirt felt strange. He normally wore T-shirts or polos to work. He tucked it into his pants and found a belt. He decided not to wear a tie, but found the maroon sweater his parents had sent him last Christmas. He'd only worn it twice since then, both times to church. He slipped it on. The doorbell rang as he went back to the bathroom to check out his reflection one last time. He straightened his shirt collar and ran his hand through his hair. He could hear voices down the hall.

Ginny's here.

He'd told her to wait in the driveway, honk the horn, and he'd come out. He was already nervous enough without adding his sister to the mix. He had no doubt Louisa would pick up on his feelings for Ginny, no matter how hard he tried to hide them. She knew him too well.

He yelled down the hall before he trotted back to his room to get his dress shoes, "I'll be right there!"

A chorus of giggles echoed back at him. He took a deep breath as he put his shoes on. Be calm. *Remember to breathe. She's only a friend.*

He paused one more time at his bedroom door before he walked down the hall to the living room. The lights from the Christmas tree in the corner twinkled like fireflies. Ginny sat on the couch, her red hair swept softly away from her face and clipped somehow behind her head. The deep green of her coat complemented her coloring beautifully. She grinned as she caught sight of him.

"Hey there, stranger. You look great!"

"Thanks. You do, too."

"How can you tell? I could be wearing sweats under this coat!"

Katy and Maria, who sat on the floor at Ginny's feet, both laughed. Katy pointed to Ginny's shoes. "You're wearing a dress. I can see your legs and heels."

Ginny cocked her head and squinted her eyes. "Maybe I'm wearing shorts."

"No!" grinned Katy. "That would be silly!"

"Yes, it would." Ginny nodded. "But, I could be a very silly person – you never know."

Chester got his coat from the closet and caught his sister's gaze. She stood in the kitchen threshold, watching the scene unfold in front of her. When she noticed Chester's stare, she gave him a quick nod and a smile.

What did that mean? Wals that a sign of approval?

He put his coat on. "Let's go."

Ginny stood, her long legs looking even longer in the heels she wore. "I'm glad I got the chance to meet you all. Chester talks a lot about you."

Louisa took a step into the room. "We're actually on the way out ourselves. Maria has a concert tonight." She shooed the two girls down the hall. "Brush your teeth, and Maria, pull your hair back."

Chester hoped to scoot Ginny out the door before his sister could say anything more, but Louisa beat him. "Chester doesn't talk much about the people at work, except for the residents. How long have you been at Marigold?"

Ginny picked up her purse. "A little over a year. I work in Activities."

Louisa nodded as her eyes conducted a quick overview of Ginny's appearance. Chester knew she was taking in everything she could: the fact that Ginny didn't wear a wedding or engagement ring, the fact that in her heels she stood a little taller than him. Louisa's eyes flickered from Ginny's face to Chester's, and her smile faded almost imperceptibly. He reached over and opened the front door.

"Have fun at the concert tonight, Sis. Be careful on the roads. They might get icy."

"You, too."

Ginny stopped in the doorway. "I haven't been to one of these before. Do they go late?"

Chester shook his head. "It depends. We have the room for the night, but dinner is over by nine."

Ginny pulled her gloves out of her pocket and slipped them on. "Do you usually stay?"

"You're the driver. It's up to you." He ushered her out the door. "You don't have to decide now. Wait and see how you feel at the party. I'm flexible." He glanced over his shoulder at Louisa. She gave him the "What's up with this?" look. He shrugged with an "I have no idea" kind of reply.

I caught a whiff of Chester's cologne as he closed the passenger-side door. It smelled wonderful. Would it be weird to mention it to him? Probably. I focused on backing out of his driveway. The Christmas lights outlining the house reflected like a rainbow on the windshield of my car. "Thanks for going to the party tonight. I didn't want to have to brave this alone."

"You know people. You wouldn't be alone."

I cranked up the heat as we headed down the road. "I hang out with the residents, not the employees. I don't really talk to anyone but Karen the head nurse and Susan the administrator. Oh, and Patty the secretary. They're all bringing their boyfriends and husbands. It'll be nice to have a friend to sit with."

My defogger was having trouble starting up. I had to wipe the windshield with my arm to see the road. Chester did the same on his side. White icicle lights sparkled merrily from several of the houses while "Jingle Bell Rock" played on the radio. I smiled as I pulled up to a stop sign. The owners of the house on the corner must have taken stock in inflatable decorations. A giant merry-go-round twirled precariously as it struggled to stay landlocked against the brisk December wind. Santa popped up and down from a chimney on the other side of the house. Lighted candy canes lined the driveway, and multicolored bulbs hung from the porch and bushes. I sat at the stop sign longer than necessary as I took in all the decorations that adorned the house.

"You all right?" Chester asked.

"Yeah, sorry." I pulled the car out onto the road. "It's fun to see someone who enjoys the holiday."

"It's a tough time for you, isn't it?"

"It's getting easier." I glanced at Chester. "I went nuts the first Christmas I moved into my house. I couldn't afford the inflatable stuff, but I had lights everywhere. I remember my mother being appalled when she saw it."

"Why?"

"My parents always had the classy kind of displays. Single white candles in every window, or a flood light on the front door wreath. I put lights on everything. The porch, the trees, the bushes. It was great."

"I didn't want to put the lights out this year. It's been so cold. But, Katy insisted."

"She's the little one, right?"

Chester nodded.

"She's a cutie."

"She's a handful." He laughed. "And very creative."

"How long have you lived with your sister?"

"Almost five years now. Ever since her husband split."

I shifted lanes. "That stinks. What happened?"

Chester looked out the passenger window. "We don't know where he went. Louisa said he packed up while she was at work one day. He left Katy in her crib and brought Maria over to the neighbor's house and left."

"Wow." I pulled up and stopped at a red light. "She hasn't heard from him since?"

Chester looked back at me. "Not a word. I'd already decided to get out of the Navy. I thought I'd come out here and give her a hand for a while."

"You're a good big brother." The light changed, and I headed back down the road.

"You have any brothers?"

"Two. James is a lawyer out in Massachusetts, and Simon works for a counseling house over in Iowa. How about you? Is Louisa your only sister?"

He chuckled. "No. I have an older sister, Teresa, and a younger brother, Michael."

"I have to ask. How did you get a name like Chester?"

"My grandfather."

I glanced back at him. "I thought your family was Mexican? That's not a common name, is it?"

"Actually, my grandfather was American through and through. A rancher in Texas."

"Really?"

Chester nodded.

"So, your last name is really Martin then? Patty said she thought you'd shortened it from Martinez or something."

"Nope. My grandmother came to work at my grandfather's house when they were both teenagers. They married in '47."

"I'm sorry. I thought Susan told me your family was from Mexico."

"It gets confusing, because after my grandfather died, my *abuela*, my grandmother, couldn't make a go of the ranch anymore. Too many prejudices about a woman rancher and Hispanics. She took my father and my aunt back to Mexico in '62. My father was twelve and still a U.S. citizen. As soon as he turned eighteen, he came back to the states."

"And your mother? Did he meet her here?"

"No. They fell in love in Mexico. My father brought her here once he'd gotten established in Colorado."

We stopped at another red light. I groaned. "The elves don't like me tonight."

Chester gave me an odd look. "What?"

"It's something my grandfather used to say when he drove around town. He tried to convince me there were elves living in the traffic lights, and they were in charge of switching them around."

"Okay...."

I pretended to be serious. "Now, you'd better not tick them off, or we'll be stuck here even longer. You have to be nice and ask them to give you a green light."

Chester stared at me.

I turned to the light. "Please Mr. Elf, we're trying to get to our party on time. Would you please turn the light green now?" I couldn't have planned it any better, as the light switched over. I lifted my hands in a "What did I tell you?" gesture. Chester laughed.

I guided my car onto the highway, careful to ease into traffic. "What do your parents do?"

"They own a restaurant."

I flashed him a quick look. "Then why—"

"Why don't I work for them?" Chester focused on the cars ahead of us. "I guess I needed to break away. Prove myself, you know?"

"Sometimes we need to see if we can make it on our own."

The lights from the oncoming traffic glowed across his face. "It was more than that. They have a good life, and they're good people, but they cook Mexican food, and I wanted to cook more than that. I want to own a gourmet restaurant one day. But, one where everyone feels welcome." His voice filled with excitement. "So many people get lulled into thinking that the chain restaurants are the only way they can afford to eat out. I want a place that'll serve unique foods from all over the world, but at a decent price."

"That sounds really cool."

"It will be. Someday."

We exited off the highway and merged onto the road. I made the appropriate quick turns to get us into Johnny's parking lot. The steak house had been a staple in Omaha for decades. I had to park in a lower lot, so we had a bit of a walk to get to restaurant. I'd enjoyed the drive with Chester, but now that we'd arrived, I dreaded going in to the party. I slowed my steps as we approached the main door.

"You forget something?" Chester asked.

I shivered in the cold Nebraska wind. "No. Just trying to get my nerve up."

"What are you worried about?"

"I don't know." I shrugged. "Maybe it's because at all of my mother's parties, I always end up leaving either angry or in tears. It's been awhile since I've been to a normal party."

He linked his arm in mine and pulled me up the front stairs. "This is not one of your mother's parties. These are your friends. You'll have a drink, eat dinner, get a present, and go home."

"I don't drink."

"Not even soda?"

I shoved my shoulder into his. "You know what I mean."

"So, have a Coke or Pepsi, eat dinner, and get a present." He opened the door and led me inside. We were greeted immediately by Karen, the head nurse. She reminded me of Paula Dean with her poofy gray hair and round face. She wore an emerald green pantsuit and bright gold earrings.

"Hi there, you two! I didn't know you were coming together."

"Chester needed a ride," I said as I took off my coat and handed it to him. He brought it over to the coat check girl.

Karen smiled at me. "I don't think I've ever seen you in a dress before! You look fabulous!"

I did a little twirl in the foyer. My black chiffon skirt spun up around me. I'd always loved how I looked in simple, classic styles. Chester stood staring at me. A tiny smile formed on his lips. I stopped spinning.

"Do I really look that bad normally? You all seem floored that I even own a dress."

Chester seemed frozen for a moment; then he shook his head. "I'd been expecting sweats is all."

"What?" I asked.

"You told Katy you were wearing sweats under your coat. The dress is a bit of a surprise."

Karen laughed and pointed down the hall. "We have the room on the left. They'll be serving in a couple of minutes, so get down there."

"What about you?" I asked.

"I'm the official greeter for the night. Making sure everyone knows where we are. I'm waiting for a couple more people to show up."

Chester held out a numbered tag from the coat check. "Do you want me to keep this?"

"Sure. You won't catch a ride home with someone else, will you, and leave me coatless?" I wondered at the strange look that flashed across his face. He seemed almost sad. Then he grinned.

"How much?"

"How much what?"

"What's it worth to keep me hanging around tonight instead of leaving with someone else?"

I smacked his arm. "You wouldn't dare!"

"You're right," he said as he stepped into the reserved dining room. Then, under his breath I thought I heard him say, "I wouldn't."

༄

The glow from the television spilled out of the living room window and painted the snow-covered ground in a light blue hue.

Louisa's up. Chester glanced at Ginny as she pulled into the driveway. "Thanks for the ride."

She smiled. His heart stopped momentarily. He fought back the urge to reach across the seats and take her face in his hands. *I wonder what her lips feel like?*

"Thanks for coming with me. I would have been miserable without a friend there."

A friend. That's what I am, a friend. Chester turned away. "Any time." He opened the door.

"Wait!"

He shifted back into the car, excited at the thought she might need another favor. "What?"

Her arm stretched toward him but then moved to the backseat. She struggled with a large, colorful bag. "Don't forget your prize."

He had won a three-foot resin bear covered in fiber-optic lights. Katy would love it. Ginny tried to maneuver her body to get a better grasp on the bag, and their arms brushed together. She giggled.

"I think my arm is stuck!"

She sat so close her breath warmed his cheek. Again, he fought the desire to kiss her. He opened the door. "You let go. I'll get it from the back."

He retrieved his gift as Ginny positioned herself properly in the front seat.

"Thanks again for the ride."

She gave him a wave. "I'll see you bright and early Monday morning. Have a good Sunday."

"You, too," he called as he slammed the door shut. Ginny waited until he'd made it to the front door before she backed out of the driveway. He waved as she turned onto the street. He unlocked the door, and Louisa sat up on the couch.

She stretched her arms over her head and yawned. "How was your night?"

Chester put his prize down and hung his coat in the front closet. "Don't pretend you fell asleep there. I know you were waiting up for me."

Her eyes opened wide as she shook her head. "No, I wasn't."

"Fine." He walked into the kitchen and opened the refrigerator. He stared at its contents for a moment before pulling out a gallon of milk.

Louisa's slippers made a scuffling noise on the hardwood floor as she came in behind him. "I'll take a glass of that, too, if you're pouring."

Louisa sat at the kitchen table. Chester poured two glasses then put the milk away.

Louisa's eyes narrowed as she watched him. "Is she the reason you won't go out with Tina?"

Chester grimaced. "No."

Louisa sipped her milk and stared at him.

He stared back then drank his milk in three huge gulps. "Well, thanks for the chat. I'm off to bed." He wiped his mouth with the back of his hand, then put his glass in the sink.

"How long have you been in love with her?"

His shoulders slumped. "I like her. We're friends."

"She may be friends with you, but . . . ."

He turned around and leaned against the counter. "But what, little sister?"

"I don't want to see you get hurt."

He snorted softly. "Ginny wouldn't hurt anyone."

"She might not mean to, but she'll break your heart, big brother."

She already has.

Louisa ran her finger along the rim of her glass. It let out a quiet chime. "She looks like she comes from money." His sister looked up at him. "Does she?"

He shrugged. "I really don't know. We haven't talked much about our families. Surface stuff is all."

"Is that why you like her?"

"What do you mean?"

"She doesn't look like any of the girls you've dated before."

He paced away from the counter. "She isn't like anyone I've ever been with. She's funny and smart and incredibly nice." He whirled back to face his sister. "I mean, she's nice to everyone, from the crabbiest resident to the meanest co-worker. She always has a smile." He put his hands on the table and leaned on them. "I don't know if she has money or if she's poor as dirt, and it really doesn't matter one way or the other." He collapsed into a chair and ran his hands over his face. "All I know is she's had her heart broken once before, and as much as I like her, I know I'm not the right guy for her."

Louisa reached over and grabbed his hand. "And, why do you think that?"

"Because she deserves someone as good and honest and nice as she is."

She squeezed his hand. "You're honest and nice."

He let out a pathetic laugh.

"That was the past. You're a different man now. A better man."

"Am I?" He searched his sister's face. "Am I really?"

"I know you are."

Chester pushed himself away from the table and stood. "I used to think that. I used to think that I'd changed, and then . . . ." He struggled to find the right words, then remembered he was talking his sister. "And my love life, or lack thereof, is probably not something I want to talk with you about in detail."

Louisa chuckled. "I must have caught you off guard. You've never been so open before." His sister went to the freezer and took out a package of chocolate mint cookies. "This is the last of them. Good thing the girls will be selling more next month." She opened up a sleeve and popped one into her mouth. "What are you going to do about it?"

Chester slouched in his chair. "Nothing."

Louisa's voice rose. "You have to do something!"

"She doesn't think about me the same way. She had a fiancé who died. She still hasn't gotten over him. I don't think she ever will."

"Well, I'm torn." Louisa nibbled on another mint wafer. "I don't think she's the right girl for you, but I don't want to see you sell yourself short, either." She finished the cookie. "If anyone can mend a broken heart, it would be you, big brother. That's what you do. You fix things."

He let out a long, slow breath. "I don't know. I don't think the time is right."

"Maybe if you dated someone else, it would get your mind off of her."

Chester grabbed a handful of cookies. "No. I don't want to just date someone. Not when I know it can be so much more."

Louisa finished off her milk. "Poor Tina. She'll be disappointed."

CHAPTER NINE

The sign on the wall read *Silent Tears Ministry 7:00-8:30.*
I stood outside the door to the classroom, peeking through its
narrow window. About eight people milled around with
coffee cups and snack-filled napkins. A few sat in chairs
arranged in a circle in the middle of the room. *I don't want to
be here.*

"None of us do," said a voice behind me.

I turned around and found myself face-to-face with a
woman probably in her mid-to-late fifties. "Excuse me?"

Her gentle smile softened her appearance. "None of us
wants to be here. But, it helps."

My face grew warm. "I didn't think I said that out loud."

She chuckled and extended her hand. "I'm Beverly."

"Ginny."

Beverly opened the door. "Come on in. I promise we
won't bite."

Nancy spied me as soon as I stepped into the room.
"Ginny! I'm glad you came!" She embraced me before I had a
chance to say anything. "Do you want some coffee or
something to eat?" She dragged me over to a table in the back
of the room. "Sally Ann made a wonderful zucchini cake."

She handed me a thick slice of what appeared to be chocolate cake.

"This is the way I want to eat all my veggies." I took a bite. "Drowned in chocolate."

Nancy addressed the group. "Okay, gang, let's get started."

The cake turned to lead in my stomach as my nerves got the best of me. Beverly caught my eye and nodded to a chair at her side.

"Relax." She patted my knee after I sat. "You don't have to talk if you don't want to."

The group consisted of eleven people, ranging in age from teens to their seventies. Every segment of society was represented as well, from preppy to grunge. *I guess grief is no discriminator.*

Nancy opened the session with a prayer and then asked those in the group to introduce themselves. The well-coiffed woman to her right spoke first.

"I'm Vanessa." She turned to the Goth teenager sitting next to her. "This is my daughter, Monica. My husband committed suicide."

The businessman beside them spoke next. "I'm Tom. I lost my wife to cancer six months ago."

The sad litany continued around the room. It was a little odd, like some weird variation of Alcoholics Anonymous: *Hello, I'm Ginny, and I'm a griever.*

"Sally Ann. My twin brother, back in August."

"Merideth. My mother last year."

"I'm Nancy. I lost my daughter to leukemia three years ago."

"I'm Steve, and this is my wife Laura. We lost our son to SIDS."

"Terry. My husband died of a heart attack in October."

"I'm Valerie. My best friend was killed in a car wreck."

"I'm Beverly," said the well-dressed woman next to me. "My son killed my husband five years ago." Beverly patted my knee again. "Take your time."

I took a deep breath. "I'm Ginny. My fiancé was killed two years ago in a car accident."

For the next hour, people opened up about how they were trying to move on with their lives with varying degrees of success. Terry, an older woman of probably sixty-five or so, had lost her husband of forty years to a heart attack a couple of months ago. *I have no reason to complain. She's lost everything, not only the love of her life, but her income and security as well.* But, she laughed as she related how her son had taught her to pump gas the other day.

"You've never pumped gas before?" Monica, the Goth teen, asked.

"No." Terry smiled. "My son was very patient, walking me through the steps then making me do it on my own."

Monica still shook her head. "Never before?"

"When the service stations went to self-serve, Andy insisted on pumping my gas. Every Saturday morning, he'd fill my car up and run it through the car wash." At this, Terry's smile faded. "He was old-fashioned that way. Certain jobs were a woman's work, and others were a man's responsibility."

Nancy peeked up at the clock. "I think you deserve our award of the week for that." She walked over to the table and picked up a trophy. It stood about a foot high, with a gold figure on top dunking a basketball. "I should explain to our newcomer. Each week, someone gets to take our trophy home in honor of something they've done to reclaim their lives." She held a fist to her mouth and blew air out, creating a kind of kazoo fanfare. "To Terry Preston, in recognition of learning new skills!"

Everyone clapped and cheered. Sally Ann insisted that people take the leftovers of her zucchini cake home. She'd even brought plastic baggies to put pieces in.

Nancy came over as I put on my coat. "Do you need to leave right away, or can we talk a minute? I'd like to get your e-mail and phone number. It's good to have this time of year, in case we have to cancel because of snow."

Beverly shook my hand before she left. "It was good to meet you, Ginny. I hope you come again."

"Thank you. I'm sure I will."

The room cleared out, and Nancy sat down then handed me a notepad and pen. I wrote down my work e-mail and my cell phone number and passed her back the information.

"What did you think?" Nancy asked.

I shrugged.

"What's that mean?"

"I don't know. I feel weird."

"Why?"

"I feel guilty finding comfort hearing about other people's pain."

"Don't. That's what these meetings are all about. Realizing that you're not the only one feeling crummy."

"Makes my problems seem small."

"I don't want you to negate your own grief." Her forehead wrinkled as she stared at me. "Everyone's pain is different, and you need to experience and work through what you're feeling. You can't force it away."

I looked up at the ceiling. "That's the truth."

"I don't like to ask people to share the first week with the group, but. . . ." she paused. "Do you need to talk about something?"

I played with the buttons on my coat. "Not really."

Nancy cocked her head like a dog listening to a high-pitched whistle. "That wasn't convincing enough. What's on your mind?"

"Nothing important."

She leaned forward, resting her elbows on her knees. "I don't care if it's not important. Let's hear it."

I shook my head. I really didn't want to admit how much I'd been crying lately. It'd just make me start up again. "Maybe some other time. It's getting late, and I have to be in early tomorrow."

She pursed her lips in mock-anger. "Dan said you were a tough nut to crack. But, I like a challenge." She gave me another hug after I stood to go. "You can call me anytime when you're ready to talk. Okay?"

I nodded. "Thanks."

Chester took off his gloves and stuffed them into the pocket of his coat. He slid the zipper down but left the jacket on as he sat down in the lobby of Abundant Grace Church. The clock on the wall read 8:27. He looked around to see if he knew any of the myriad adults milling about the lobby. He did a double-take as Ginny Stafford came up from the basement stairs. She blinked several times before she seemed to recognize him.

"Chester?"

He waved. "What are you doing here?"

She took a seat next to him. "I was going to ask you the same question."

"I'm picking up my nieces. They're in the Christmas pageant this weekend. Tonight was the big dress rehearsal."

She smiled wistfully. "I never got to be in a pageant."

"No?"

She shook her head. "My parents never bothered taking us to church. I was twelve when I went with my Grandma and Grandpa. Too old by then." She nudged him with her shoulder. "How about you? Did you get to be a shepherd?"

He straightened himself up and looked down his nose at her. "I'll have you know I was Melchior." He clarified when he saw her confused expression. "One of the three wise men."

"Well, now, a starring role. I'm impressed."

He chuckled, then furrowed his eyebrows. "What are you doing here?"

She looked down as if studying the carpet.

"You don't go here, do you? I've never seen you here before."

"No." The toe of her boot rubbed against a stain on the floor as if trying to scrub it out. "I came here to a grief counseling group."

"Oh." *Stupid, stupid, stupid! Now what do I say?* He was saved by the appearance of two harried-looking women who opened up the sanctuary doors.

"Thanks for waiting," announced the taller of the two. "We need to have you come inside and sign your kids out before you take them home."

The shorter woman read from her clipboard. "Please, have the children here by eight-thirty Sunday morning with their costumes. We'll do the pageant for both services, so make sure they get a good night's sleep on Saturday."

"*Tio* Chester!" Katy squealed as she peered out from behind the advisors. The tall one put her hand on Katy's head.

"He has to sign you out first."

Katy spied Ginny. "Hey! I know you!"

The rest of the adults crowded into the sanctuary to retrieve their children. Chester rose to collect his nieces. Ginny buttoned her coat as she stood.

"Wait! Don't go yet!" pleaded Katy from the door. "I want to talk to you!"

Chester gave her an apologetic look. "Do you mind?"

She grinned. "Not at all."

Chester made his way through the melee and took Katy's hand. "Let's find your sister and get you signed out."

"The pretty lady's not leaving, is she?" Katy pouted.

"No, she said she'd wait." He wandered through the sanctuary until he found Maria talking with a group of her friends. "Come on, we have to get going."

Marie gave an exasperated sigh and frowned at her friends. "Bye."

Chester signed the girls out, then led them into the lobby. Ginny stood looking out the window. Katy pulled her hand from her uncle's and ran over to her.

"You came to my house!"

Ginny laughed. "Yes, I did."

"You were silly."

Ginny gave the girl a shocked expression. "Me? Silly? I think you must have me confused with someone else. I'm never silly."

"No." His niece's face got serious. "It was you. I'm sure."

Ginny squatted down to Katy's height. "You're right. It was me. How've you been?"

"I'm good. I'm going to be a sheep in the play. You want to come see me? I'm going to sing 'Away in a Manger.' Do you know that song?"

Ginny laughed. "I think I may have heard it before."

"Will you come see me? I have a solo!"

Chester put his hand on his niece's shoulder. "It's kind of last-minute, honey. She probably has plans already."

Ginny smiled weakly. "I can't promise, but I'll try and come."

Katy beamed. "You promise? You'll try?"

Ginny nodded. She stood and flexed her knees.

Chester leaned over and whispered, "You don't have to come. There'll be tons going on Sunday. She won't know if you're here or not."

Katy looked up at Ginny with her eyes wide. "Will you hold my hand?"

"Sure."

Chester turned to get Maria and found her missing. "Give me a minute. I have to find the other one." He spied her in the corner, talking with her friends again. Their heads were down, but they were looking over to where Ginny and Chester stood. "Maria! Let's go!"

When he looked back, Ginny was squatting again in front of Katy, this time zipping up her coat. The little girl got her mittens on and then thrust her hand into Ginny's.

Maria led the way out to the parking lot. She glanced back. "You don't go to this church, do you?"

"No. I was here for a meeting."

"Oh." Maria scrutinized Ginny with the same gaze her mother had.

Chester shivered. "Feels like snow."

Maria looked up at the sky with a hopeful look in her eyes. "Maybe we won't have school tomorrow."

"But, I want school," Katy whined. "Mrs. Prescott said we were going to work on special projects tomorrow."

Ginny stopped. She pulled Katy's hand up with hers and pointed. "My car is down this way." She turned to Chester. "I'll see you at work tomorrow."

He shook his head. "No, you won't."

"Why not?"

"I took the day off, since I'm working all day Saturday. I took Monday off, too." He leaned toward her and said under his breath, "Santa needs to get some shopping done."

"I guess I'll see you Saturday, then, for the open house."

Katy pulled on Ginny's hand. "And Sunday, too! Don't forget!"

"I'll try." She glanced over at Chester. "What time are services?"

"At nine and eleven."

"All right." She pried her hand from his niece's. "I have to go now, but I'll try and come on Sunday."

"It's going to be really good. You'll like it a lot."

Maria waited by the car. "It's freezing! Hurry up!"

"Bye." Ginny waved.

"Good night," called Chester as Ginny made her way in the opposite direction.

He picked Katy up and walked toward the car. She placed her mittened hand on his cheek. "She's beautiful."

He lifted his eyebrows. "You think so?"

"Uh-huh. What's her name again?"

"Ginny."

Katy turned her head and yelled, "Goodbye Ginny! Please come see me again on Sunday!"

Ginny's voice drifted up from the lower parking lot. "Bye, Katy!"

Chester lowered Katy as they got to his car. He pressed the key fob to unlock the doors. Maria blew on her fingers. "I'm freezing."

Chester shrugged. "I told you to wear more than your jean jacket. It's winter, you know?" Maria slid into the front passenger seat. Katy climbed up into her booster, and Chester buckled her in. He gave her a kiss before shutting the door and getting behind the wheel.

"Ginny's going to come to see the pageant on Sunday!" Katy exclaimed from the back seat.

Maria scowled. "No, she's not."

"She said she'd come!"

Chester glanced over his shoulder. "She said she'd try, honey. Don't get your hopes up."

"Yeah, that's what grown-ups always tell you when they're not going to do something," Maria said.

"Why do you have to be like that?" Chester turned out of the parking lot. "If Ginny said she'd try, then she'll try. She doesn't lie."

"Yeah!" Katy stuck her tongue out at her sister.

They rode with Katy singing "Away in the Manger" as the only noise for several minutes. Maria stared out the side window while Chester's mind swam with the hope that Ginny might come to his church on Sunday.

Maria's voice broke through his thoughts. "Do you like her?"

"Who? Ginny?" Chester asked.

"Duh."

"She's a nice lady."

Maria gave him the look that only an annoyed tween can give. "Please. I'm not dumb. You *like* her like her, don't you?"

Although it seemed important to his niece to know, he couldn't bring himself to discuss his feelings about Ginny with an eleven-year-old. "I don't know."

Maria kept silent until Chester stopped at a red light. "Will you ever leave us?"

"What?"

His niece's face grew solemn. "If you ever did find someone you really liked. Would you leave us?"

The car went silent as Katy stopped singing and listened for his answer. "No matter what happens, whether I find someone I want to marry one day, or if your mom finds someone, I will never leave you. *Comprendes?*"

Neither girl answered him. He turned to face them. "I mean it. I don't know what the future holds. I may have to move to another house someday, you guys might move away, but you're stuck with me in your life. I'm your *Tio* Chester. I'll be with you forever."

The car behind them honked as the light turned green. Chester waved his arm. "Yeah, yeah, I'm going."

"You promise?" whispered Maria.

He reached over and squeezed her knee. "I promise, *chiquita*. I promise."

CHAPTER TEN

"It looks wonderful, Ginny," said Susan, our administrator, as she surveyed the lobby and dining room. Her brown eyes gleamed with the excitement of meeting prospective residents.

"Thanks." I could still see things I would have done differently if I'd had a bigger budget, more time, and about twenty more hands, but overall, I was satisfied with my work. I'd put up the lobby's eight-foot Christmas tree at the beginning of the month, but I'd added an oversized lighted wreath over the fireplace. I'd gotten a great deal on poinsettias and filled every bare corner with one of the red flowers. The main office now sported elf and Santa decals, and the coffee tables both had gold baskets with scented pinecones. I frowned as I scanned the room one more time. *At least they're supposed to have baskets.* "Can someone check Margaret Ann's room? I think she's run off with one of the table decorations again."

Susan laughed. "I'll go up in a minute."

I'd removed the round game table where my grandmother and Frank seemed to have taken up residence lately and replaced it with two long buffet tables. A chocolate fountain had already been set up at one end with platters of fresh fruit, marshmallows, and pretzels ready for dipping. Susan's teenaged son stood guard over it, making sure none of the residents dug into the dessert before the party began in another forty-five minutes. Chester was busy preparing hors d'oeuvres and punch for the open house. My mouth watered at the smell of Swedish meatballs and chicken wings emanating from the kitchen.

Susan and I backed up from the doorway as several men came through, pushing a cart loaded with various boxes and instrument cases. A round man with no hair but a huge smile walked up to us.

"I'm Johnny Miles."

"I'm Ginny Stafford. I spoke with you on the phone." I shook his hand. "This is Susan Abels, the facility administrator."

Johnny's grip was firm on my hand, and he pumped it rapidly. "Good to meet you! Good to meet you! Where do you want us to set up?"

Susan left us while I walked the musicians into the dining room. I'd rearranged the tables along the walls to make a space for their portable dance floor. I'd also put up another eight-foot tree. The white lights twinkled from the corner of the room, reflecting off the blue and silver ribbons I'd wrapped around it. I'd never seen musicians work as efficiently as Johnny and his band. The fifteen-by-thirty wooden parquet dance floor appeared in minutes. They set up a stage at one end, with old-timey placards in front of their seats. Johnny Miles' Swing Band was emblazoned on the boards in sparkling red letters.

Chester and his kitchen staff appeared with trays of food. They followed their leader like the pied piper, dodging the various family members and residents who were already making their way down to the party.

Susan tapped me on the shoulder. She held up an empty gold basket. "Margaret Ann had it. I don't know what she did with the pinecones."

I sighed and grabbed it from her. "I'll stick it in my office."

Susan's eyes surveyed me. "You going to change before the party starts?"

I looked down at my jeans and sweater. "Yeah. I brought a dress."

"Go change. I'll hold down the fort until you get back."

Chester straightened the silver chafing dish so it aligned with the one beside it. He looked up at Marianna and Jose behind the table. "Keep an eye on all the dishes. If we start getting low on something, one of you run back to the kitchen and get another tray of it."

Marianna nodded in what appeared to be frustration. "And, when we refill, make sure to take the used tray away. We know, boss. We know."

Chester scowled good-naturedly. "This is an important party. Hopefully, we'll get a lot of outsiders coming to check out the facility. The more people we get in, the more likely you get to keep your jobs next year, *comprendes?*"

Jose and Marianna stood up straighter. "*Comprendo.*"

"*Bueno.*" Chester turned from the table as Ginny came around the corner. He forced his mouth not to drop open at the sight of her. She wore an emerald-green velvet dress that fell below her knees. If it had been any longer, he would have sworn she'd stepped out of a turn-of- the-century painting.

Chester didn't know much about women's clothing, but he knew what he liked, and he liked the way the dress seemed to accentuate Ginny's slender waist and round hips. A cameo necklace hung around her neck on a green ribbon. A few wisps of red hair fell free of the French braid she'd put it in, and they framed her face nicely.

"Ay yi yi," whispered Jose.

"*Si,*" mumbled Chester.

Ginny didn't seem to notice the attention she was drawing as she made her way through the lobby and back into the dining room. The band was already warming up, and Johnny had put on a CD of their music as they finished some last-minute tuning.

Chester continued to watch Ginny as she flitted about the dining room, straightening tables and helping several residents find seats. Bill startled him.

"When can we get some grub?"

Chester tried to pull his thoughts away from Ginny and back to the job at hand. "Right now. Plates are down on the other end. Help yourself!"

Frank stood as Edith made her way toward him. "You look festive." White snowflakes glittered on her black sweater. She wore red Christmas light earrings to match her red skirt.

"Ginny bought me this outfit last year. We both agreed the earrings would give my daughter Joyce a conniption. I can't wait to wear them to her house!"

"You are so bad." Frank chuckled.

Edith raised an eyebrow. "You haven't met my daughter. I don't know how such an uppity, self-centered creature ever came from me or my husband."

Frank pulled a chair out for her to sit on. "I don't know how someone like that could raise a daughter as nice as Ginny."

"Ginny's always been a special girl, even as a child. Very loving. I don't know if she could have survived it, though, if her parents had stayed together."

Frank sat down. "What do you mean?"

"Neither has empathy for anyone else. When they divorced, Joyce said she couldn't handle the children on her own. Ginny and her oldest brother Simon came to live with Lloyd and me on our farm out in Iowa. James went to live with his father."

"That's why Ginny turned out so good!" Frank smiled fondly. "She had you to help her."

Edith nodded slightly at the compliment. "A lot of it was God's hand on them, but I must admit, Simon and Ginny did blossom under our care. The two of them are wonderful people. Simon worked as a missionary to the inner-city when he first graduated from high school. He went on to college and got a counseling degree. He works in a church-sponsored halfway house now. And Ginny . . . ." Edith glanced over to where her granddaughter stood in the dining room threshold, welcoming guests. "Well, you know all about her."

"What happened to her other brother? James, was it?"

Edith shook her head. "Turned out like his father. He's successful, at least in the world's eyes." She toyed with the green napkin on the table. "But, as a human being, he leaves a lot to be desired. He's over thirty, drinks heavily, has been in a string of relationships and even fathered a child he never sees."

"Funny how kids can turn out so different, isn't it?"

"Funny...."

Frank leaned forward. "So, you ready to put our plan into action?"

"Of course." She looked at the empty dance floor. "But what if no one dances? Can we still pull it off?"

"I know I can get Chester to dance with you." Frank nodded. "Even with no one else out there. He's a softy, and I'll claim my bum leg hurts too much to dance with you myself."

"What bum leg?" asked Edith.

"I don't have one." Frank laughed "But, Chester doesn't know that!"

She swatted his arm. "You're awful!"

"You want to get Chester and Ginny together, don't you? A little white lie might be necessary. I'll only tell it if I have to. Now, what about Ginny?"

"Oh, I know she'll dance with you if you ask her. She loves to dance." Her smile faded. "At least, she used to."

"Don't worry," Frank placed his hand over hers. "She will again."

∽

"I'd say this party has been a success, and it's not even over yet!" crowed Susan as she caught my arm in the lobby.

"Everyone seems to be having a good time." I glanced at the clock. Three-thirty – another half-hour to go.

"Karen and I have both given tours, and I have another two scheduled for next week!"

"Excellent!"

Susan nodded. "You done good, kid." She pointed to the dining room. "Looks like you're wanted by someone."

Bill waved me over to his table. "Hi, doll. I'd like you to meet my grandchildren."

He introduced me to the two girls and one boy at his table. They all appeared to be college-aged.

"You home on break?" I asked

They nodded, and we talked briefly about what schools they went to and what they were studying. I couldn't help notice Bill swaying to the music and singing along with the band. Although the dance floor had been crowded earlier, many of the residents had headed back to their rooms, not used to being active for that long in the afternoon. I glanced back at Bill.

"You look like you want to dance."

He smiled impishly. "You offering, doll face?"

I shook my head. "Why not ask one of these young ladies?"

The two girls gave me the classic "deer in the headlights" look. "I don't dance," they said simultaneously.

"Come on," pleaded Bill. "Humor an old man."

I stood and pushed his walker out of the way. "All right, but no dipping!"

He laughed. "You got a deal!"

We did a kind of modified two-step along with the band's rendition of "Beer Barrel Polka" that segued into "Roll Out the Barrel." I did my best to support Bill while still letting him lead.

"Now's our chance," said Edith as she eyed Bill and Ginny on the dance floor. "Where's Chester?"

"Over there by the kitchen, watching her of course."

"Let me see if I can woo him with my feminine charms. Then you won't have to lie." Edith smiled coyly as she stood from the table. She walked toward Chester. "Excuse me, young man, but I'd like to ask a favor."

"There's no more cheesecake, if that's what you're asking for." Chester lifted his hands in exasperation. "You'd be the fifth person to ask me."

"No, it's not that." She looked down at the floor. "I was wondering if you might be willing to dance with me. I can't seem to get my tablemate interested."

Chester shot Frank a look. "Is that so? Being stubborn, is he?"

"Yes. And I'd dearly love to dance."

Chester held out his hand. "I would be honored, my lady."

Edith placed her hand in his. "Why, thank you, young man."

They arrived on the dance floor as the music changed into "Moon River." Chester smiled. "Oh, good. I'm much better at the slow songs than the polkas."

Out of the corner of her eye, Edith spied Frank cutting in on Bill and her granddaughter. She kept Chester's back to them so he couldn't see Frank maneuvering Ginny across the dance floor until they almost bumped into each other.

Edith looked down her nose at Frank. "Well, fancy meeting you here. I thought you didn't want to dance."

Frank's eyes twinkled. "That's before I saw you up here with another man. I got jealous." He nudged Chester with his shoulder. "Would you mind trading partners?"

Chester looked down at Ginny. "What do you think?"

She gave him a mischievous smile. "It'd be fine with me."

Chester glanced at Edith. "Would you like to dance with this old coot?"

"I suppose so," she said with an exaggerated sigh.

☙

Chester took my right hand and placed his other hand on the small of my back. "Thanks for doing this." I told him. "I'm really hoping Frank and my grandmother might develop a relationship."

"It's my pleasure," he said as he led me away to the strains of "Moonlight in Vermont." I kept my focus on Edith and her partner. My grandmother had a huge smile on her face, and Frank grinned like the Cheshire Cat. "Something's up."

"Hmmm?" mumbled Chester.

"My grandmother and Frank. They look very satisfied about something."

"Maybe they're happy to be together. That's what you want, isn't it?"

"Yeah." I turned toward him. My breath caught in my throat. I'd never seen Chester look at me the way he was now. It only lasted a moment before a kind of curtain dropped, but that moment was electric.

He watched me, his eyes now guarded. "What's wrong?" His hand pressed against my back to turn me across the floor. Tiny shivers shot up my spine. I gripped his hand tighter and tried to take a breath. He slowed his steps until we merely swayed. "Are you all right?"

I nodded. "Fine."

"You sure?"

"Uh-huh." I couldn't stop watching his face. Would I see it again? Did I want to see it again?

Someone came up behind Chester and tapped his shoulder. "Do you mind if I cut in?"

A look of annoyance crossed Chester's eyes, but he graciously stepped aside. "Sure."

The tall, older man who took my hand seemed familiar. "My name's Patrick. I'm Rachel Johnson's son.

"I met you briefly in the hall last week. I'm Ginny." He didn't have the same grace that Chester had, and I regretted his intrusion. I tried to hide my frustration. "How long are you visiting?"

He grinned. "I'm not visiting. I'm moving back to Omaha."

"That's right. Your sister told me. Your mother will be happy."

Patrick pulled me in a shade closer. "I hope she's not the only one."

I turned away from him, watching Chester as he walked toward the kitchen. "I'm sure your sister is glad as well. It will take some of the burden off of her with your mother."

"I plan on being a frequent visitor. Especially now."

I didn't acknowledge his not-so-subtle flirtation. Instead, I let my gaze roam around the room, checking to see who remained and how much cleanup I'd have to do. I noticed Rachel was nowhere to be seen. "Where's your mother?"

"She's back in her room, taking a nap."

"And your sister?"

"Gone home."

My stomach tightened into a knot as I realized I was the reason he'd stayed. He stood several inches taller than me, and when I looked up, I found his hazel eyes watching me. He attempted to spin me out and back into his chest, but I managed to keep a respectable distance between us. Patrick's advances added to my already jangled nerves. I couldn't get the look in Chester's eyes out of my mind. He'd looked at me the way Mark used to. A rock lodged itself in my stomach. *Did I imagine it? Am I making more out of this than I should?* I sighed with relief when Johnny announced that the last twenty minutes would be a carol sing. "That's my cue. I have to get started on the cleanup."

Patrick held onto my hand. "That other guy. Is he your boyfriend?"

"Who? Chester?"

"Was that his name? The guy you were dancing with?"

I nodded.

"Are you seeing him?"

"No." I shook my head. "We're friends." I tried to move away, but Patrick kept a firm grip on my hand.

"Are you dating anyone?"

"No. I mean yes." I shrugged. "Kind of."

He laughed. "What does that mean?

I shook my head again. "I've been on a couple of dates with this guy, but it's nothing serious."

"So, could I stop by sometime? Maybe take you to dinner?"

"I don't know." I pulled my hand from his. "I really need to go." I hurried off the dance floor and made my way to the lobby. Karen and Susan stood by the doorway, shaking hands with the guests on their way out.

"Oh, look!" Karen grinned when she saw me. "It's the belle of the ball!"

Susan nodded. "You had them eating out of your hand. Lucky duck!"

I didn't know why her comment bothered me, but it did. Against the laws of nature, the rock in my stomach grew in size until it obstructed my breathing. My heart pounded. My palms sweated.

"Are you okay?" Karen asked. "You don't look good."

I put my hand on my chest and tried to suck in some air. I made a horrible gasping sound.

Karen came up and placed her arm around my shoulder. "Let's get you a seat."

I shook my head. "Not here. My office." My breath came in short, rapid pants. *I'm hyperventilating! This has never happened to me before!*

Karen helped me away from the crowd of curious onlookers and back to my office. She sat me on one of the chairs in front of my desk while she took the one opposite. "Put your head between your knees."

I followed her command. *At least the room's stopped spinning.* My breath slowed a bit. "What happened to me?"

She pressed her hand on the back of my neck. "I'm not sure, but I think you had a panic attack."

My head popped up. "What?"

She forced me down again. "The hyperventilating and sudden sweating are symptoms. Was your heart racing?"

"All of a sudden."

She picked up my hand and checked my pulse. "You feeling better now?"

"Uh-huh."

"I'm going to get you a glass of water. You stay there."

I waited until she returned.

"Try sitting up."

I lifted my head slowly. Besides a few brightly colored dots buzzing around the periphery of my vision, I felt okay. Karen handed me a cup of water. I took a sip. "I don't get it. I've never had a panic attack before. Why now?"

The head nurse shrugged. "Stress, probably. It's been a crazy month and an extra-busy day. More than likely, your body needed to release some tension."

"Stress, huh?"

"That's my guess. Once the holidays are over, you ought to take a couple of vacation days. Maybe go someplace warm and relax."

"You think?"

"Couldn't hurt." She patted my knee. "You going to be okay?"

I nodded.

"I'm going to help with the cleanup. I'm sure we can handle it. Why don't you stay here a bit longer, catch your breath, and then head home?"

"I can help," I offered.

Karen scowled. "I'm the nurse, and I'm telling you to go home. You've done enough today." She stood to leave. "Really, I'm sure we can handle it."

I took another sip of water. "All right."

Chester wiped down the last of the countertops and threw the washcloth into the laundry basket. He stepped out into the dining room, pleased to see his kitchen staff had vacuumed the floor, washed down the tables, and reset the room for breakfast tomorrow. He wheeled out the carts holding sack dinners for the residents. After the full meal served at lunch, as well as the buffet throughout the afternoon, sandwiches were all the dining staff would serve from now until Sunday morning.

Susan approached him and shook his hand. "Good job today! The food was excellent. Everyone raved about the meatballs. Were they from the food service?"

"No." Chester grinned. "My own secret recipe."

Susan's eyes grew wide. "Even the sauce?"

He nodded.

"Well, my friend, you could make a mint off of those. They were awesome."

"There's some left in the fridge." He gestured with his head to the kitchen. "Behind the middle door on the lower shelf."

"I might take a few home for dinner tonight!" She smiled. "Thanks again for everything."

"*De nada*," he replied. He walked out into the lobby, looking for Ginny. He hadn't seen her since their dance, and he wanted to say goodbye and give her Katy's plea that she attend the pageant tomorrow. Frank and Edith sat at their corner table, the backgammon board laid out in front of them. "Have you seen Ginny?"

Edith frowned. "No, but I don't think she's left yet."

Frank looked up at him. "You're quite the dancer, young man. Where'd you learn to move like that?"

"It's a gift." Chester grinned and swayed his hips. "It's my natural Latin rhythm."

Frank and Edith chuckled together.

Susan came out from the dining room, carrying a ball of tinfoil. She lifted it toward Chester. "Thanks for dinner!"

"Have you seen Ginny?" he asked.

The administrator glanced quickly at Edith. "I think she might have left already."

Edith shook her head. "She wouldn't have left without saying goodbye. She must be here somewhere."

A worry crease formed along Susan's forehead. "She might be in her office."

"Can I talk to you a minute?" Chester asked. He turned back to the couple at the table. "Have a good night."

"*Adios, amigo!*" said Frank. Edith didn't say anything, but a look of concern spread across her face.

Chester and Susan walked down the hallway. He spoke in a hushed tone. "What's wrong?"

"It's nothing. I don't want Edith to worry about her."

"What happened?"

Susan paused by her office door and slipped off her shoes. "Sorry, these heels are killing me." She picked them up and let them dangle off her fingertips. "I don't know what happened. We teased her about all the attention she'd been getting, and the next thing I knew, she looked like she was going to pass out."

Chester turned toward Ginny's office as Susan said, "I was going to check on her. . . ." Her footsteps whispered on the carpet behind him as he knocked on the door.

"Ginny?"

A muffled groan came from the office. Chester fought back his own panic and pushed open the door. "Ginny?"

She spun her chair around to the wall. He couldn't see her face.

Susan came in behind him. "Are you okay? Should I try and find Karen?"

Ginny's head shook. "No." She took a deep breath. "I'm fine."

Chester stepped around to the side of the desk, trying to get a look at her. "What's wrong?" She hid her face in her hands, but not before he'd seen her puffy eyes and the tears still on her cheeks. It broke his heart. "*Por favor,*" he pleaded, "let me help you." He put his hand on her shoulder. Her chest heaved.

"I'll be okay." She turned around and grabbed a tissue. "Really. It's just hormones. The holidays."

Chester didn't believe her. "Did that guy say something to you to get you upset?"

She actually let out a giggle. "No. No. I don't know what's wrong." She blew her nose. "I'm being irrational. I'll be fine after a good night's sleep, I'm sure."

Susan took his arm. "Let's leave her alone."

He couldn't take his eyes off of Ginny. "Are you sure you'll be okay? You want someone to drive you home?"

She didn't meet his gaze but shook her head. "No. I'll stay here a bit longer. I'll be fine in a minute."

Susan pulled him from the room. "You take it easy tomorrow, kiddo. If you're still not feeling up to snuff on Monday, you take the day off. We'll manage without you somehow."

Chester and Susan left my office, shutting the door behind them. *Well, that was humiliating. I'm sure he thinks I'm a total lunatic now. But, then again, what does it matter? I wasn't looking for a relationship, was I?* More tears came from I didn't know where. *What is the matter with me lately? I've never cried like this. Not even when Mark . . . .*

I froze, in the middle of reaching for another tissue. *This has something to do with Mark, doesn't it? But, what?* I sat in my chair for a while. It wasn't until the snot running from my nose tickled my upper lip that I actually completed the act of grabbing the Kleenex. I couldn't get a grip on my thoughts or my emotions, and I didn't know what to do about it, when Nancy Donaldson's name popped into my head.

Nancy?

Call her.

I barely know her. She'll think I'm a freak. Besides, she's probably busy. It's a Saturday night, and she has a husband.

Call her.

I pulled my purse up from under the desk. *If I find her number right away, I'll call her.* I had pulled her card out of my wallet before I'd gone to the meeting on Thursday. It had probably floated down to the bottom of my bag by now. I unlatched the flap and saw the purple card with silver lettering sitting on top of the stuff in my purse. *It's probably her business number, anyway. A line at the church. I'll have to leave a message.*

My hand trembled as I picked up the phone. I dialed with care, not wanting to face the humiliation of a wrong number on top of everything else today. The phone rang. *I should hang up.* It rang again. *I'll give it one more ring, then I'm hanging up.*

"Hello?"

In my head, I swore. "Nancy?"

"This is Nancy."

"It's Ginny Stafford." I tried to steady my voice. I was going to add, "Father Dan's friend," but she interrupted me.

"Oh, hi!"

She sounded glad to hear from me, at least. But, maybe she was a good actress.

"Sorry if I sounded rude at first. I couldn't figure out what 'Marigold Manor' could mean on the Caller ID."

My hand stopped trembling. "Sorry about that. I'm calling from work."

"What can I do for you?"

What could she do?

"Ginny? You okay?"

"I'm not sure."

"What's wrong, sweetie?"

Sweetie? Nobody'd called me Sweetie in a long time. Maybe never.

"Ginny?"

"I don't know what's wrong. I can't seem to stop crying, and all I could think of to do was to call you. I'm sorry."

"It's fine." I heard the clatter of silverware and the beep of an oven or microwave timer. "Marigold is off of 370, isn't it? In Papillion?"

I nodded, then realized she couldn't see the gesture. "Yeah."

"I'm only about ten minutes from you. Why don't you stop by?"

"I don't want to bother you."

She chuckled. "It's no bother. Luke is out with the youth group tonight, and I'm home alone, listening to Christmas carols and making cookies. I'd love the company."

"Are you sure?"

"I wouldn't ask if I weren't sure. Let me give you directions."

CHAPTER ELEVEN

I slipped out of Marigold with only a wave to my grandmother. I'd have to call her later and explain. I found the Donaldsons' house without a problem. White icicle lights hung from the second story eave, and a Christmas tree stood in the center of a picture window. I walked up the front steps to the split-level house and rang the bell.

"Come on in!" Nancy yelled.

The comforting smell of warm cookies greeted me when I stepped inside the small foyer. A flight of stairs to the right led to the second floor. A flight to my left must have gone down to the basement. Nancy poked her head around the corner of the kitchen.

"Sorry! Make yourself comfy. I have to get another batch into the oven!" She disappeared behind the wall. I hung my coat over the stair railing and slipped off my shoes. An oven door closed, and I heard the beeping of a timer being set.

"There." Nancy sighed. She came out of the kitchen and wrapped me in a hug as I got to the top of the stairs. She rubbed my back as she squeezed me, and I couldn't believe more tears started to fall.

"I'm sorry."

Nancy continued to rub my back. "What are you sorry for?"

"For barging over like this. For weeping uncontrollably." I half-giggled, half-sobbed as I backed away from her. "I'm a mess."

She took in my appearance, then tilted her head to the side. "Well, I must say, being in the ministry I've seen my share of distraught people, but never one that looked so classy."

I looked down and realized I hadn't changed out of my green velvet dress. "We had an open house at work today."

"I wish I was tall like you and could carry something like that off. I'd drown in all that velvet." She led me into the kitchen and pulled out a chair next to a table covered in mixing bowls and various baking supplies. Opening a drawer, she found an apron and threw it toward me. "Better put this on. I'd never forgive myself if you ruined that dress."

I slipped the apron over my head and tied it around my waist. Nancy handed me a wad of tissues, then turned and pulled a spoonful of dough from one of the bowls. She rolled it in her hands. "Now, tell me what's going on." She plopped the dough ball on a baking sheet and dipped the spoon in the bowl for more.

I blew my nose. "I don't know what set me off. One minute I'm dancing, the next I'm having a panic attack."

"Dancing?"

I nodded.

"With who?"

"First it was Frank, one of our residents. Then Chester." My breath caught in my throat and I made a kind of hiccupping sound. "And then this guy Patrick. He's the son of one of the residents."

"All this was this afternoon?" Nancy rolled the dough balls she'd made in powdered sugar and placed them back on the cookie sheet.

"Uh-huh."

Her hands kept working on the cookies, but she kept her focus on me. Her eyes narrowed as she finished rolling the last dough ball. After switching out the pan with one in the oven, she wiped her hands on a dish towel, and sat down at the table. Then, resting her elbows on her knees, she leaned toward me. "Tell me about Chester."

"What?"

"Who is he?"

My heart skipped erratically. "He's the chef at Marigold."

"And?"

"What?" I rubbed my chest, trying to loosen the muscles so I could breathe right again.

Nancy sat back in her chair. "There's something going on with this guy Chester. What is it?"

"I don't know what you mean."

Nancy didn't say anything. She just sat there, staring at me with those big brown eyes of hers.

I picked at some dried dough stuck on the table, scraping it off with my fingernail. "I think he goes to your church." I could hear gears whirring in her head as she tried to make the connection.

"Chester Martin? Medium height, dark complexion, mustache?"

"That's him. Frank wanted to dance with my grandmother, who was dancing with Chester. We switched partners."

"And?"

I flicked the dough off my fingers. More unwanted tears rolled down my cheeks. I grabbed another tissue and dried my face. "He looked at me."

Nancy shook her head. "Looked at you? How?"

"I can't be sure. It happened so fast. I'd been watching Frank and my grandmother dance and then I turned . . . ." The rock was back in my stomach. "Chester was looking at me . . . the way Mark used to." I tried to take a deep breath but only succeeded in several small gasps. "I never thought I'd see that look again."

"Why not?"

"It would be too much to find that kind of love twice."

"With God, all things are possible."

I stood and took a step toward the sink. Pointing to the stack of bowls and utensils piled in the basin, I asked, "Can I wash these for you?"

"If it'll keep you talking, sure."

I pulled the stuff out and ran the hot water. I added a couple of squirts of dishwashing liquid. Once the bubbles got nice and high, I turned off the water and drowned the dishes. "Can I say something to you? I'm not sure how to say it without it offending you, and I don't mean to do that. It's mostly things that I've been thinking about and need to get off my chest."

"Go ahead."

I pushed the sleeves of my dress up past my elbows, then plunged my hands into the hot, soapy water. "I don't trust God."

Nancy got up from the table. She took the warm cookies from the sheet on top of the oven and dipped them in powdered sugar again. "What do you mean?"

"I can't risk being with someone. How do I know God won't take him from me again?" I scrubbed a bowl, then rinsed it out in the adjoining sink.

She put the newly dipped cookies onto a rack to cool. "God didn't kill Mark."

My hands attacked another bowl. "But, he let it happen."

"But, he didn't kill Mark."

"He could have stopped it."

Nancy finished with the cookies as the timer buzzed. She pulled the last batch out of the oven and placed them on top of the other cookie sheet while I continued to wash dishes. She wiped her hands on her apron. "Ginny, look at me."

I turned to face her.

"Can you say it? Can you tell me that God didn't kill Mark?"

My whole body shivered.

"Why do you think God killed him?"

My mind filled with images of Mark's body in the hospital. Pictures I'd imagined of the man I loved on the side of the road. Dying alone.

"Why, Ginny? Why would a good God kill the man you love?"

"I don't know!" I wanted to get away before my grief and anger consumed me. I brushed past Nancy. She stumbled back and hit the baking sheet. The pan rattled against the stove. I reached forward to keep the cookies from falling, but I was too late. The tray clattered to the floor. Russian tea cakes rolled everywhere. I dropped to my knees.

"Nancy," I sobbed. "I'm sorry. I didn't mean to." I grabbed several cookies and held them out to her. She threw them onto the counter. Using a dish towel, she picked up the baking sheet and put it back on the stove. We sat on the floor amidst crumbs and powdered sugar. Nancy leaned against the oven door, then quickly sat back up.

"It's still hot." She put a hand on my knee. "I'm sorry, too. I shouldn't have pushed you so hard."

"It's okay." I picked up a cookie. I stared at it for a moment before glancing at Nancy. "Does the five-second rule apply to your kitchen floor?"

She gave me a quizzical look then giggled. "Sure." She found a cookie and popped it in her mouth.

I ate the one I had in my hand. "These are really good." I reached for another that had rolled by my knee.

"They're not bad, are they?"

Between the two of us, we ate a half-dozen tea cakes as we sat on the floor.

"You want some milk?"

"Sure."

She went to the refrigerator, while I surveyed the cookie carnage around me. I tried to scoop up some of the crumbs.

"Leave it." Nancy pulled a gallon of milk from the fridge. "I'll get the broom in a minute."

I pulled my legs up to my chest and rested my chin on my knees. "Do you trust Him?"

"Who? God?"

I nodded.

"Oh, yeah."

"But...what if it happens again? What if you have another kid, and . . . ."

"And the baby dies? Or is killed in an accident?" She passed me a glass of milk. "I wouldn't understand it. But, I would trust God."

"How?" I chewed on my lower lip. "I mean, why does He let this kind of pain exist?"

"Because we chose it."

I put the milk down. "I didn't choose this."

"You're choosing it now."

I looked up. "What?"

Her face wrinkled with worry. "Now, it's my turn to ask you not to get angry, okay?"

I steadied my breath. "I'll try."

"You're choosing to live inside yourself, trapped with this pain. Alone." She sat down in front of me. "It sounds like God might be offering you the chance to experience love again, and you're too afraid to take the risk."

"I know this pain. I can live with it." I closed my eyes. "I can't handle any more. I'll break."

"I don't think that's true." She must have scooted up beside me, because her arm wrapped around my shoulders. "Besides, it's a crummy way to live your life. Always afraid."

"Why does it have to hurt so much?"

"That's why they call it faith, sweetie. We can't understand it all." Her arm squeezed me tighter. "And it helps to know that God's been through it, too. He suffered. He experienced grief. He knows what you're going through, and that's why Jesus died on the cross, so that we could have the promise of a better life."

"I used to believe that." More tears fell.

"I think you still do."

"I don't understand what's been happening to me." I wiped my eyes. "I've cried every day since Thanksgiving."

Nancy took her arm from my shoulders and leaned back against the cupboards. "I think you're going through some survivor's guilt."

"Huh?"

"You're feeling guilty because you're still alive. You get to live your life, while Mark doesn't."

I pondered that for a minute. I guessed she was right in some respects, but there was something else. *How can I explain it when I don't understand it myself?*

Nancy watched me. "What are you thinking?"

"I had a plan before. With Mark. I knew who I was. What I wanted." I brushed powdered sugar off my dress. "I feel like a part of me died, too. I think I'm mourning for the person I was before all this happened. Does that sound crazy?"

She shook her head. "Not at all."

I sighed. "I went on autopilot when Mark died. I took my finals, then started the spring semester right away because I'd already made out my schedule before the accident. I couldn't tell you what classes I took, but I went to all of them."

I crossed my arms over my knees and rested my head on the crook of my elbow. "You want to hear something strange?" I didn't wait for her answer. "I didn't cry. Only the first night, at the hospital. But not at the wake, not at the graveside." Not in the weeks and months that had followed.

"When did you quit school?" asked Nancy.

"After that spring semester. I had a job in the admin office. I did that for a while but by July, I'd sort of turned into a zombie. The only thing I kept doing was going to Marigold to visit with my grandmother. I'd help out with the activities. That's how I got my job."

"It's normal to grieve what you've lost. It's a part of letting go."

I ached. My head hurt. My eyelids were puffing shut from all the crying I'd done over the past couple of hours. "Will it last much longer?"

Nancy chuckled softly. "I don't know, sweetie. Everyone is different. But, it helps that you're talking about it now."

"What do I do about Chester?"

"What do you want to do?"

"I'm too tired to think anymore. I'm not sure whether I really saw what I think I saw, anyway."

She leaned forward so her face was level with mine. "You want my advice?"

I nodded.

"Play it cool for a while, until you know how you feel about him. Get to know him better as a friend."

"Sounds like a good plan."

Nancy smiled. "Besides, it'll give me time to probe Luke to find out anything about him. Whether he's dating anyone, stuff like that."

"Okay." I tried unsuccessfully to stifle a yawn. "His niece wants me to come see her in the pageant tomorrow. Should I go?"

Nancy's grin widened. "Of course I think you should come!"

"I'm nervous about sitting with Chester, though."

"Then sit with me. I'll wait for you in the lobby."

We were interrupted by the sound of the front door opening. Luke's voice called up the stairs. "Hey, honey! I'm home!"

"We're up here!"

Luke appeared as he made his way up to the second floor. His brow furrowed as he stared at his wife and me sitting on the floor covered in powdered sugar and cookie crumbs. "Everything okay?"

Nancy looked around the kitchen and giggled. It was contagious. Luke seemed to get more confused.

"It's my fault." I tried to speak through my laughter. "I tossed her cookies!"

Nancy snorted and grabbed her sides. I started to cry again, but for the first time in weeks it wasn't because I was sad.

⁓

"It's your turn," said Frank.

Edith blinked. "What?"

He pointed to the board. "It's your roll."

Edith looked down at the backgammon board and sighed. "My mind's not on the game tonight. I forfeit."

Frank sat back in his chair. "What's wrong?"

She pursed her lips. "It's Ginny. I think we pushed too hard."

"It was only a dance."

"Did you see the way she ran out of here? With only a wave goodbye? That's not like her at all. She was upset. And, it's my fault. It was too soon."

Frank reached over and took her hand. "She'll be fine. If she was crying, it was probably for the best."

"How do you figure that?"

He rubbed his thumb along the back of Edith's hand. Even with the wrinkles of age her skin felt soft. "Sometimes people need to cry before they can let go of someone."

"You could be right. I cried every night for months after Lloyd died."

Frank continued to stare at their joined hands. "I didn't cry much after I lost Lucy. She'd had Alzheimer's for so long...I guess I'd already said my goodbyes to the woman who'd been my wife. The person that was left was only a shell of the woman I'd loved."

Edith tightened her grip. "How long were you married?"

"Fifty-one years." He lifted his gaze. "You?"

Her eyes met his. "Forty-three."

"Long time."

"Yes."

"Do you think it's possible . . . ." Frank took a deep breath. "For a person to find love again after a lifetime with someone else?"

Edith blinked. "I don't know." Her cheeks turned a rosy color. "I'd like to think it's possible."

The corner of Frank's mouth rose in a half-smile. "I'd like to think so, too."

The grandfather clock across the lobby chimed eight times. Edith sighed. "It's been a busy day. Perhaps we should call it a night?"

"If you insist." He stood and picked up the remains of the sandwich they had shared earlier, putting them into the brown paper bag. "Do you want to take the cookie home for later?"

"No, thank you." Edith rubbed her stomach. "I can't put on any more weight this holiday, or I won't fit into any of my clothes."

"You look terrific."

"You're being too kind, but I know what's true. My pants won't zip up soon if I keep eating like I've been doing."

Frank watched her for a moment, wanting to say more but not having the courage. "Shall we play again tomorrow? After church?"

"That would be fine." She turned to go. "Oh, wait. Our church is having pot luck tomorrow."

"We could make it later. Say three or four?"

"Let's say four and then we can go in for dinner."

"It's a da – deal" He almost said date, but at the last moment changed the word. "I'll see you then. Four o'clock."

She gave him a little wave. "Goodnight."

"Goodnight."

He watched as Edith walked down the hallway toward her room. *She is still a fine- looking woman.* He sighed, grabbed the cookie from the table, and threw the sack into the garbage. He picked up the backgammon board and headed back to his apartment.

Am I being a sentimental old fool? Frank took one more glance at Edith as she turned the corner. *What's the point of falling in love at my age?*

CHAPTER TWELVE

Katy bounded toward Louisa and Chester. The white cotton balls on her headband jiggled as she ran. "How was I?"

"*Muy bueno*," said Louisa.

Chester swept her up into his arms. "Terrific." He kissed her cheek. "You were the prettiest lamb up there."

Maria walked over. She'd returned her wings and angel halo to one of the directors but still wore the white cotton tunic. "I'm glad that's over."

Louisa gave her eldest daughter a hug, which Maria quickly squirmed out of.

"Did Ginny come to see this one?" Katy asked.

Chester sighed. "I didn't see her. She wasn't feeling well yesterday. She's probably still in bed."

Katy pouted. "I wanted her to come."

"I know, sweetheart." Chester kissed the top of her head. "Would pancakes help?"

The little girl nodded. "And hot chocolate."

"I want waffles," said Maria.

Chester grinned. "Pancakes and waffles and chocolate! Oh my!"

Maria shook her head. "You are so weird." She pulled off her angel's tunic and dropped it in the pile by the stairs.

"Are you sure that's where it goes?" asked Louisa.

"Yes, mother," Maria sighed. "Mrs. Hill is going to take them home to wash before they pack them away."

"I was just checking," said Louisa as the family made their way back up to the lobby through the crowded stairwell.

"There you are!" a voice called as they marched up the next flight. Nancy waved at them. "There's someone here who wants to see the pageant stars!"

Katy giggled. "Who is it?"

"Come see." Nancy leaned over to Chester. "She had kind of an emotional night last night. Head's a little sore. Thought I'd look out for you rather than have her try and wade through this madhouse."

His eyes followed to where Nancy's were focused. Ginny sat at the back of the sanctuary. Another woman tapped Nancy on the shoulder.

"Can I talk to you a moment?"

Nancy excused herself as Chester and his family walked toward the sanctuary. Ginny stood when she spotted them.

"Hi there! I have something for you." She turned around and lifted two packages of tissue paper off of the seat behind her. She presented one to Maria and one to Katy. "I always liked seeing my friends get flowers after a performance."

"Wow! Yellow roses!" Maria exclaimed. "They're beautiful."

Chester had to duck his head as Katy grabbed her bouquet. He set his niece down so she could have more room to examine the flowers. He glanced up at Ginny. "You didn't have to do that."

She raised one shoulder. "It was my pleasure." She looked at the girls. "I enjoyed the pageant. You two were great."

Maria sniffed her flowers. "I didn't do much."

"I had a drama teacher who insisted that there are no small parts, only small actors," said Ginny. "I watched you. You were never late on a singing cue, and you followed what was going on. That's important."

Katy tugged on Ginny's coat. "What about me?"

Ginny crouched down beside the girl. "You, my dear, sang beautifully. Your solo in 'Away in the Manger' was truly magnificent."

"Is that good?"

Ginny nodded. "That's very, very good."

Katy embraced her, squishing her flowers between them. "I'm glad you came. I knew you would."

Ginny rose. She smiled at Louisa. "You have two talented daughters."

"Thank you."

Ginny started to button her coat. "I won't keep you. I wanted to tell the girls how much I enjoyed their performance."

Katy grabbed her hand. "Come to breakfast with us!"

Louisa pulled her away. "Now, honey, she probably has things to do."

"Everyone has to eat!" Katy pleaded.

Chester stepped forward. "Would you like to come? We're going to Village Inn for brunch."

Ginny's eyes met his then lowered quickly. "I don't want to intrude."

He smiled broadly. "We wouldn't have invited you if we didn't want you to come." He glanced at his sister. "Right?"

"I'd love to get to know you better." Louisa grinned slyly toward her brother.

Katy tugged on Ginny's coat. "Please?"

Even Maria commented. "Please, come. Then I won't have to entertain her."

Ginny laughed. "If you're sure."

Chester clapped his hands together. "Good. That's settled. We're going to the Inn over on Fort Crook. Do you know where it is?"

She nodded. "I'll meet you there."

They trooped out to the parking lot together. The sun shone pale yellow against a gray sky. Chester and his family piled into Louisa's van while Ginny went to her car.

Minutes later, Chester sat at a large corner booth, watching Ginny walk through the parking lot. She stopped, dug her cell phone from her purse, then answered it with an annoyed look on her face. After talking for a moment, she threw the phone back in her bag and came into the restaurant.

Katy jumped up on the cushioned bench and waved. "Over here!"

Ginny wove through the waitresses and customers. "Busy place." She slipped off her coat and slid in next to Katy. Chester sat opposite them, next to Maria. Louisa occupied the middle spot, mostly to act as referee between her girls.

Katy played with Ginny's hair. "I've never seen anyone with orange hair before."

Ginny laughed. "I like to call it red, but you're right. It's more orange."

"It's pretty," said the little girl as she ran her fingers through it.

"Leave her hair alone," Louisa chided.

"It's okay," Ginny said. "I don't mind. It's a mess, anyway."

Chester shrugged. "It looks fine to me."

Ginny made a raspberry noise. "That's because you're a guy. Guys don't notice stuff like hair. I need to get it cut, but I haven't had the time."

"My mom could cut it for you," offered Maria. "She works in a salon."

Ginny looked surprised. "Really?"

Louisa nodded. "*Serendipity*. Off of Q Street."

Ginny puffed her cheeks and let out a long sigh. "Maybe after the holidays I'll give you a call." She pulled a piece of hair away from her face. "I need to do something."

Louisa eyed her for a moment. "You're like Chester, aren't you? You never take time for yourself. Always working and helping other people first?"

Chester tried not to squirm as Ginny looked over at him. "I knew Chester was like that at work, but he helps out around the house, too?"

His sister grinned. "Helps out? The man cooks dinner almost every night. He babysits the girls on the weekends when I'm at the salon. He's renovated my entire house."

"*Tio* Chester is the best!" crowed Katy.

Ginny bent toward the little girl. "The best, huh?"

"Uh-huh."

Chester let out a sigh of relief when the waitress came over to take their drink orders. They took a moment to peruse the menus before she returned. He and his family ordered large platters of waffles, eggs, and pancakes. Ginny opted for an English muffin to go with her coffee.

"You sure you don't want something more?" asked Chester. "It's my treat."

"No, thanks." Ginny shook her head. "I ate about a dozen Christmas cookies last night and I have to go to my mother's house tonight for dinner. I'd better give my stomach a little break."

The waiter brought their drinks, and Ginny dug through her purse and pulled out a small bottle of aspirin. She popped two and swallowed them with a mouthful of coffee.

"Headache?" asked Chester.

"Yeah." Ginny's cheeks pinked. "Yesterday was a little stressful."

He sipped his coffee. "The open house went well, though. Susan was real happy with the turnout."

Ginny smiled. "I was surprised. Lots of outside interest for once. I guess Johnny Miles is more popular than I thought with that generation."

Their food arrived, and the girls dominated Ginny's conversation with questions about what she'd like to do with her hair and what clothes she liked to wear. Chester enjoyed watching Ginny interact with them. She chuckled as she picked at her muffin, and only the occasional rubbing of her temple indicated that she didn't feel the best. For a moment he let his mind wander, thinking about what it would be like to have brunch every Sunday after church with the beautiful red-haired woman across from him. He pictured coming home and cooking dinner for the two of them, enjoying an evening cup of coffee on the couch, and talking about their days.

"Earth to Chester," called Louisa. "Are you in there, big brother?"

He shook his head to clear the daydream from his mind. "What?"

The four females at the table giggled.

"Where'd you go?" asked Louisa.

"I guess I zoned out for a minute. I must need some more coffee." He poured another mug from the pitcher and took a long swallow.

The waitress came over to the table. "Can I get you anything else? A slice of pie?"

Everyone groaned.

"Just the check, please," said Chester.

Ginny reached for her purse. "Let me give you something for the muffin."

He raised his hand. "Nope. My treat. I insist."

"I'll bring in bagels or something one day next week to make it up to you."

Katy jumped up and gave Ginny a kiss on the cheek. "Will you come out with us again?"

Chester held his breath, waiting for her to answer.

Ginny laughed. "You'll get sick of me if I hang around too much."

"No, we won't!" The little girl argued.

Louisa smiled a knowing grin. "I know we won't."

Ginny ducked her head and shot a quick glance Chester's way. "We'll see." She picked up her purse and coat. "But, on that note, I really have to go. I'm hoping a short nap and another round of aspirin might help me knock out this headache before I go to my mother's this afternoon." She inclined her head toward the table and in a mock British accent said, "Thank you all for a simply wonderful morning of entertainment and refreshment." She gave them a queenly wave of her hand as she turned to leave. "Ta-ta. Ta-ta." She gave Chester one last look and a smile. "Thanks again."

The table went quiet until Ginny was out in the parking lot; then, all three girls started talking at once.

"I like her," Maria said.

"She's pretty," chimed in Katy.

"She likes you," Louisa offered.

Chester raised his hands in surrender. "Stop! There's nothing going on between Ginny and me."

"There should be," Maria said. "She's really nice."

"And pretty!" yelled Katy.

"And pretty." Maria nodded.

Chester leaned in toward his sister. "You really think she likes me?"

She smiled. "I got that vibe."

"What's a vibe?" Katy asked.

"A feeling," explained her mother. "I think Ginny likes *Tio* Chester."

The little girl looked confused. "Of course she likes him. They're friends."

Maria sighed dramatically. "Don't be stupid. She means Ginny *likes* him likes him."

Katy's eyes grew wide. "You mean like…." She put her index fingers together and made kissing noises.

Louisa frowned. "You, stop that. And you, don't call your sister stupid. And you…." she looked at Chester. "I like her, too. I think you ought to ask her out."

"Maybe after the holidays. When things quiet down a little."

Louisa eyed him. "Don't wait too long. A girl like that is hard to find."

~

I took a deep breath and rang the doorbell to my mother's house. I didn't normally attend the Sunday-before-Christmas dinner, as that was the time Roger's children celebrated the holiday with their dad. This year, however, Tony had invited Brad along for the festivities, and the two of them had insisted I come, too.

"You sure you're okay?" Brad asked me for the umpteenth time since he'd picked me up. My morning headache had dulled to a slight throb with a nap and some aspirin, but it still hurt.

"My mother and I don't exactly get along. These dinners never end well for me."

He put his arm around my shoulder. "Don't worry. This year, you have me."

Why doesn't that make me feel any better?

My mother opened the door, and for once a huge smile spread across her face when she saw me. "I never thought I'd see the day!" She backed up to let us in. "You two look wonderful together!"

Roger came up behind me and took our coats. "It's good to see you, Ginny. Brad."

Brad shook my stepfather's hand. "Great to see you again too, sir. Thank you for having me over."

"It's our pleasure," said my mother. "Everyone is in the family room." I could see the slight irritation in her eyes. My stepsister's children had to be running around somewhere; it always caused my mother to twitch.

Tony pounced as soon as he saw us. "Dude! How are you?" He pulled Brad down beside him on the couch. I wanted to sit in the chair in the corner, but Brad grabbed my hand.

"There's room here, babe."

Babe? I shivered. When had he decided to call me that? I sat next to him but turned my attention to Roger's daughter, Elaina, who sat on the loveseat across from me with her husband, Peter. "How've you been?"

She tucked a lock of her blonde hair behind her ear. "Busy. And you?"

"Busy." I nodded. I shifted my focus to Peter. "And how's your company doing?"

His round face exploded with a grin. His brown eyes gleamed. "We are doing great! Even in this economy. It's hard to believe." He leaned forward and gestured excitedly with his hands as he told me about his plans to expand his computer consulting business. I tried to focus – honest, I did – but Brad's hand reached over and rested on my leg and I got distracted. *What is up with him? First calling me "babe" and now this touchy stuff. He's never acted like this before.*

Roger interrupted the conversation. "Ginny, would you like a soda?"

"Yes, thank you."

He turned to Brad. "And what can I get you? Soda, beer, wine?"

"A beer, please."

My mother sat down in the chair next to Elaina, her eyes surveying the scene on the couch. "So darling, tell me how you are."

I glanced down at my knee, where Brad's fingers were busy caressing my leg. "I'm fine." I wished I'd worn the wool slacks I'd originally put on instead of the short plaid skirt. I looked over at Brad, but he seemed engrossed in a conversation with Tony about the Nebraska Cornhuskers. I turned to my mother. "And you? How are you holding up through the holidays?"

She let out an exaggerated sigh. "It's difficult. So many functions to attend. If you don't go, people feel like you've snubbed them. It can be exhausting."

Elaina nodded. "We're running everywhere on the weekends, trying to keep all of Peter's clients happy. And then, there's the kids' activities."

As if on cue, Alexis and Adam screamed into the room. My mother stiffened and grabbed her wine glass from the end table.

Alexis's blonde hair flew about her face as she tried to wrench a large red bow from her brother's hand. "Give it back!"

My stepsister ignored the cries of her children while my mother boiled. Roger delivered our drinks, then reached over and put a hand on each child. Immediately, the noise ceased. He'd put on his Marine officer face, and it was apparent to everyone in the room that he was in charge.

"Follow me." The kids winced as Roger tightened his grip on their shoulders. "Now."

The two did as they'd been commanded. Elaina frowned. "Remember, they're children, Dad. Not recruits."

Roger ignored her.

The conversation, such as it was, returned to normal after the minor interruption. My mother extolled us all with the hardships of finding good clothes nowadays. Elaina complained about the difficulties of keeping a decent manicurist. Peter moaned about the cost of country club fees. Brad and Tony talked about the local nightclub scene. I sat on the edge of the couch, trying to seem interested in any one of these inane topics while attempting to ignore Brad's hand, which seemed to have a life of its own. He rubbed my knee, my hand, my shoulder and my hair, all while in animated conversation with my stepbrother.

When the time came to eat, Brad stood first then helped me off the couch. He pulled me into his chest and kissed me on the lips. Right there in the living room. We'd only been on three dates, and he'd only kissed me on the cheek before. I resisted the urge to slap him but let the rest of the family make their way out toward the dining room.

"What was that?" I whispered when the coast was clear.

Brad looked perplexed. "What?"

"All of it." I waved my hand toward the couch. "What's with the touching? The kissing?"

He pulled me close to him again. "Loosen up, babe."

I pushed him away. "And don't call me that. All I can think of is that pig from the movie. I'm not your babe."

"I like you," Brad sighed. "I thought you liked me. And I can tell your mom is into the idea of us dating. She's looking at us and picking out china patterns."

"Well, I'm not. Cool it."

He tilted his head in a kind of resigned acquiescence. My mother called from the dining room. "Come on, you two lovebirds. We're waiting for you!"

The rest of the afternoon passed without too many incidents. Brad's hand still found a way to touch me, but not to the extent it had before dinner. The kids were relatively well-behaved; Roger must have threatened them with something drastic. After dinner, we retired into the family room, where the blue and silver Christmas tree glowed festively from the corner. My mother put on some Mannheim Steamroller to set the mood while Roger's family exchanged gifts. Peter was thrilled with a certificate for new golf clubs while Elaina gushed over the diamond necklace my mother had picked out from Borsheim's Jewelers. Tony seemed a little disappointed in his thirty-two-inch plasma television.

Roger folded his arms and leaned back into the couch. "If you want to return it and go for something bigger, you can pay the difference."

Tony nodded. "I might. I think a forty-two-inch would work better."

"Can I have your old TV?" asked Brad.

"You know the deal."

Brad glared at him. "Don't you forget it."

Tony glanced at me, then gave him a grin. "I won't."

"What deal?" I asked.

Brad put his hand on my leg. "Tony has this deal with all his friends about who gets his castoffs. We gamble for them. Poker, that kind of thing."

"Do you want your gift this week, darling?" my mother asked. "Or when your brother is here?"

"I can wait until New Year's." Mom's side of the family always celebrated the holiday on New Year's Day, so my brother Simon could have Christmas at home with his family or with his in-laws.

Next, we dutifully trooped out to the garage so Elaina's kids could open their presents. Five-year-old Alexis shrieked with delight when she opened up her Barbie jeep, and eight-year-old Adam did the same with his new ATV. Lucky for everyone, the temperatures had warmed up to above freezing the past couple of days, making the roads clear of ice and snow. Roger had wisely charged up the cars' batteries as well. Peter, Tony, and Brad offered to watch the kids drive around the cul-de-sac while the rest of us stayed warm inside.

Roger took my arm as we stepped back into the house. "Can I talk to you for a minute?"

"Sure. What's up?"

He led me to his study and shut the door behind us. I took a seat on one of the leather wingback chairs. He walked over to the wet bar in the corner. "You need anything to drink?"

"You have anything diet over there?"

He rummaged through the cans in the small fridge underneath the counter and found a suitable soda. He prepared a scotch, neat, for himself then sat down on the chair next to me. He passed me my drink. "Here you go."

"Thanks." I took a sip while Roger sat there. "Everything okay?"

He put his drink down on the desk and turned his chair to face me. "I've been wanting to say something to you for some time, but I haven't had the chance." He paused. "When your mom and I married, what? Twelve years ago now? I didn't think much about being a dad. My ex-wife had done most of the raising of our kids. I can't say I like how they turned out, but I have no place to complain. I wasn't around for most of their lives, so . . . ." He lifted his hands in a sign of resignation.

I wondered where this conversation was going but kept quiet.

"Anyway, I tell you all this because I want to let you know that one of the best things that's happened to me in this marriage with your mother is that I've had the privilege of watching you grow up. I first saw you, and you were this awkward—"

"Fat," I offered.

"Plump." He smiled. "Shy teenager. You barely spoke to me when you first came to live with us." He shrugged. "My kids, when I did see them, were always loud and demanding. You liked to sit in the corner and read. You know what my favorite times were?"

I shook my head.

"In the mornings, when we'd both get up early. Do you remember? Joyce didn't have the cook come in until lunchtime, so you and I would get our breakfast and sit at the table together."

I smiled at the memory of Roger in his bathrobe with the striped pajamas underneath. He'd pour a cup of black coffee for himself and then fix one up super-light for me. He always made me drink a glass of juice as well, even though I'd have been happy with just the coffee. During the week, when time was short, we'd wolf down a bowl of cereal or piece of toast while sharing what was on our schedules for the day. On the weekends, we'd trade cooking duty. I liked to make pancakes and French toast, while Roger liked eggs.

"I miss those mornings," he said softly. "Your mom doesn't get up until ten most days."

"We should get together on Saturdays sometime. Trade houses. One week here, one week at my house."

"I'd like that." Was that all he wanted to tell me? He grabbed his drink from the desk and took a sip. Then another.

"What's the matter, Roger? You look uncomfortable."

He nodded. "I need to say something to you, but I don't want to offend you."

I chuckled.

Roger's eyebrows furrowed. "What?"

"I said that to someone last night." I laughed again. "Say what you want. I promise I won't get mad."

He took another drink, then replaced the glass on the desk. "Let me first tell you how glad I am that you're dating again." His hand reached over as if to touch me, but then he pulled back. He'd never been a huggy type of guy. "It broke my heart to see how unhappy you were after you lost Mark. It really did." He shifted in his chair. "You'd come out of your shell. You were finally showing the world the pieces of yourself you'd shown me while we ate breakfast. Your intelligence. Your humor. Your sensitivity. And then, it was as if someone shut the light off inside you again. Every time I saw you, you looked like that shy teenager who wanted nothing more than to be left alone with her book in the corner."

"I know. I'm sorry I worried you."

He lifted one shoulder. "I felt helpless."

I didn't know what to say.

"I'm glad I'm starting to see the life again in your eyes. To see you smile."

"But?" I could tell there was something more he wanted to say.

"But, how serious are you about Brad?"

The muscles in my shoulders relaxed. *Is that what he's worried about?* "I'm not."

"Good." He nodded. "I don't think he's right for you. You deserve better."

I grinned. "Thank you for your concern, and the compliment, but you don't have to worry. Brad's nice enough, but I know it's nothing serious."

Roger raised his eyebrows. "Does Brad know that? He looked very possessive of you today. It got me worried."

"He's never acted like that before."

"Be careful."

"I will."

Roger seemed more at ease. He stood, went around to the other side of his desk, and sat down behind it. "There's one more thing."

"Shoot."

He pulled a business envelope out from the top drawer. "Your mother doesn't know I'm doing this." He passed it over to me.

I stared at it.

"Go ahead. Open it."

He hadn't sealed it, so I lifted the flap and pulled out the check inside. *$100,000?* I raised my head.

I'd never seen Roger look so happy. He rested his elbows on the desk. "It's for medical school."

"But...I'm not...you don't...."

"I know, I know. You're not in med school right now, and I don't have to do this." He leaned toward me. "But, I want to do this, and I believe in you. Out of all our kids, you're the one I want to see succeed the most. You have so much to give." He folded his hands. "Put that check in the bank until you're ready to go back. I know you will someday. Soon, I hope. And then, you'll have it."

"I don't know what to say."

"You don't have to say anything. Just use it like I asked. Make this world a better place."

"Thank you." This time, tears of happiness rolled down my cheeks instead of pain.

Roger looked away. "Enough of that." He stood. "We'd better get back to the others. They'll wonder what we've been up to." He waved me over to the wall. "Take a look at my new acquisition." He pointed to a frame containing a letter on yellowed paper. "It's from a soldier in the Confederate Army. I got it from an auction last month. We'll tell your mother that's what I was showing you in here."

I wiped away my tears. "Sure." I looked up at him. "I don't think I ever told you this, but I'm really glad my mother married you."

He might have been a tough old Marine, but I saw his eyes grow moist as he swallowed. "Thank you."

I leaned up and gave him a kiss on the cheek. "I love you." I turned quickly and left the room, but not before I glimpsed Roger smile and wipe his eyes.

CHAPTER THIRTEEN

Margaret Ann's blue hair bobbed up and down as she shook her head in disgust. "This is the worst card I've ever had."

I bit the inside of my cheek. *If she says that one more time today, I may have to take her out.* I pulled another ball out of the Bingo cage. "N-fifty. N, five-zero. Fifty."

Sam made a soft raspberry sound. "She's called that number six or seven times today already." She looked over at Margaret Ann. "I have forty-nine and fifty-one. Everything but fifty."

"I know how you feel," said her friend. "This is the worst card I've ever had."

I had to laugh. It was either that or whip a Bingo ball at her.

"What was that number?" called another resident. "Sixty?"

"No." I sighed. "Fifty! Five-zero!" I glanced at the clock, relieved to see it was almost three. After this round, I could call the last game. I picked out another number. "I-twenty seven. That's I, two-seven."

"Bingo!" shouted Bill.

Thank God. "What do you have?" He read off his numbers. "That's a Bingo. Clear your cards." I lifted the prize basket full of cookies, chips, and candy then walked it over to Bill.

Chester came out from the kitchen as Bill pulled out a pack of sugar wafer cookies. "Bill! You won?"

The old man smiled. "It's been a good day for me." He pointed to the three other packages of cookies on the table.

Chester raised his eyebrows in exaggerated surprise. "You and me should hit the casinos tonight, *amigo*."

Bill waved his hand. "Nah. I don't like 'em since they went all electronic. I miss the sound of the coins coming out."

Chester laughed, then nodded his head toward the basket. "Can I carry that for you, ma'am?"

I shook my head. "It's not heavy."

"But, you look tired." He took the basket from me, then looked around the room. "You guys must be wearing her out." He brought the basket over to where the Bingo cage sat and put it on an empty chair. "There you go." He offered me a quick smile before turning back to the residents. "*Adios, amigos! Hasta mañana!*"

"Thanks," I said as the rest of the room called out their goodbyes.

Chester winked at me. "*De nada.* Don't work so hard."

I chuckled at the way his mustache curled up when he grinned. "This time of year, that's all I'm doing. Working hard."

He gave me a wave, then headed out for the night. I replaced the Bingo numbers I'd called from the previous game and picked a new one. "This will be blackout Bingo. Cover the whole card."

I finished calling the last game at about 3:10. Agnes Pendleton won the jackpot of fifteen dollars. As I handed her the money she asked, "What's this for?"

"You won at Bingo."

She shook her head. "But, I don't play Bingo."

I took a deep breath. "You just played a game, and you won."

"Really?"

"Yes. This is your money." I picked up her purse. "Why don't you put it right in your wallet, so you don't lose it?"

Agnes nodded and did as I asked.

"Don't forget," I called to the residents as they started to make their way out of the dining room, "we have a troop of Girl Scouts coming in a few minutes to sing carols and bring cookies."

"Where?" asked Sam.

"They'll be in the lobby," I said as I turned away from the table.

"Why did I get my wallet out?" asked Agnes.

I shook my head. This had been the longest Wednesday of my life. Fortunately, I'd already set chairs up in the lobby. I had to direct residents that way so they'd remember to stay for the carolers. I packed up the Bingo gear and brought it to the activity room to lock up. Susan called to me as I came back to the lobby.

"Ginny! Come here!"

"What is it?"

She had a huge grin on her face. "You have an admirer."

"What are you talking about?"

She moved away from the doorway, and I slipped by her into the office. On Patty's desk sat a huge bouquet of red roses. I looked from the roses to Susan, to Patty, and back to the roses again.

"Are those for me?"

Susan nodded. "The card has your name on it."

I stepped toward them. There had to be two dozen long-stemmed red roses in a crystal vase, along with sprays of baby's breath and ferns. "Who are they from?"

Patty stood with a bemused look on her face. "We didn't open the card. We're not that rude. We waited for you."

Susan came up behind me as I took the card out. "Is it from that guy you've been seeing?"

I slipped the note out of its tiny envelope. *Ginny, I enjoyed our dance on Saturday. The prospect of moving back to Omaha was an unhappy one for me, until I saw you. I hope you'll give me the opportunity to know you better. Patrick Johnson.*

Susan read the card over my shoulder. "Patrick Johnson?"

"Rachel's son?" asked Patty.

I nodded.

"Wow, that must have been some dance." Susan sat down on one of the office chairs. "What did you guys talk about?"

"I don't even remember." I sat down next to her, flipping the card between my fingers. "He told me he was moving back to Omaha. He asked me if I was seeing anyone."

"He's a nice-looking man."

I shrugged.

"I thought he was married," said Patty. "Doesn't he have kids?"

I toyed with the card. "He didn't mention anything about a family."

Patty snorted. "They never do." The phone rang, and she turned to answer it. "Good afternoon. Marigold Manor Assisted Living. This is Patty. How can I help you?" She smirked. "Let me see if I can find her for you – one moment." She pressed the hold button. "It's him."

"Patrick?"

"Yup. What should I tell him?"

This can't be happening. How did I go from being alone to having two, maybe three guys interested in me?

Patty tapped her foot. "Well? Do you want to talk to him?"

Susan swatted me on the arm. "You have to at least thank him for the flowers."

I stood. "Let me go back to my phone."

"Aw," Susan groaned. "I want to know what you say to him."

I ignored her and made my way to my office. Shutting the door behind me, I took a deep breath and picked up the phone. "Hi. this is Ginny."

"Hey there. It's Patrick Johnson."

My palms were sweating. "Yeah, hi…uh…thanks for the roses. They're beautiful."

"They came, then?"

There was a knock on my door. "Yeah, I just got them."

Susan entered, carrying the bouquet. My boss put the flowers on my desk, then stood next to me, trying to hear what Patrick was saying. I pushed her away, but she crept back to my side.

"I didn't know what flower you liked best. I figured I couldn't go wrong with roses."

"I like roses."

"But, they're not your favorite, are they? What's your favorite flower?"

I turned away from Susan. "I don't know. Maybe irises."

He let out a throaty chuckle. "I'll try and remember that next time."

"Oh, no." I tried again to maneuver away from my nosy boss. "You don't have to send me more flowers."

"Does that mean these ones worked?"

Susan whispered, "What does that mean?"

"What do you mean?" I asked Patrick.

"Will you go out with me?"

Susan looked at me sternly. "Ask him about his wife."

"About that." I sat on the edge of my desk. "Some of the girls in the office thought you were married."

He didn't answer right away.

"I'm sorry. When they found out who the flowers were from, they started talking."

"That's all right. We're separated. The divorce will be final in February."

I let my breath out slowly. "Well, maybe we should wait and see how things are going in February."

"There's no chance we're going to reconcile, Ginny. My wife is staying in California."

"Call me old-fashioned," I said. "I'd rather wait."

He sighed. "Will you consider it, then? When it's final?"

"Sure." I said, relieved that this was one problem I could put on the back burner. "I'll think about it."

He let out another low chuckle. "And I'll be thinking about you."

I stuck my finger down my throat and pretended to gag. Susan stifled a laugh. "Thanks again for the flowers."

"Next time, it will be irises."

"Really, you don't have to do that."

"I know, but I'd like to."

"Well, I have to run. Goodbye."

"Bye."

Susan played with a rose, running her fingertips over the blood-red petals. "You think you'll go out with him?"

I shook my head. "No. He's not my type."

"Why didn't you tell him to forget about it?"

"I avoid confrontations. And, he just moved here. I hate to dash his hopes completely before the holidays."

Patty's voice came over the intercom. "Your carolers are here."

I ran out and met the Girl Scouts at the door. They passed out baggies of cookies with Christmas bows on them to the residents, chatting as they did so. I loved seeing these eight- and nine-year-olds interacting with the older generation. They talked about Christmases past, and the girls asked about the kinds of toys and foods the residents had enjoyed. Agnes Pendleton had one girl by the hand, explaining how she'd used to raise their own turkeys on her parents' farm. Bill had several girls listening with rapt attention as he told his favorite story of the Christmas he spent on the German front during WWII. Edith and Frank were explaining the rules of backgammon to another group of scouts. I spied Helen Franklin leading her husband down the hallway toward the commotion. I directed her to a couple of chairs in the corner.

"Here you go."

"Thank you, dear."

"What's going on?" asked George.

"Some girls are here to visit with us," explained Helen. She glanced up at me. "Our great-granddaughter is here somewhere." At that moment, one of the younger looking scouts ran over.

"Gi-Gi!"

I left them to their reunion and scanned the room to make sure everyone was engaged. Satisfied, I approached one of the leaders.

"You'll want to begin singing by four, because they start bringing the residents down for dinner by 4:15."

The woman nodded. "We need to be done by 4:30."

"That's perfect." We chatted a little longer before she got the girls gathered around the piano to begin the caroling. As this was the sixth group we'd had in this month, with another two expected before Saturday, I excused myself and ducked into the main office, closing the door behind me. "If I never hear "Jingle Bells" again, it will be too soon."

Patty laughed. She gestured to a candy bowl on the corner of her desk. "Indulge. It will ease the agony."

"You think?"

She shrugged and flipped her blonde ponytail behind her. "It can't hurt."

I picked through the bowl until I found something gooey. I turned around to look out of the office's glass windows to check on the festivities outside. Bill caught my eye. He had slumped over in his chair as he listened to the girls sing. Was he sleeping? He often dozed after reading the paper, or sometimes after lunch he'd take a nap by the fireplace, but this seemed unusual. I chewed on the caramel in my mouth and took a step closer to the window.

"Is Susan in her office?" I asked.

"She's on a conference call."

"How about Karen?"

"I can buzz her. What's up?" Patty walked over to my side.

"Take a look at Bill." His body seemed to collapse in on itself. I swore under my breath. "What'll we do? With all the girls out there?"

Patty ran to the phone and buzzed Karen while I slipped out of the office and over to one of the leaders. "We have a slight problem," I whispered, nodding toward Bill. "Can you maybe have the girls walk toward the back of the room as they sing? I don't want to alarm them."

The leader's eyes grew wide. "Sure thing." She turned to the troop with a big smile as they finished "Frosty the Snowman." "Follow me, girls!" She led them around behind the fireplace while they sang "Rudolph the Red-nosed Reindeer."

Karen sat by Bill's chair, feeling his neck and wrist for a pulse. I ran over to her. A look of exasperation flashed across her face. "Can you get me a wheelchair? We'll need to move him out of here."

"Is he?"

"Oh, yeah. And, he's a DNR, so we just need to call the coroner to verify." She looked around the room. "We have to get him out of here before the girls realize what's going on."

DNR. Do not resuscitate. I hurried to the front atrium and grabbed one of the extra wheelchairs we kept out there for transferring patients. I wheeled it over to Karen. In the year I had worked here, no one had died while in house. All of them had been transferred out and died in hospitals. "Now what?"

"Help me lift him into the chair."

I froze.

Her face showed her aggravation. "Come on! Put your arm under his and we'll lift him into the chair."

The girls went into "Hark the Herald Angels Sing," as we maneuvered Bill so that he sat hunched in the wheelchair.

Margaret Ann reached out and grabbed my arm. "What's the matter with Bill?"

"He's not feeling well." I whispered, trying not to sound as panicked as I felt. "The nurse is going to check on him in the office." A few other residents glanced our way, but our carolers kept most of the residents' attention.

Karen put one hand on Bill's shoulder to keep him from falling off, then pushed him into the office. We closed the door behind us and brought him into the conference room.

I looked at the shell of Bill Watson slumped in the wheelchair. It had been awhile since I'd seen a dead person. Mark had been so disfigured in the accident, they hadn't let me see him at the hospital. My Grandpa Lloyd had had an open-casket funeral, but somehow it was different looking at Bill. You expected dead people in a funeral home. A cadaver in the office was another story. I shuddered. "I have to get out of here. I'm sorry."

I ran down the hall and back to my own office. My cell phone chirped at me. I rummaged through my purse until I found it. *Brad.*

"Hello?"

His voice sounded perky. "Hey there. I wanted to make sure we're still on for tonight. Pick you up at seven?"

My eyelid twitched. I tried to relax it by massaging it with my index finger. "I'm not sure."

"Don't back out on me. It's my last night in town before I leave for Missouri."

I took a deep breath. "I'll meet you there. I may have to come straight from work."

I sensed rather than heard him groan. "O'Brien's at seven. See you there."

"Bye." I hung up the phone and finished off the last mouthful of cold coffee in my mug. Catching my breath, I went back out to the lobby to thank the Girl Scouts for their visit.

"Were they suspicious of anything?" I asked the leader.

She shook her head. "Did that man . . . is he dead?"

I nodded.

She swallowed hard and put a hand on my shoulder. "I'm glad there are people like you. I couldn't work in a place like this." She turned her focus to the girls in the lobby. "Let's go, troop. Time to head out."

The girls said goodbye and lined up by the front door as the coroner's car pulled up.

Great timing.

The scouts marched out as the somber-looking official came through the front door. Immediately, the residents set upon me.

"Was it Bill?" asked Rachel. "I saw you wheel Bill out. Was it Bill?"

I took a deep breath. "Everyone, head in to dinner. We'll make an announcement soon."

⌇

Chester pulled into the church parking lot a little before five. Candy, the church's secretary, walked out as he opened the trunk of his car.

"Is the office still open?" he called to her.

The gray-haired woman nodded. "Pastor Luke's in there."

"I've been driving around with this box of gifts and food items for the Angel Tree and I figured I'd better drop it off tonight while I was thinking of it." He grunted as he pulled out the large cardboard container. "Where should I put it?"

"In the office. Tammy will be by tomorrow night to pick everything up." The older woman walked up beside him. "Can I close the trunk for you?"

"That would be great." Chester struggled to keep his balance on the icy blacktop.

"Let me get the door for you as well." Candy returned to the building and let him into the office. "There you go." She pointed to several boxes stacked in the corner. "Put it with the rest of them."

"Thanks." He put his burden down.

"You coming back out?" asked the secretary.

Chester hesitated. "I think I might see if the pastor has a minute to talk."

"Goodnight, then." Candy waved.

"Goodnight." Chester watched to make sure the older woman made it to her car without slipping before he approached Luke's door. He knocked softly. When there was no answer, he knocked a little louder.

"Come in!"

Chester opened the door. Luke sat behind a desk cluttered with papers, books, and a computer; behind him hung a portrait of him, Nancy, and their daughter. It always made Chester pause when he saw the girl's cherubic face smiling out at him.

"Wow," Luke said. "You're the last person I expected to walk through my door tonight. What can I do you for, my man?"

"Stopped in to say hi. See if you needed anything done before the big services on Christmas Eve."

The young pastor leaned back in his chair and put his hands behind his head. "I think we have it covered. Candy's been a saint, getting everything organized for the luminaries and the three services."

"Good." Chester nodded and looked around the room. A tall metal filing cabinet stood in the corner of the cramped office. On top of it sat a dying houseplant and a plaque. From where he stood, Chester couldn't make out what the plaque said, but the picture of a boat on the water at sunset seemed to indicate it would be something inspirational.

"Have a seat." Luke gestured to the vinyl armchair opposite his desk. "What's on your mind?"

Chester moved toward the chair but didn't sit. "Do you have a minute? I know things are busy for you. I can come back some other time."

The pastor rocked forward in his chair and rested his elbows on the desk. "Actually, you're an answer to prayer. I've been struggling over the Christmas Eve message, and you are the distraction I've been looking for."

Chester sat down and studied the man behind the desk. It had taken him some time to get used to such a young pastor. Growing up, the priests in the church he'd attended with his parents had been much older. Chester had always thought they probably knew Jesus when he walked on earth. At this moment, though, he was grateful that Luke was the same age as him. It would make what he wanted to talk about much easier. At least, a little easier.

Luke's laughter brought Chester out of his thoughts. "You look uncomfortable. Please, just tell me whatever it is."

Chester sighed. "I'm worried."

"I can tell."

The cook tapped his fingers against his knees. "I haven't really talked to you. About my life before I came to this church."

Luke shook his head.

Chester's fingers moved over to the arm of the chair and kept tapping. "Pastor Gary and I . . . we talked quite a bit."

Luke's brow furrowed. "Go ahead."

Chester threw up his hands. "Before I came to Christ, I wasn't such a nice guy. There's a lot of stuff I don't need to go into right now, but I have a potential problem, and I don't know what to do about it."

"I need a little more info. What are you dealing with?"

Chester slouched back into the chair and pulled a piece of lint off the knee of his pants. "Let's just say I used to have a problem with women." He flicked the lint to the floor. "I used women. A lot of women."

"I see." Luke nodded. "But, you don't anymore?"

"No!" Chester looked up quickly. "I haven't since I started following Christ." The pastor waited for him to continue. "I think about it and I realize that I just haven't been tempted again. Before now."

"What do you mean?"

"I mean, the dates I went on since I accepted Christ were never a challenge. I may have liked the girls, but it was easy to not let things go too far, because I knew I wasn't in love with them."

"But, you think you're in love with someone?"

Chester shook his head. "I don't know. It's different than anything I've ever felt before. I look forward to work every day because I know I'll see her. At least for a minute. And, when she's near me . . . it's like . . . ."

"Like what?"

Chester looked Luke straight in the eyes. "I've wanted a woman before. I mean, I've lusted after a woman. But, with Ginny, I want to be with her because everything about her intrigues me." *The way her hair shines when the sunlight hits it. The way her eyes seem to change color when she's sad.*

Luke leaned forward. "You're talking about Ginny Stafford, right?"

"Yeah."

The blond-haired man let his breath out slowly. "Boy, God's really putting you to the test, isn't he?"

"What do you mean?"

"I only know a little about her history, but to fall for a woman who's going to need special care...for a man who has a whole different set of issues with intimacy...." Luke lifted his hands. "It's going to be a trial for you, my friend."

Chester's heart sank. "I'm not even sure how she feels about me. I think she likes me, but I don't know."

"Ginny's emotionally confused right now. She's finally dealing with a lot of stuff in her past."

"You mean her fiancé?" asked Chester.

"Exactly." Luke folded his hands. "I don't know what kind of relationship she has with God, but she could lead you somewhere you shouldn't go."

An ominous shiver ran down Chester's spine. "What do you mean?"

"I'm assuming you want to remain abstinent until you're married. That's what you're worried about?"

Chester nodded.

Luke picked up a pencil and doodled on the large calendar on his desk. "If something does...develop...between the two of you, I think you're going to have to discuss the subject of sex early in the relationship." He looked up as Chester shifted in his chair. "It might be awkward, but it will keep you out of temptation."

"What would I say?"

"I think you'll have to let her know where you stand on the idea of sleeping together before marriage. Do you know what her beliefs are on the subject?"

Chester shook his head. "I haven't even asked her out on a date yet."

Luke put down the pencil and leaned on his elbows. "I'd talk to her before you go out on your first real date. Before either of you gets so emotionally committed to the relationship you can't see clearly."

"I don't see clearly now," muttered Chester. "I just want to be with her. Is that wrong?"

"Not if you can keep yourself in check. I know you're not some young kid who's never experienced the power of sex before. But, if you've only encountered it outside of marriage, you've never known it the way God intended." The corner of Luke's mouth lifted into a wistful smile. "And, let me tell you, it's worth the wait."

Chester stared out the window into the early-evening darkness. His heart felt lighter, for having talked about his concerns, but now a whole new set of problems had developed. "I've never talked with a woman like that before. It's not that I lied to them. I've just never been so honest. So .
. . ."

"Vulnerable." Luke picked up the pencil and colored in the "0" before turning his full attention on Chester. "Honesty's the key. If you're serious about wanting a relationship with Ginny, if you're thinking she might be the person you want to spend your life with, then you have to be as open as you possibly can, and you have to communicate your concerns to her." He chuckled under his breath. "And not just this one time, either. It's a never-ending cycle of problems and communication. Get used to it."

❧

Edith reached over and took Frank's hand. He'd gone pale as the winter sky while he watched the coroner wheel out the body of his friend.

"I'm sorry," she whispered. "I know you were fond of him."

Frank continued to stare as they put the stretcher onto the hearse and drove away. "We were supposed to go to Europe together in the spring. He wanted to see Germany."

Edith didn't press Frank to talk more. He'd do that when he was ready. Instead, she sat at his side, hoping her presence brought him some comfort. Residents shuffled through the lobby on their way into the dining room, but she waited until the kitchen staff began serving before speaking again.

"Do you feel up to dinner? I'm sure we could bend the rules and you could sit at my table tonight." She hesitated. "Or, I could sit at yours."

At this, Frank finally looked at her. The pain in his eyes brought tears to her own. "He was a good friend. A decent man." He choked back a sob. "I'm going to miss him."

"I know, dear." Edith patted his hand. Comforting came naturally to her. She stood, walked behind his chair, and wrapped her arms around the big man's shoulders. "He went peacefully, though." She chuckled. "And he went happy. He's never won so much at Bingo before! You heard what Ginny told us. He'd just finished telling a story about his army service. It was a perfect day for him."

Frank snorted softly. "You're right there. He couldn't have been happier." He put his hand to his chest and covered Edith's with it. "It'll be tough for his son, Jimmy, though. So close to Christmas."

Edith sighed. "The holidays do make it harder." She placed her free hand over Frank's. "Come into the dining room. I'll sit with you."

He leaned his head against her arm. "I'm not really hungry."

"I know, but come have coffee. It's better than stewing about things out here."

Frank sighed. "You'll really buck the rules and sit with me?"

"I'll flaunt the powers that be this once. Seating assignment? What seating assignment?"

That actually produced a laugh from Frank. "Edith MacPherson, you rebel, you."

She unwrapped her arms from around his neck. "You have no idea. I can be quite the maverick."

"You?" He shook his head. "But, you're always so proper." He stood, and they walked toward the dining room. "I can't imagine you being a renegade."

She lifted an eyebrow. "Still waters run deep, Mr. Leno. You'll find I'm full of surprises."

∽

I made it to O'Brien's Bar and Grill by ten minutes after seven. Brad waved me over to the booth where he waited. A mug of beer sat half-empty on the table along with a tall glass of water and an unwrapped straw. He stood, helped me out of my coat, and hung it on the hook on the side of the bench. He kissed me on the cheek.

"Tough day at work?"

I slid into the booth. "Well, I got a bouquet of roses, and a resident died while the Girl Scouts were caroling."

His eyes widened. "What?"

"Right during "Frosty the Snowman." He keeled over."

The corners of Brad's mouth twitched. I could tell he was trying not to laugh. I shook my head. "It's not funny! Those girls could have been traumatized."

He let out a short chuckle. "I'm sorry. The image that keeps popping into my head is pretty funny." He got himself under control. "I'm better now."

A short, blonde waitress approached the booth. "Can I get you something to drink?"

"A diet cola."

Brad frowned as she left. "Is there a reason you don't drink?"

"There's a history of alcoholism in my family. I saw how much my parents drank when I was younger." I shrugged. "I wouldn't say they were alcoholics, but they're definitely alcohol-dependent. I like to be in control."

Brad took a sip of his beer. "In moderation, it can be a good thing."

"I never thought it was worth the risk."

"Who were the roses from?"

"What?"

"You said you got roses from someone." He eyed me over the rim of his glass.

"Oh, that." I ripped the wrapper off the straw and stuck it in the water. "He's the son of one of the residents. He's in the process of divorcing his wife, and I guess he likes me."

Deep lines creased Brad's forehead. "Should I be worried?"

"About Patrick?" I chuckled. "No. He's not my type at all."

He leaned back against the bench. "Good." He changed the topic, bringing up our plans for the holiday. I would spend Christmas Eve with Edith and Christmas Day with my father. Brad was leaving the following afternoon for Missouri to celebrate with his family. When the waitress returned with my soda, we ordered our meals.

I watched Brad as he interacted with the waitress. I could tell she found him attractive. She joked with him as he struggled to decide between a burger and a chicken sandwich, then smiled broadly when he handed her the menu.

"Don't hesitate to call me over if you need anything. Remember, my name's Audra."

He flashed a cockeyed grin at her. "Thank you very much."

She tilted her head toward him and spun away from the table.

I couldn't tell if Brad was flirting with her on purpose, or if he naturally exuded that kind of charm. It didn't seem forced. He turned his attention back to me.

"I enjoyed having dinner with your folks the other night. I really like them."

I smiled, remembering Roger's lack of affection for Brad. "My mother was in a very good mood."

Brad lifted his hands. "Mothers like me, what can I say?"

We shifted topics for the next couple of minutes, alternating between holiday memories, politics, and the various cold and stomach viruses plaguing the Omaha area. Once Audra arrived with the food, our conversation dwindled to almost nothing as we ate. I especially enjoyed the spicy fries served on the side of my turkey club, and Brad commented again that he was glad I didn't count my carbs.

Audra returned to clear our plates. "Can I get you anything else?" she asked Brad.

He glanced over to me, and I shook my head. He smiled up at Audra. "Just the check."

"I'll have that right up to you." She bounced away from the table as Brad reached across to take my hands.

"I'm going to miss you while I'm gone."

"You'll be too busy with your family." I didn't want to tell him that I probably wasn't going to miss him much at all. He was nice enough, but I didn't feel anything other than friendship for him.

"I'll be back on the twenty-eighth, but I have to work that night and the next. I got New Year's Eve off, though. I thought we could spend it together."

"I don't care much for New Year's."

"We could do up the First Night celebration. It's a blast."

I shook my head. "I'm not into drunken crowds."

Brad leaned back against the booth. "How about this? My friend Robbie is having a party at his house. It'll be small."

I could tell he wasn't going to give up. "Okay."

Brad left some bills on the table to cover the check and helped me put on my coat. "Let's go for a walk."

"It's freezing outside."

"It's not too bad tonight. I have an extra hat in my car, if you want it."

We stepped outside into the crisp night air. He'd been right; for Nebraska, the temperature wasn't too bad.

Brad gestured with his head. "I thought we could stroll down to the mall and see the lights. What do you think?"

A stiff breeze whipped through the parking lot. "Can I have that hat?"

He laughed. "Wait here." He jogged over to his car. After a moment, he hurried back and handed me a black knit cap with a bright red N emblazoned on the front.

"A Cornhuskers cap? Really?"

He gave me a shocked look. "You're not a fan? Is that even legal here?"

I stretched the hat between my hands. "I don't think so. I've never confessed it openly before."

He took the cap and stuck it on my head before I could protest. He stepped back and grinned. "You look adorable."

I groaned. "I can't believe I'm wearing this thing." I put my hands into my coat pockets to keep warm. "Let's go before I change my mind."

We walked down 15th Street until we got to Farnam, then took a left. The Gene Leahy Mall illuminated the center of the city like a fairy land. Brad grabbed my arm and pulled me across the road so we could see it better. Every tree on the green had been wrapped from the tip-top to the trunk in white lights. They twinkled against the night sky like fallen stars.

Brad squeezed my hand. "I have something for you."

"What?"

He pulled a flat, square box wrapped in gold paper with a velvet ribbon from his pocket. My heart dropped.

"I haven't finished my shopping yet. This month's been crazy."

Brad passed the box to me. "Don't worry about it."

"You really shouldn't have got me anything."

He grinned impishly. "I wanted to. Go ahead. Open it."

I reluctantly tore the paper and pulled out a black box stamped with the name of a boutique in the Old Market. I lifted the lid and pulled out a stunning bracelet made with silver block beads stamped with flowers. "It's beautiful."

Brad's smile broadened. "I thought you'd like it." He took it from my hand. "Let me put it on you." He undid the clasp and placed it around my wrist. He fumbled a few times before he got the clasp to reclose. "There." He pulled my hand to his lips and kissed it. "Merry Christmas."

I felt like a heel. He really seemed to like me. I had little experience with casual dating and wasn't quite sure what etiquette required I do now. "I feel bad that I haven't gotten you a present yet."

"It's okay. Really. I don't need you to buy me anything. Promise you won't run off with that other guy before I get back from Missouri."

It took me a moment to remember I'd told him about Patrick sending me roses. "You don't have to worry about that."

Brad stared into my eyes. "Good. It's not that I don't like a little competition, but I'd like to know what I'm up against."

I turned and started to walk back toward the restaurant. "I don't date married men, even if they are 'separated.'"

"A woman with strong morals." He caught up to me. "I like that."

"Would you date someone who was still married?"

"I don't know." He shrugged. "Probably. I mean, what's the problem if they're already getting divorced?"

"Getting a divorce means they're still married." I glanced at him to try and read his face. "Doesn't that mean anything to you?"

It took him a moment before he answered; it seemed like he was formulating what response I wanted to hear. "I guess, when you put it that way, it wouldn't be right."

I nodded. "Thank you."

We chatted about insignificant things until we arrived back at the restaurant parking lot. I reached for my keys, but Brad stopped me before I could unlock my door. Gently he pressed me up against the side of my car. He lowered his face close to mine.

"I really will miss you while I'm away," he whispered.

"Thank you for the bracelet."

He cupped my face with his hands and kissed me. Softly, but with purpose. The kind of kiss that would have melted my socks off if Mark had given it to me. Unfortunately, Brad wasn't Mark.

He pulled back and looked into my eyes. "Merry Christmas. I hope Santa is good to you." He kissed me again, then backed away so I could unlock my door.

"You have a good Christmas, too," I said. "Call me when you get back in town."

"I will. I'll see you on New Year's Eve."

"See you then." I shut the door and waved goodbye.

My thoughts wandered as I drove the back streets of Omaha before pulling onto the highway. Would I ever love someone again? The same love I had for Mark?

CHAPTER FOURTEEN

'Twas the night before Christmas Eve, and Marigold Manor was a madhouse. Staff rushed about, trying to get medications ready for residents to take with them before they left with relatives for the holidays. Those residents who weren't going anywhere complained that there would be no Bingo on Saturday or Monday afternoon.

"It's because of the holiday," I explained again, this time to Rachel Johnson.

She scowled up at me from her wheelchair. "But, why no Bingo on Monday?"

"Because Christmas is on a Sunday, the federal government takes the day off on Monday. That means the staff gets Monday off as well."

"It's not fair. If Christmas was on Monday, would you take Tuesday off as well?"

At this point, I want to take all of next week off. "No, Rachel. Only if a holiday falls on a weekend."

"Where will you be? Can't you come in and call Bingo?"

"Afraid not. I have plans." *They involve sleeping in past six and finding my bedroom floor again by doing my laundry.*

Rachel pushed her wheelchair away. "Why do I pay for care in this place, if everyone's going to take a vacation and leave us here alone?"

"You can play this afternoon," I called after her. "At one."

I stood in the lobby and let my breath out slowly. *Not long now, and you can go home.*

I jumped when Patty came up behind me.

"Didn't mean to scare you, but I don't want everyone to know," she whispered.

"Know what?"

"There's chocolate, cookies, and popcorn in the conference room. You look like you could use a treat."

I smiled at the reindeer antlers she had on. "Where did you get those?"

"I've had 'em for years." She motioned with her head toward the office, making the antlers bobble wildly. "Come on and feast for a minute. You have time before Bingo, right?"

I followed her through the main office and into the conference room off to the side. The six-foot table sat buried under a smorgasbord of treats. "Where did all this come from?"

Patty leaned her thin body against the doorframe. "Everyone brings in stuff this time of year. Visiting nurses, Hospice, physical therapy, families." She pointed to a festive tin. "Check out the fudge. The Franklins' daughter makes it. It's fabulous."

I took the lid off and was engulfed by the scent of chocolate and peanut butter. My mouth watered. I offered the tin to Patty first.

"I've already had two pieces, but I can't resist it. Guess I won't have dinner tonight." She took a square.

"I didn't have lunch, so...." I picked a big piece and shut the lid. I took a bite. My mouth exploded with the flavor of sweet chocolate and rich peanut butter. Closing my eyes, I savored the experience of melting wonderfulness. "If there's food in heaven, this fudge will be there."

Patty nodded.

I ate a cookie and then took a Styrofoam bowl full of popcorn. "I'll bring this back to my office to snack on later."

"There's plenty here. Come back if you want some more."

I left the conference room and plowed into Chester as I walked into the main office. The popcorn flew everywhere. *Great.*

Chester stumbled backward. "I'm sorry."

"My fault," I apologized. "I wasn't looking where I was going."

Patty stood laughing in the doorway. "That's a picture."

I got on the floor to pick up the kernels. I seemed to be spending a lot of time lately on the floor picking up food. First the cookies at Nancy's, and now this. Chester knelt to help me.

I looked back at Patty. "You could help, too, you know. Instead of enjoying yourself at our expense."

She tossed her blonde hair over her shoulder. "That wouldn't be as much fun."

Nancy walked in and stared at Chester and me on the floor. "One of you lose a contact or something?"

"No, popcorn," Chester explained.

We got most of the mess up, and I threw away the bowl.

Nancy picked up a stack of phone messages from the slot on Patty's desk. "Did you need something else?"

Chester stood. "I wanted to check in before I left on vacation."

Chester is going away? Is he going alone? "Where?"

He shook his head in confusion. "What?"

I tried to act casual. "Are you going somewhere special?"

"Louisa and I are driving the girls out to Boulder to spend Christmas with my parents."

I realized I had been holding my breath. I let it out and smiled. "Sounds like fun."

Nancy shuffled through the memos. "You have someone to fill in for you while you're gone?"

"Jose is on for Saturday and Sunday. He needs the holiday pay. Ana will cover me for Monday and Tuesday. I'll be back on Wednesday."

"Good." Nancy patted his shoulder as she walked by him toward her office. "Have a great Christmas. Enjoy the time with your family."

"*Gracias.*" He looked at Patty and me. "You two have a good Christmas."

"Thanks," said Patty.

I shrugged. "I'll try."

He frowned. "You don't sound convincing."

"I have to spend Christmas down in Lincoln with my father. He's not exactly warm and fuzzy."

"I'm sorry."

"Not your fault. Have fun with your family. Tell them I said hi."

"I will." A funny look crossed his face. He reached out toward me, and my heart skipped a beat. "You have popcorn in your hair."

"What?"

He chuckled as his fingers pulled a puffed kernel from my head. He held it out to me.

"Now, that's attractive, isn't it? Is there any more?"

"One." He removed another piece and tossed it into the garbage. He turned back to me. "There. Beautiful."

I saw it again, for a moment. The look. My heart fluttered, and I swallowed. "Thanks."

He looked away. *"De nada. Adios, amigas."* He walked to the door. *"¡Feliz Navidad!"*

Patty and I called after him. *"Feliz Navidad."*

"Oh, great." Patty groaned as I turned to go.

"What?"

"I'll be singing that stupid song for the rest of the day now." She plopped down in her chair, whistling the Spanish carol.

Nancy appeared in the doorway of her office. "Hey, did I ask you yet about Bill Watson's memorial service?"

I shook my head.

"His son Jimmy called this morning. They're taking the body down to Kansas tonight, and they'll bury him on Tuesday. He wants to know if we can have a memorial service in the chapel sometime after New Year. Maybe that Monday or Tuesday?"

"I don't see a problem with that."

"He'd also like to use the activity room for a gathering place afterward. He'd get someone to provide punch and cookies and stuff, but he wondered if they could use our tables."

"I'll check the book and see what we have going on. Do you have a number I can reach him at?"

Nancy disappeared into her office and came back a moment later with a piece of paper. "Here you go. Let him know as soon as possible, okay? Then leave me a note if I'm not here."

"You leaving early, too?" I asked.

"If I can. I want to stop at the mall this afternoon."

"I have to do that, too," I admitted. "But, I'll probably wait and go in the morning."

"Good luck finding a parking spot on Christmas Eve."

"I know." I pushed the note with Jimmy's cell phone number into my pocket. "If I don't see you, have a great Christmas."

"You, too. Take anything from the conference room you want home. Except the fudge. I'm bringing that to my mother's tomorrow and telling her I made it!"

I waved goodbye and left to the sound of Patty still whistling the tune to "*Feliz Navidad*" while she worked on the computer.

Frank watched Edith move her game piece across the backgammon board. "My son Michael is picking me up around four. I'll drive out with him and his family to my daughter Angela's house in Peoria."

"When will you be home?" Edith passed him the dice.

Frank took his turn. "Monday afternoon."

She tried not to show her disappointment. "Oh."

"What are your plans for the holiday? Going to your daughter's?"

Edith shook her head. "No. Joyce and Roger always spend Christmas away from home. I think this year they're in London. They'll be back next Wednesday. We celebrate on New Year's Day."

"That's odd."

"It's easier for Joyce's son Simon to come on New Year's. That way he can spend Christmas with his wife's family."

Frank looked up at her, concern written on his face. "What will you do for the holiday? You're not stuck here alone, are you?"

She smiled at his worry. "No. Ginny and I will go to church on Christmas Eve, and my friends Donna and Harvey have adopted me into their family. I'll go to their house on Christmas Day."

"Good." He patted her hand. "I'd hate to think of you here alone."

"I'll be fine."

They played backgammon for a few more minutes before Edith moved her last piece off the board. "There! I win again!"

Frank sat back in his chair. "You're a lucky lady, Mrs. MacPherson. I'll give you that much."

She put the pieces away. "I have been lucky over the years, I have to admit. I've had a good life."

Frank grew quiet.

"Thinking about Bill?" she asked.

Frank nodded. "It hasn't really sunk in yet. I keep thinking he's visiting his son for the holiday, and we'll be back reading the paper together on Monday."

"It'll do you good to get away this weekend. Take your mind off things."

"I suppose." He looked over at Edith. "I'll miss seeing you, though."

"Pishaw! You'll be so busy with your grandbabies, you probably won't even think of me."

Frank sat up. "That's not true. I'll miss our talks. Family is fine, but it's not like. . . . "

Edith tilted her head. "Not like what?"

"I don't know. Not like being with a friend."

Friend. Yes, a good friend. "I know what you mean."

Frank's gaze shifted away. "I have something for you. For Christmas."

She couldn't help the grin that spread across her face. "Frank Leno! You shouldn't have!"

He smiled but still couldn't meet her eyes. "It's nothing much. Would you like it now or when I get back?"

Her stomach fluttered. "Why not now? It'll give me something to remind me of you while you're gone."

Frank stood. "Wait here."

"But, if I wait, I can't get you your gift."

He stopped and turned back. "You bought me something?"

Edith nodded. "Ginny took me out Monday night to finish my shopping."

"I'll meet you back here in ten minutes, all right?"

"Sounds good." Edith rose and walked down the hallway to her apartment, glad she'd given in to her impulse to buy a gift for Frank. She'd bought it on the sly while Ginny had been looking in another area of the store. She hadn't originally thought to buy him something, but when she'd seen the cardigan on the model, she hadn't been able to resist. The deep heather blue color would complement his eyes, and the soft knit would be sure to keep him warm. She'd had it wrapped at the store so Ginny wouldn't see it.

Entering her apartment, she pulled the box out from under the small Christmas tree Ginny had set up in the corner by the couch. Frank was already sitting at their table by the time she made it back to the lobby. A brightly colored gift bag with silver and blue tissue paper peeking out of the top sat in front of him.

"Wow." Frank smiled. "You bought me something big!"

"Perhaps I put something small in a big box. You won't know until you open it." She handed him the gift.

He shook it. "Hmmmm, doesn't rattle. It's not another backgammon board."

Edith took a seat by his side. "Go ahead and open it."

He tore the wrapping from the package, then took the lid off the box. He fingered the fabric of the sweater. "It's soft." He held it up. "It's a great color."

Edith's hand trembled as she straightened one of the sleeves so it hung nicer. "Do you really like it? I saved the receipt if it's not the right size or you hate it. Don't worry about hurting my feelings." She drew her hand back. "I saw it and thought of you."

Frank unbuttoned the cardigan and slipped it over the shirt he wore. He stood up and modeled it for Edith, turning from side to side to show it off. "What do you think?"

"I think it looks wonderful."

He rubbed his hands along the sleeves. "It feels great. I'll bring this to my daughter's house. She always keeps the thermostat low."

Edith put a hand to her face, trying to hide the blush she could feel in her cheeks.

Frank sat back down and pushed the gift bag toward her. "Your turn."

She shivered with excitement. "What is it?"

"Open it, and find out."

She dug through the tissue paper and pulled out a chocolate-brown teddy bear. "He's adorable!" She rubbed the bear's head. "And he's so fluffy!"

"There's more," Frank said. "Take a good look at him."

Edith held the bear out and noticed it held a small jewelry box. "Frank Leno? Whatever did you do?"

"Now, don't get too excited. It's just a little something."

She pulled the box from the bear's arms and opened it to find a pair of gold earrings in the shape of roses. Her eyes moistened. "Oh, Frank. They're beautiful."

"You like them? I thought they'd remind you of springtime."

"I love them." She took out the small hoops in her ears and replaced them with Frank's gift. "What do you think?"

"Lovely, Mrs. MacPherson. Just lovely."

She picked up the bear and cuddled him. "Well, I guess Mr. Bear and I will have to get to know each other while you're away this weekend." She held the bear up to her face. "Isn't that right, Mr. Bear?"

"What's he saying?"

Edith raised an eyebrow at him. "A lady doesn't discuss private conversations with other people, Mr. Leno. But, you should know that Mr. Bear has made his intentions for this weekend clear to me, and you may have competition for a backgammon partner."

༄

I stared at my computer. The words on the screen blurred together. *I'm too tired for this.* I had to get a jump on the newsletter before I could go home. Three days off. Thank God. I wondered what this holiday would hold. My life had been a rollercoaster of change since Thanksgiving — dating, grief share meetings, even going to church again. I wasn't sure I could handle any more excitement.

I grabbed my coffee mug and took a sip of the lukewarm liquid. Someone rapped on the door.

"Come in."

I did a double-take as Patrick Johnson stepped into my office.

"I'm glad you're still here," he said with a warm smile. "The rest of the office staff is gone."

"I'm finishing up some stuff." I sat back in my chair. "What are you doing here?"

He came further into my office. "I wanted to thank you for taking such good care of my mother." He pulled a gift from behind his back. "I know she's not the easiest person to deal with."

Didn't I just say I didn't want any more excitement? "You shouldn't have."

He shrugged good-naturedly. "I was wandering aimlessly through the stores last night looking for presents, and you're the only one I found something for."

I had to admit, he was handsome for an older man. *How old is he, anyway?* I knew his sister Paula was in her fifties, but she'd told me she was much older than Patrick. I tried to study him casually. A hint of silver highlighted his dark-brown hair. Dimples popped through when he smiled while deepening the lines around his eyes. *Late thirties, early forties maybe*. He held the gift out to me.

I stood and took it from his hands. "Thank you."

"You don't even know what it is."

I undid the metallic gold ribbon tied around the maroon paper. Slipping my finger under the tape, I undid the package. *A book?* I turned it over. *A Study of Van Gogh.* I let out a shocked breath.

"What is it?" he asked.

"I can't believe this."

The smile faded from Patrick's face. "Did I do something wrong?"

"No!" I opened the book and flipped through the pages. "When I turned sixteen, my mother took me to New York for my birthday. We spent one afternoon at the Metropolitan Museum of Art. Not exactly fun for a teenager. Until I saw this." I turned the book around to show him the picture. *Irises.* I put the book on the edge of my desk. "I sat on a bench across from that painting for at least a half-hour. You can't see it in the photo." My finger traced the outline of the vase holding the flowers. "But, he used layers and layers of paint. It was incredible. Disturbing. Beautiful." I looked up at Patrick. "Sorry. I don't mean to go on and on like that."

"I'm glad you like it." His blue eyes seemed to twinkle. "I saw it and knew it would be perfect for you."

My finger continued to trace the picture. "I don't know what to say. Thank you."

"You're welcome."

I realized he stood very close to the edge of my desk. A warning bell went off in my head. I stepped back and sat down. I saw the flash of disappointment behind his eyes.

"Are you here to take your mom home for the holiday?"

Patrick shook his head. "I'm just visiting today. Paula will bring her over to her house tomorrow."

"Good. Then she won't miss Bingo." I explained the conversation I'd had with his mother earlier.

"That sounds like her." He pointed to the book. "That's why you deserve something special. That, and I'm hoping you'll change your mind about going out with me."

My tongue seemed to swell in my mouth, and every last ounce of spit evaporated. "I'm sorry, call me old-fashioned, but I wouldn't feel comfortable dating you." I wanted to say "ever," but I couldn't. He looked so hopeful.

"Not until everything's final." He gave me a rakish grin. "The wait will make the first date more exciting."

CHAPTER FIFTEEN

I brought my grandmother to my house for a late Christmas Eve lunch, then to the five o'clock service at Cornerstone Lutheran Church. I sat in the pew and tried not to think about Mark. We'd attended service every Sunday together at this church. Old friends and acquaintances made sure to come up during the greeting time to tell me how glad they were to see me. I met them all with a smile and a lump in my throat.

"You're doing well, dear," Edith whispered. "I know this is hard for you."

I made it through the service, even letting myself enjoy singing the carols. Candles were passed out at the end as the lights dimmed in the sanctuary. We sang all the verses to "Silent Night," then filed out into the lobby. We blew out the flames and put the candles into a recycling bin for the next service. Pastor Robert stood shaking hands at the door.

"Edith." He smiled when he saw my grandmother. "You look wonderful, as always." His eyes registered surprise when he glanced my way. "Ginny." He took my hand. Instead of shaking it, he placed his other hand on top, sandwiching mine between his. "How are you?"

I started to give him the standard "fine," answer, but I could see from his face that he wanted to know more. "It's hard, but I'm doing better."

He gave me a genuine smile of affection. "I'm glad to hear it." He squeezed my hand. "Please, call me. If you ever need to talk. Or just to say hello. We've missed you around here."

"Thanks."

A line had formed behind us of people wanting to speak with the pastor. He let go of my hand. "I mean it. Call."

Edith and I buttoned up our coats. I took her arm, and we headed out into the frigid air. Luminaries flickered along the shoveled pathways, giving the night a magical glow.

Edith patted my elbow as we walked with care along the icy path. "People ask me every week how you are."

"I'd have thought they'd forgotten me by now."

"You're unforgettable."

I chuckled. "Now you've got me thinking about Nat King Cole."

She swatted my arm. "Don't change the subject. You should come back to church. You can't stay mad at God forever, you know."

A huge puff of condensation rose as I exhaled. "Not tonight, Grandma. Okay?"

She lifted an eyebrow at me but kept quiet.

Edith and I shared a cup of hot chocolate in her apartment while we exchanged gifts. I'd bought her the new Karen Kingsbury novel and a mystery by Mary Higgins Clark, plus a collection of her favorite body lotions from the local bath boutique. She opened one of the bottles and sniffed.

"Heavenly!"

I giggled.

"Your turn." She took a small box from under her tree and passed it to me.

I eyed her with suspicion. The box was shaped like one that came from a jewelry store. "What did you do? We agreed, no expensive gifts."

She stuck her tongue out at me. "Actually, it didn't cost me anything. It's something I wanted to give you."

I opened the box and lifted out a crystal and gold heart suspended on a long gold chain. "It's beautiful."

"Look closely at it."

Something tiny sat suspended within the crystal heart. I stared at it.

"Turn it over," Edith ordered.

I flipped the pendant over and read the inscription on the back. "If you have faith as a grain of mustard seed, nothing shall be impossible unto you."

Edith smiled. "My parents gave that to me when I was confirmed. I wanted to make sure it went to you."

I put on the necklace. "Thanks, Grandma."

"It's true, you know." She finished her cocoa. "All you need is a little faith, and nothing is impossible."

I sighed. "I'm trying."

She nodded. "I know."

"I'd better get going." I gave her a kiss on the cheek. "I'll call tomorrow."

"I'm going to Helen's at one. I should be home by six or so."

"Merry Christmas!"

She gave me a big hug. "Merry Christmas. Be careful driving to your dad's tomorrow."

"I will."

I walked out to the lobby and ran into Rachel Johnson and her daughter. They seemed agitated. "Is everything all right?"

Paula's mouth tightened into a hard line. I could see the tears welling in her eyes.

Rachel pounded on the arms of her wheelchair. "I want to be home. I don't want to be with strangers!"

"She lost it at dinner." Paula said. "Didn't recognize anyone. Couldn't remember that I'd told her about my brother's divorce." She pushed her mother's chair toward the elevator

"Patrick!" Rachel called. "Don't leave me alone!"

"Patrick didn't come with us, Mom." Paula pressed the button for the elevator. "It's just me."

"I'll call a med aid," I offered. "Then stop by and see if you need some help getting her ready for bed."

"Thanks."

I tracked down one of the girls on duty. She wasn't too pleased about actually having to do something on Christmas Eve, but she came with me to Rachel's room. When we got there, Paula was kneeling in front of Rachel, trying to reason with her.

"Mom, please, calm down."

"You should have told me Kristen and the kids weren't coming. You should have told me."

Paula rubbed her mother's knee. "I did. Before Patrick came."

"No, you didn't. I would have remembered. You didn't say anything."

Paula crossed to me. "She's never been this bad before. She couldn't recognize any of the grandkids."

The med aid stooped down by the wheelchair. "Rachel, would you like me to get you ready for bed? I bet a good night's sleep will help you to feel better."

The old woman nodded. "I want to go to bed. I don't feel well."

The med aid stood and pushed the wheelchair toward the bedroom.

"Paula?" Rachel looked over her shoulder. "Paula, are you here?"

Her daughter hurried to her mother's side. "Yes, Mom. I'm right here."

Rachel took her hand. "Don't leave me."

"I'll stay while you get ready for bed, don't worry."

"Promise you won't leave me?"

Paula patted her hand. "I promise."

Rachel's voice trembled. "I need you."

"I'll be here for you, Mom."

The med aid brought Rachel into the bedroom then closed the door. As Paula stood, a tear ran down her cheek. "She's never said anything like that to me before."

Chester sat between his sister Theresa and his father in the pew. It had been a while since he'd been to church with his whole family. They took up two rows with all the siblings, their spouses, and their children. The Martin family had definitely taken the "Be fruitful and multiply" commandment to heart. *Except me.*

He knew his being single at thirty-two disappointed his mom. She never said anything, but it was the way she stared at him when she thought he wasn't looking. He'd seen the faraway gleam in her eye that betrayed her feelings.

An organ played the opening notes to "Hark, the Herald Angels Sing." The congregation stood. Chester sang the words from memory while his mind drifted back to Nebraska.

I wonder what Ginny is doing tonight? Who does she spend Christmas Eve with? It hurt him to think of how little she seemed to enjoy the holiday. Between thoughts of Mark and the stress with her parents she didn't seem able to experience the joy of the season.

His older sister Theresa pushed him with her shoulder. "Pay attention!" She pointed to the verse on the hymnal. "We skipped 3 and 4."

He focused on singing the last verses, then sat down. Katy and her cousins were sprawled along the pew, coloring the handouts given to them by the ushers. Maria and his niece Brenda stared up at the ceiling, while all around the sanctuary candles flickered and sputtered with the changing air currents caused by so many people breathing.

I bet if Ginny spent Christmas here, she'd learn to like it again. Chester tried to focus on the readings and the homily to no avail. He couldn't stop the daydreams of Ginny enjoying Christmas Eve with his family.

I sat in the pew of St. Andrew's Catholic Church, staring at the ornate alter as parishioners made their way outside. A huge stained-glass mosaic of Christ on the cross shimmered behind the altar. Candles and poinsettias decorated the raised platform. Evergreen boughs had been tied to the front pews, and satin banners hung along the side walls. I'd stopped in on my way home from Marigold, not quite ready to be alone on Christmas Eve.

"Hello, stranger." Father Dan slid beside me on the pew.

"Hey there."

His eyes twinkled in the candlelight. "How're you doing?"

I shrugged.

"Nancy said you'd been to one of her meetings. I'm glad."

"Keeping tabs on me, huh?"

"I've been concerned. How was the meeting?"

"Good. Weird, but good. I really like Nancy."

Father Dan smiled. "She and Luke are great people. I'm sure they can help you, if you let them."

I turned away and stared at a candle on the altar. "I went on a date. A couple, actually, with a friend of my stepbrother."

"And? How'd that go?"

I let out a loud sigh. "He's not Mark."

Dan didn't say anything for a while. "No one is going to be like Mark."

"I know."

"But, maybe someone will bring something new to your life. Something different, but special."

The candles sputtered as another priest opened a side door to the sanctuary. I glanced at Father Dan. "I guess I should get going. I just wanted to wish you a Merry Christmas."

His blue eyes clouded with concern. "You okay?"

I nodded. "Yeah."

His eyes narrowed. "You sure?"

"I'm sure." We stood up together, and he walked me to the door. "Thanks for everything."

He gave me a hug. "Don't forget what I told you about the trees, Ginny. Things look barren now, but there will be a spring. You just have to hope."

"I'm trying." I waved goodbye as he returned to the sanctuary. The sand-covered sidewalk crunched under my feet as I made my way out to the parking lot. A halo glowed around the moon, and ice crystals in the snow sparkled under the street lights. A picture-perfect Christmas Eve. I wiped away my tears as I started my car and headed home.

CHAPTER SIXTEEN

I woke up Christmas morning at 4:00 a.m. with a killer headache, the kind I usually get after a particularly nasty carnival ride. My bed rocked as if I'd set sail on rough seas. A sharp cramp in my stomach doubled me over. I managed to roll out of bed and stumble into the bathroom before my bedtime snack of sugar cookies and milk reappeared in my toilet bowl. I remained on the floor for several hours, only getting up to let my stomach heave. By nine, the floor stopped rocking long enough for me to crawl to the phone and call my dad.

A female voice answered. "Merry Christmas!"

My head throbbed, and my stomach cramped again. "Brittany?"

"Yeah. Who is this?"

"It's Ginny."

"You sound terrible."

"I've got some kind of stomach bug. I won't be coming down today."

Brittany whined, "Emma will be disappointed."

"I don't think she'd want to see me right now. Nobody wants to be sick over Christmas vacation."

"I guess you're right. When will you come down, then?"

I clutched my stomach as another cramp stabbed me. "I don't know. Look, I gotta go. Bye!" I barely made it to the bathroom before whatever had made me vomit now attacked my intestines.

∽

Chester stood in the driveway of his parents' house wearing his sweats and a coat, holding a cup of coffee. He'd walked outside to grab the newspaper and been distracted by the brilliant red and peach hues of sunrise over the mountains.

Lord, you are good, and your mercies are new each morning. How could anyone believe this was an accident? His coffee let off little wisps of steam, and he took a sip. Someone crunched on the gravel behind him.

"*Feliz Navidad, mi hijo.*" His father, Alex, shivered in the freezing air.

"*Feliz Navidad,* Papa."

Alex Martin stared at the mountains as he stood beside his son. "*Es muy bonito,* no?"

"*Si.* I forget how beautiful the mountains are sometimes, living in Nebraska. They take your breath away."

His father put a hand on his shoulder. "What are you thinking about?"

Chester passed his father the paper. "God."

Alex nodded. "A good thing to think about. Especially today." The two men watched as the sun crested the peaks and the sky melted into blue. Only the glow of a couple peach clouds remained from the glorious sunrise. "Your mother will yell at us if we stay out here too long in the cold." He patted his son's back and turned toward the house.

Chester took one last look at the view, then followed his father down the long gravel driveway to the house. It was a testament to Alex Martin's perseverance and ingenuity. His parents had bought the land twenty years ago, before the housing boom in Colorado. Over the years, they'd put away a little money each month, until eight years ago, when they'd finally started building their dream house: two stories, four bedrooms, a huge kitchen big enough for their four children and seven grandchildren to eat in together. Almost every room offered at least a glimpse of the Rocky Mountains.

Chester and his father wiped their feet on the straw mat outside the door. They slipped their shoes and coats off, depositing them on the mud room floor before stepping into the kitchen. Chester's mother, Rita, stood at the counter, whisking eggs. Although she'd lived in America for forty-eight years, she still preferred to speak Spanish in the house. Chester had spent his youth jumping back and forth between both languages so that he hardly noticed now.

His mother looked up as they came into the kitchen. She spoke in rapid Spanish. "A.J., Maria, and Brenda are awake. I let them take their stockings into our room to open. I told them they had to let the little ones sleep a little longer before they wake them." She poured some milk into the bowl and kept mixing. "I can't believe they let the children stay up until midnight. They'll be tired this morning."

"They'll be fine," said Alex, also in Spanish. He poured himself a cup of coffee. "I'm going to take my shower now, while there's still some hot water."

She glanced at her son, then back to her husband. "Have you spoken to him yet?"

Alex shook his head.

Chester leaned against the counter. "Spoken to who?"

His father switched back to English. "You. She's worried about you."

"Me? Why?"

"Because, there is something not right," his mother said in heavily accented English. "You are worried about something. What is it?"

Chester gave his mother a hug. "Don't worry, Mama. Everything is good."

Her eyes searched his. "You're not in trouble again, are you?"

"No, Mama."

She put the bowl of eggs on the counter. "And Louisa? She is fine, too?"

"Yes, Mama. Everyone is fine."

She swatted his arm. "Then why are you worrying me?"

He chuckled. "I'm sorry. I don't mean to."

"You look lost. Your thoughts are somewhere else." She paused for a moment before he could see comprehension cross her face. "Ah! I know! It is a girl!"

His father leaned back on the counter. "A girl? Is that it?"

Chester took an opportunity to refill his coffee cup. When he turned back around, his mother's eyes were bright with excitement.

"Who is she?"

He sighed as he sat down at the table. His parents sat on either side of him, breakfast temporarily forgotten.

"Is there a problem with the girl?" His mother whispered, "She's not pregnant, is she?"

"Mama! No." Chester took a sip of coffee. His parents both let out sighs of relief. "I'm not seeing anyone."

His father frowned. "But, I thought you said—"

"You said. I didn't." Chester took another drink.

"No, there is a woman. I can tell." Rita folded her hands on the table.

Chester nodded.

"So, what is the problem?" Alex shrugged. "There is a woman you're not seeing. Have you ever met her, or is she a dream?"

"She's not a dream, Papa. She's a friend."

"A friend?"

"Yes. And I don't know how to make her more."

His mother reached across the table and took his hand. "You must tell her how you feel."

He looked into her eyes. "How?"

"What do you mean, how?" his father interrupted. "You talk to her."

Chester shook his head. "It's not that easy."

His father furrowed his eyebrows. "Why not?"

Chester couldn't put his thoughts into words. *Why is it when I think about Ginny nothing makes sense? I'm a complete idiot.*

A huge smile formed on his mother's face. "Because he is in love with her."

Alex glanced between mother and son. "So?"

Rita patted Chester's hand, then sat back in her chair. She gestured toward her husband. "You couldn't speak to me when you first saw me."

Alex scowled. "That's not true."

Rita's eyes sparkled. "He watched me for weeks before he spoke to me. I had come to work my uncle's fields for the harvest. Your father would spy on me as I brought the corn in to sell." She laughed lightly. Chester could see the young girl she used to be hiding beneath her wrinkled skin. "I would see him trying not to look," she continued, "but always his eyes would turn to me. Like a...a...."

"Magnet?" Chester suggested.

Rita nodded. "Yes. But, he wouldn't speak to me."

Alex looked at his wife. Chester could see the deep love the man had for her. "How could I? She was so beautiful." He brushed the back of his hand down her cheek. "She still is."

Chester waited until they broke the tender moment themselves. "What did you do? When did you finally meet?"

Alex beamed. "One day, she tripped as she walked past me. Her basket of corn flew out of her hands. I had to help her pick it up."

"I didn't trip."

"Of course you did," Alex said. "You fell right in front of me. I had to help."

"I did it on purpose."

Silence fell in the kitchen as Chester and his father contemplated what she'd said. A deep chuckle rose from Chester's throat, while his father looked scandalized.

"You fell on purpose?" asked Alex.

She raised her hands out to her sides. "It was the only thing I could think of to do. I wanted to meet you, and you wouldn't speak to me. I knew if I pretended to trip you would help me." She gave her husband a loving smile. "I knew."

His parents held hands across the table. *Does Ginny know? Can she tell how I feel?*

"Look over here, Dad," called Frank's daughter-in-law Annette. She pulled her auburn hair out of her eyes, then squinted into the camera lens. "That's perfect!" She snapped a picture.

"Wait! Wait!" His son-in-law Peter waved his arm. "I have to get a shot, too."

Frank sat on his daughter's sectional couch surrounded by his three children, nine grandchildren, and four great-granddaughters. In his arms he held his first great-grandson. *I've been truly blessed. Thank you, Lord.* He wished his wife Lucy could have survived to meet this son of their granddaughter. He stared down at the baby's sleeping face. Little Jonathon Franklin.

I bet Edith would eat this cutie right up. It surprised him how easily Edith's face kept popping into his head over the weekend. He'd thought, being around his family, he'd be consumed with thoughts of Lucy, but the two women seemed to flow effortlessly together. *They're similar in many ways. Both strong, intelligent ladies with wicked senses of humor.* Physically, they couldn't have been more different. Lucy had been small and dark, a whirlwind of passion and temper. Edith stood an inch or so shorter than him and had that beautiful head of silver-white hair.

His son Michael interrupted his thoughts. "I'll take the baby, Dad."

Frank relinquished the squirming bundle in his arms. "He's beginning to smell a bit fragrant."

Michael lifted the baby, and sniffed. His nose wrinkled. "Jennifer! Come and change my grandson!"

Frank stood and stretched his legs while the rest of his family sat talking around his daughter's large family room. Although the new baby, Jonathon, was the first great-grandson, there were plenty of great-granddaughters scurrying around. Frank had given up trying to remember which lacy-frocked girl belonged to which parents as they squealed and laughed together on the floor. He stepped over a pile of discarded gift wrap and made his way to the kitchen.

His daughter Angela looked up from the sink as he entered the room. Her dark eyes showed her concern. "Everything okay?"

"Wonderful. You cook like your mom." Frank rubbed his stomach in appreciation.

Angela beamed. "The highest praise I could hope for. Thanks, Dad." She pushed a rogue strand of black hair back against her head.

Frank poured himself a cup of coffee and grabbed a thin Italian cookie from the plate next to it. "I'm not used to all the noise is all. Wanted to sit somewhere quiet for a minute." He took his mug and sat down at the oak table while Angela went back to washing dishes. "You want any help with those?"

Angela shook her head. "You relax. I like the quiet as well."

A random shriek broke the calm, but other voices cooled the tantrum. Frank decided his help was unnecessary. He drank his coffee and ate the cookie he had grabbed.

Angela let the water drain from the sink. She turned to her father as she picked up a dish towel to dry the items dripping on the counter. "So, how are you doing? Are you happy at Marigold?"

"I am." Frank felt his cheeks lift as he grinned. He couldn't stop another picture of Edith from floating across his mind. "It's finally beginning to feel like home."

"Good." She put down a pot she'd rubbed dry. "How's Bill?"

His heart sank at the mention of his friend. "I forgot to tell you. Bill died last week."

Angela leaned against the counter. "I'm sorry. That must be rough for you. I know you were good friends."

"We were at that." Frank nodded. "But, it's to be expected at my age."

"Don't say that!" His daughter waved the dish towel in his direction. "You still have a lot of good years ahead of you!"

"Do I?"

She walked over to the table. "I knew there was something bugging you." She leaned over and gave her father a hug. "Don't let this get you too down. You still have a lot of life to live, Dad." She sat next to him. "That's why I hate you living in there. It makes you think you're old, and you're not!"

"I'm seventy-six, Angela. That's not young."

"But, it's not old, either. Not with your health." Her brown eyes stared at him. "Come live with Peter and me. We've only got James left in the house now, and that's only when he's home from college. We could renovate the basement for you."

Frank shook his head. "Now is the time for you and Peter to be enjoying your time alone. Exploring and seeing where you fit together now. You don't need me in the middle of things."

Her lips formed a hard line. "You wouldn't be in the middle of things. I know you can take care of yourself."

"But, for how much longer? Sure, I'm good now, but you never know when something is going to happen. You don't want to be stuck taking care of me."

"We wouldn't be stuck. We love you."

He put his hand on her knee. "I know you do. I love you, too. Don't worry about me. I'm fine at Marigold."

"But, Bill was your only friend."

Frank snorted. "Whatever gave you that idea?"

Angela looked surprised. "He's the only one you've ever mentioned."

"I have other friends. I can still drive my car. I go over to Veterans' home and visit Martin and Thomas. I still volunteer with the Red Cross at the bloodmobiles." He patted her leg. "I have plenty to keep me busy."

"Are you sure? You're not saying that to make me feel better?"

Frank smiled. "I'm sure." *Three months ago, I almost called to see if you'd take me in. Now, I wouldn't dream of leaving Marigold.*

∽∾

Edith paced in her apartment. She dialed Ginny's home phone number for the fourth time since she'd returned from Donna's house two hours ago. She glanced at the clock as the answering machine picked up again. 8:45. Edith didn't leave a message. She dialed Ginny's cell phone number and again hung up when the voice mail message came on.

This wasn't like Ginny at all. There'd been no phone call this morning to wish her a Merry Christmas, no messages on the machine when she'd gotten home, and now no answer. Ginny never stayed at her father's for long. *And even if she is there, why isn't she answering her cell phone?*

Panic set in. *What if she never made it home last night? What if she hit a patch of black ice and lost control of her car?* Horrible images of twisted metal and shattered glass filled Edith's imagination. *I wish Frank were here.* She stopped her pacing and took a deep breath. *Now, Edith, you don't need a man to solve this problem. What else can you do?*

She grabbed the phone and dialed information. "Lincoln," she told the computer when it asked what city she wanted. "Gregory Stafford." She opted to let the computer connect her for a small fee on her phone bill.

"Merry Christmas," answered a female voice after a few rings.

Edith took another deep breath. "Hello. Is this the Stafford residence?"

"Yes, it is. Who is this?"

"I'm Edith MacPherson. I used to be Gregory's mother-in-law. I'm looking for my granddaughter, Ginny. Is she still there, by any chance?"

There was a pause. "No. She didn't come down today."

Edith reached out and balanced herself on the counter as the blood drained from her head. "What?"

"She called this morning and said she was sick."

"Is Gregory there, please? I'd like to speak to him."

The phone clunked as the woman set it down. A minute later, someone picked it up again.

"Edith?"

"Gregory, I'm worried."

"What's wrong?"

"Ginny didn't call me this morning. She's not answering either of her phones."

He let out an irritated sigh. "She's sick. She's probably in bed asleep."

"I didn't know she was sick. I've called her house four times now. Don't you think the phone would have woken her up?"

"Maybe she turned the ringer off."

"What did she say was wrong with her? How did she sound this morning?"

"I didn't talk with her. Brittany said she sounded sick. Something about a stomach bug."

Edith tightened her grip on the phone. "You need to check on her."

"What?"

"You need to see if she's all right."

Ginny's father grunted. "And, how am I supposed to do that? I'm down here in Lincoln, Edith. What do you propose I do?"

Edith fought to keep her anger down. "I propose you act like a concerned father, Gregory. Try and think about what little you know of your daughter." Edith's voice trembled. "You know how close she and I are. You know this is Christmas. You know if Ginny were well she would have called me at some point during the day."

"Edith, I—"

"Don't you 'Edith' me, Gregory Stafford. You get in your car and check on your daughter. I would, but I don't have a car. I can't even call a cab, because my money is locked up in the office. Be a father for once, Gregory." Edith took a deep breath. "Be a father to your daughter for once, and find out what's wrong with her."

Only silence answered her for several seconds. "Give me some time. I'll figure something out."

"Thank you. I'll be waiting for your call."

ᴄᴏᴄᴏ

I tried to open my eyes when I heard a distant pounding. Thud. Thud. Thud.

My eyelids stayed glued shut. Someone moaned. A bell rang. *My doorbell? Is that my doorbell?*

Thud. Thud. Thud.

I wanted to get up. Honestly, I did. But, someone had tied weights to my arms and legs – either that, or somehow replaced my blood with lead.

A loud crash from down the hall finally woke me up enough to lift my eyelids. The harsh light from the bulbs around my bathroom mirror made me close them again.

"Miss Stafford?" An unfamiliar voice floated down from somewhere in the house. "Ginny Stafford, are you here?"

I tried to answer. Someone groaned. *Who else is here with me? Who's making that awful noise?*

Footsteps came closer. A man's voice called out. "Ginny? Are you here?"

Again, I heard the moan. A low, almost animal growl.

"She's in here. I found her!" The man sat or knelt next to me. "Ginny! Ginny, can you hear me?" He lifted my arm. More footsteps came near. "Pulse is weak and rapid."

"Look at the blood on the counter."

Blood? What blood?

A hand gently turned my head. "Looks like she hit her head and passed out. Probably dehydrated, too. Better call the EMTs." The man picked up my hand. "Miss Stafford? Ginny? Can you hear me?"

I wanted to answer him, but I couldn't seem to summon the energy needed to make a coherent sound, never mind talk.

The voice from the other room spoke. "Dispatch, we need the EMTs out to 214 Franklin in Bellevue. Woman, late twenties, unresponsive. Possible concussion and dehydration."

More hand-patting. "Ginny? Ginny, if you can hear me, squeeze my hand."

I tried to respond.

"I felt something. Ginny? Can you open your eyes for me?"

I forced my eyes to open. A kind face stared down at me. That was all my mind could register at the moment. Whoever found me had a kind face.

The man smiled. "Hey, there. Don't worry about anything, Miss Stafford. We're going to get some help. You'll feel better in no time."

I looked into the man's green eyes and was surprised when the words "Merry Christmas" came out of my mouth before I passed out again. I have a vague recollection of fleeting images after that: being lifted onto a stretcher, the sting of an IV needle in my arm. The shock of cold air on my cheeks as they wheeled me out to the ambulance. The green-eyed man spoke to me again before they closed the vehicle doors.

"Don't worry, Ginny. These guys will take good care of you. And your father's on the way."

I closed my eyes as the ambulance took off. *I must be dreaming all this. My father doesn't care if I'm sick. He doesn't care . . . .*

By the time I got to the emergency room, the IV drip they'd given me had begun to work. At least I could keep my eyes open, and my arms didn't feel so heavy. They ran me through a CAT scan and informed me I had a slight concussion and would be admitted overnight for observation. An orderly brought me up to a private room and, with the help of the nurse on duty, transferred me over to a hospital bed.

"I'm Sarah," the nurse informed me. "Are you feeling dizzy? Nauseated?"

"A little."

"Any pain?"

"My head."

Her eyes narrowed. "On a scale of one to ten, ten being the worst pain imaginable, where are you?"

"About a four."

"That's okay, then. It's probably a combination of the bump on your head and the dehydration." She adjusted the drip of my IV. "We'll keep giving you fluids and I'm sure you'll feel better soon." She wrote something down on my chart then looked at me. "You up for visitors?"

"What?"

"There are some people who'd like to check in. You up for it?"

I nodded. Sarah stepped out of the room. A few moments later, my grandmother, father, stepmother, and half-sister came in the room.

"What are you doing here?" My voice sounded thick and slow.

Edith came to the bedside and took my hand. "Coming to see you, of course. You gave us a scare."

Emma jumped up on the foot of my bed. "Can I sit here?"

I tried to move my feet to give her more room. "Sure."

She thrust a tablet in front of my face. "I got an iPad. Want to see?"

My father pulled the tablet out of her hand. "Not right now. Go sit down on that chair in the corner."

Emma frowned, but she did what he asked. My dad stared down at me. "How do you feel?"

"Not good." I couldn't believe he was here, in the hospital. *Maybe I'm hallucinating.*

Brittany walked over to my father's side. "Why didn't you tell us you were so sick?"

"I didn't know." I closed my eyes, then opened them again to see if they would still be there. They were. "Why are you here?"

My grandmother caressed my hand. "You didn't call me. I knew something had to be wrong. I asked Gregory to help."

I shifted my gaze back to my father.

"I called a friend of mine in the police department. Asked him to check out your house." He put a hand on my shoulder. "I'll have someone fix the front door tomorrow."

"We got in the car as soon as the police called to say they were taking you to the hospital," Brittany said.

My father nodded. "I'll call my friend Jack Schaffer in the morning. He's a top-class neurosurgeon. I want him to take a look at your CAT scan and make sure everything's okay before they release you."

"Thanks." I soon lost the battle to keep awake. When I woke up sometime later, everyone had gone except for my father. He sat in a vinyl armchair watching CNN. I didn't say anything. I couldn't believe he was still there.

Sarah, the nurse, came in. "Oh, good, you woke up on your own."

My father walked over to the bed. "How're you feeling?"

I took stock of my aches and pains. "Better. My head's a little sore, but my body doesn't hurt much anymore."

Sarah took my blood pressure and temperature. "Everything's back to normal." She wrote something down on my chart. "Breakfast will be served soon. How's some toast and apple juice sound?"

I waited for my stomach to cramp up at the mention of food, but it didn't. "I'll give it a try."

She walked out of the room, leaving my father staring down at me.

"Where's Brittany and Emma?" I asked.

"I sent them home. Brittany will be back up at ten. You should be released this morning after Jack Schaffer takes a look at the CAT scan and says you're okay." He straightened out the bed cover. "We'll take you home."

"You don't have to stay."

"And, how would you get home?"

I paused to think about that. I didn't have my cell phone with me, and most of my friends were away for the holiday. "I could take a cab."

"We'll take you home, Virginia." He must have noticed me cringe. "You know why I call you Virginia?"

I shook my head.

"It was my grandmother's name. She was a wonderful woman. I'm sorry you didn't have the opportunity to meet her." He pulled a chair over to the side of the bed and sat down. "She raised me, you know. Like your grandmother helped raise you."

"But, your parents died," I said. Maybe it was the bump on the head that made me want to talk about things. Or, maybe it was because my father was actually sitting with me for once. Alone. Without a phone at his ear. "Your parents died. They didn't divorce and leave you."

My father's face remained stoic. "I suppose you're right. But, I felt abandoned all the same. A four-year-old really doesn't understand about wars overseas or pneumonia. I just knew my father left one day and never came back. My mother got sick, went to the hospital, and never came back." He shuddered. "I've never liked hospitals for that reason."

"Then why are you here?"

He paced around to the foot of the bed. "When the police called and said they were taking you to the hospital, I had to come. I had to make sure you were going to be okay. I never got that chance with my mother." He grabbed onto the railing. His knuckles turned white. "I know I haven't been a good father to you, Virginia. I didn't know how to be one. I barely knew my own, and my grandfather was a strict disciplinarian. 'Spare the rod, spoil the child,' was his motto."

"You never talked about him."

He pushed against the bed rail in a rocking motion. "I didn't want to remember him. I thought I'd be a different sort of authority figure, but I ended up separating myself from you and your brothers because I was afraid I'd do the same things."

"You don't have the same problem with Emma. Why?"

My father let out a soft laugh and let go of the bed rail. "Brittany. She pushed me to be a better father. Pushed me into therapy." He walked back over to the chair and sat down. "Your mother . . . she wasn't exactly the most giving of people."

Now, it was my turn to laugh.

He smiled. "You've noticed?"

I nodded.

"I married her because she was beautiful and ambitious. I thought that would be enough to keep me going. To inspire me. But, you know as well as anyone it wasn't."

No, it wasn't enough. I don't think I have a memory of my parents that doesn't end up in an argument.

"I take my share of the blame. I wasn't faithful to your mother. I kept looking for someone to love me for who I was, not what I could do for her."

"Does Brittany do that?"

He smiled. "Yes. She does."

"I'm glad."

"Are you?"

"I never wanted you to be unhappy, Dad." I sighed. "I wanted you to . . . ."

"To what?"

"To love me. Or at least like me."

He took hold of my hand. "I do, Virginia. I do." He took a deep breath. "I'm sorry I haven't been there for you in the past. I can't guarantee I can change overnight, but I'd like to try and be a better father to you. If you'll let me."

An orderly bustled in, pushing a cart full of trays. My father stood and helped adjust my bed. The orderly placed a tray with toast, applesauce, and apple juice on my table. He wheeled it in front of me.

I watched him leave, then looked over at my father. "I'm willing to let you, if you want to try."

"Thanks."

I laughed to myself as I dipped a spoon into the applesauce and stirred it around.

My father frowned. "What's so funny?"

"I was thinking about how this should have been the worst Christmas ever, being sick and ending up in the hospital." I lifted my gaze up to his face. "But, it's turned out to be one of the best."

✍

Frank knocked on Edith's door when he arrived back to Marigold on Monday evening. He waited patiently for her to open the door. When she didn't answer, he knocked again a little louder. He checked his watch. *It's only eight. I don't think she'd be asleep already, would she?*

Sam Taggart pushed her purple walker up next to him. "She's not there."

"Where is she?"

"Some handsome man and a blonde woman picked her up." Sam had put red highlights in her hair for Christmas. She wore an emerald-green velour track suit emblazoned with sparkling ornaments. "Edith said she had to help Ginny."

"What's wrong with Ginny?"

Sam grunted and pushed her walker down the hall toward her room. "I don't know. She was in the hospital for something. Edith's been out all day, taking care of her." Sam gave Frank a nasty look, then continued down the hall, muttering. "First she spends all day with you. Now, it's Ginny. Forgotten who her friends are, that woman."

Frank strolled back to the lobby, looking for someone in the staff who might know what had happened to Ginny. No one seemed to be around, except for George Franklin, who sat by the fireplace reading a newspaper. He glared up at Frank.

"What are you doing in my house?"

Frank ignored him and walked into the dining room. No one. He knocked on the door to the kitchen and peeked in. *Everyone's gone for the night.*

He knew it was no use looking for a med aid. They'd be running around until nine or ten, helping residents get to bed.

He stepped back into the lobby. George had gotten out of his chair and was now tottering toward him.

"What are you doing in my house? I don't want whatever you're selling!" He waved an arm toward Frank, as if to shoo him away. "Can't you read the sign? It says, 'No soliciting.' Get out of here!"

"I'm not selling anything, George. I want to sit down and wait for a friend."

"Not in my house! I'll call the cops on you if don't get out of here."

Frank hurried by the delusional man and went around to the other side of the lobby. He took a seat behind the fireplace, hoping George wouldn't see him. It seemed to work. George mumbled to himself a bit more, then settled onto the loveseat with the newspaper spread out on the coffee table in front of him. Frank picked up a magazine and thumbed through it while he waited for Edith to return.

He heard the gentle whoosh of the door as it slid open. Peering around the fireplace, he saw George asleep on the loveseat and Edith walking through the door. Frank stood up.

"Is everything all right?" he asked.

Edith looked around, surprised. "Frank! It's good to see you. What a weekend it's been."

He crossed over and helped her out of her coat. "What happened?"

"Would you be a dear and make me a cup of tea?" They walked together into the dining room. "It's freezing out there. I need something to warm me up."

Frank hung her coat over a chair. "Sure thing. You sit down and tell me the news." He picked up a clean china mug from off one of the tables.

"Ginny got some sort of stomach virus over Christmas. She ended up passing out in her bathroom, hitting her head on the counter, and getting a concussion." She smiled up at Frank as he set a cup of brewing tea in front of her along with a container of cream. "Thank God I got her father to check on her. She'd been passed out there for who knows how long." Her voice trembled. "She could have died."

"I'm sure it wasn't that bad." Frank patted her hand. "She would have woken up eventually."

Edith emptied a packet of sugar into her tea. "But, she was dehydrated, too. They kept her in the hospital overnight to get her fluids back up."

"She's home now?"

Edith nodded. "I went over today to make sure she rested. She's going to take tomorrow off as well."

"Are you planning to go back over?"

"No. Ginny told me she was tired of feeling like an invalid. By this afternoon she was up and walking around. I made her a nice pot of soup for dinner. There's enough left over for a bowl or two tomorrow. Now, if she can get a good night's sleep. I think she'll be fine."

"Good." Frank sighed. "I'm sorry that's how you had to spend your Christmas."

Edith pulled the tea bag out of the mug and placed it on a napkin. "Oh, my Christmas was fine. Donna and Harvey prepared a wonderful meal. How about you?"

"I got to hold my new great-grandson!"

"Wonderful! How old is he?"

"Two months. He's going to be a handsome one."

Edith poured the cream into her tea and stirred it. "He must take after your side of the family."

"That's what I told my grandson. I don't think his wife was too pleased."

Edith laughed lightly, and a warm feeling spread throughout Frank's body. He was glad to be back home at Marigold.

CHAPTER SEVENTEEN

My cell phone woke me up from a pleasant nap. I struggled to remember what day it was. Saturday. *It's Saturday, and it's New Year's Eve.* I stumbled up from the couch and followed its incessant ringing until it led me to the kitchen and my purse. I dumped its contents out on the counter and spied my phone before it fell on the floor. The ID flashed "Susan."

"Hello?"

"Ginny? Thank God I got you!"

"What's wrong?"

"One of the med aides called in, and a pipe's burst in the activity room. I'm stuck in Des Moines at my parents' house. Can you get down there?"

I tried to clear the nap fog out of my brain. "What about the maintenance guy?"

"Dave's out of town for the holiday, too. I left messages for Chester and Karen. You're the only one around who has a key to the storage area with the water main in it."

"All right." I threw the refuse I'd dumped from my purse back in it. "I'll get down there."

"Thank you! Thank you!" Susan caught her breath. "You remember how to turn off the water main?"

I tried to think back to my orientation tour. "Righty tighty, lefty loosey, right?"

"What?"

I found my sneakers and slipped them on. "I have to turn that big valve to the right to shut it off."

"The blue one with the tag on it."

"I'm on my way."

On an average day, it took me fifteen minutes to get to work. I made it in a little over nine, not entirely due to speeding. The light elves must have heard my prayers, because I hit green all the way. I ran into the facility and battled my way through the swarm of residents in the lobby trying to get a glimpse of the excitement. No one blocked the door, so they all stood looking into the activity room, watching as water poured out of the ceiling by the closet where I stored my craft supplies. Frank and Jose, the assistant cook, had entered the room and were off to one side, peering up and discussing the problem as if they were plumbers. I herded them out and closed the door behind me. "No one goes in. Understood?"

The residents groaned and stepped away from the door. I sprinted to the maintenance closet. I turned the blue knob as far as I could to the right then headed back down to the activity room. I opened the door and slid inside, closing it behind me to keep the residents from coming in. Throwing my coat onto a dry chair, I surveyed the damage. The carpet squished under my feet. I opened the storage closet and spotted the burst pipe right away. Water still dripped from the hole. Colored construction paper bled off the shelves. Plastic bins full of feathers looked as if Big Bird had drowned. I got a large garbage can from the kitchen and began heaving out ruined craft material.

I was tugging on a plastic bin on the top shelf when the door swung open. Distracted, I turned, and the bin fell off the shelf, dumping several gallons of water on my head and causing me to fall back on my tailbone. Chester ran over but slipped on the wet carpet as he tried to stop. His legs flew out in front of him and he landed on his back by my side.

"Are you okay?" I gasped.

He lay there, looking up at the ceiling. "I think so."

"Can you move?"

His feet wriggled back and forth. He lifted his arms. "Yeah."

"Good, because that was the funniest thing I've seen in a long time!" I burst out laughing, splashing back onto the carpet.

Chester chuckled. "You don't look so good yourself, you know."

I could barely breathe. "I bet!"

He laughed harder, and soon we both were lying on the soggy floor in tears.

"Stop it!" I pleaded as he started another round of the giggles. I slapped his arm, and it made a sound like a wet fish. I was consumed by another fit. It took us several minutes to catch our breath and calm down.

I sat up. A spray of water flew around the room as I shook my arms like a wet dog. Chester sat cross-legged on the floor opposite me. He reached over to brush a strand of dripping hair away from my eyes. I shivered at his touch.

"You cold?" he asked.

I shook my head. That wasn't why I had shivered. *Why have I never noticed how brown his eyes are before? And how thick his hair is?*

His gaze flickered down my wet clothes, and a blush crept across his dark skin. "You had . . . uh . . . you'd better . . . ." I followed his stare and saw that the water had caused my shirt to become translucent.

I crossed my arms. "Oh, dear."

He started to unbutton his shirt. "Here, take mine."

"No, that's okay." His wet clothes had already molded themselves to his body, allowing me to see the outlines of his muscles. The last thing I needed right now was for him to take his shirt off and give me a clear picture. "I'll go get something from my grandmother."

The red faded from Chester's face. He stood and reached down to help me up. I took his hand and felt the same tingling sensation as when we'd danced. Once I was standing, we didn't move but stared at each other. He finally broke the tension.

"I'll get the wet vac and start cleaning some of this up."

I nodded. "I'll get another shirt."

∽

A knock on the door startled Edith. She looked up at the clock. *2:00? Not time for my medication yet.*

"Grandma? It's me." Her door opened, and Ginny stood with arms crossed and hair dripping.

Edith pushed herself off the couch. "Lands! What happened to you?"

Ginny's teeth chattered. "You didn't hear the commotion earlier?"

Edith went to her bathroom and pulled a towel from the shelf. She passed it to her granddaughter. "No. I've been reading the new Nora Roberts book. What did I miss?"

Ginny tried to dry her hair. "Pipe burst in the activity room. There's water everywhere." She wrapped the towel around her shoulders. "Do you have a shirt I can borrow while I clean up?"

"Why don't you use my hairdryer? I'll see what I can find."

Ginny followed her grandmother into the bedroom, then into the bathroom. She found the hairdryer under the sink and plugged it in. Edith searched her bureau but didn't find anything she thought would fit Ginny. She had more luck in her closet. She pulled a blue plaid shirt from its hanger as her granddaughter came out of the bathroom.

"Wasn't that Grandpa's?" Ginny asked.

Edith ran her hand over the flannel. "I gave most of his things away but couldn't part with this one." She held the cloth to her cheek. "For the first year after he died, I'd take it out and smell it." She sniffed the collar. "It's lost his scent now, but I don't have the heart to throw it away." She handed the shirt to Ginny.

"You sure you don't mind?"

"No, dear. You go ahead and put it on."

Ginny peeled off her wet shirt and threw it into her grandmother's shower stall. She dried herself off a little more before slipping the blue flannel over her head. The shirt swam on her, but a smile lit her face. "It's so soft." She rubbed her hands up and down her arms.

"That was his evening shirt. After dinner, he'd take a shower and put that on to relax in."

Ginny pulled the ends together and tied them into a knot around her waist. "Thanks, Grandma." She picked a brush up from the bathroom counter and ran it through her hair. "I have to get back and try to clean up."

"Is the maintenance man – oh what's his name? Dave? Is he down there helping you?"

"No. He's out of town." Ginny stopped brushing for a moment. "Chester's getting the wet vac."

Edith tried to hide her interest. "Chester came down to help you?"

Ginny pulled distractedly at a snarl.

"What's the matter, dear? You look like you've got something on your mind."

Ginny tugged on the brush until it untangled her hair. "I don't know. Something weird happened."

Edith sat on the corner of her bed. "How so?"

"You know I've been seeing Brad?"

Edith nodded.

Ginny continued to brush her hair. "I realized something today."

"What's that?"

"When I come home from a date with Brad, I'm always thinking about how different he is from Mark. I end up thinking about Mark and how much I miss him."

"That's only natural. You loved him very much."

"That's not the weird part." Ginny put the brush down. "It's just, lately, when I'm around Chester." She sat next to her grandmother on the bed. "I think I'm starting to have feelings for him."

"Really?"

"And the weird thing is, when I find myself thinking about Chester, I'm only thinking about him. Not how he compares with Mark."

Edith tried not to smile too broadly. "That's a good thing, isn't it?"

"I don't know." Ginny shrugged. "I don't know how Chester feels about me. And, what about Brad?"

Edith patted her granddaughter's leg. "You've only been dating that boy for a few weeks. It's not as if you're engaged or anything."

"I guess you're right. We're supposed to go out tonight for New Year's Eve. He called on my way over here to let me know what time he'd pick me up. I told him about the pipe." She picked at a loose thread on the bedspread. "Maybe I'll call him in a little while and tell him I'm too tired." She pulled at the thread, trying to pull it loose. "I think it's time I break up with him."

Edith put her arm around Ginny's shoulders. "You do what you feel is right."

"What about Chester?"

"You do what's right there as well. If you think you like him, you should let him know."

Edith saw the fear behind Ginny's eyes. "What if he doesn't feel the same way? What if I'm reading things wrong?"

"As your grandfather always said, you can't win if you don't play." She gave her granddaughter a squeeze. "Besides, any man would love to have you for a girlfriend."

Ginny snorted softly. "You have to say that. You're my grandmother."

Edith shook her head. "You know me better than that. Look at your Uncle Richard's children. I don't really like either of them. And, your brother James is no prize, either."

Her granddaughter laughed and stood. "Maybe you're right."

"Of course I am, dear. I'm old and wise, so you'd better take my advice."

Ginny gave her a hug. "Thanks, Grandma. I'd better get back to work."

"Stop back before you leave today. Let me know how you are."

After Ginny left, Edith waited a few minutes before peeking down the hallway. When she was certain the coast was clear, she walked over to Frank's apartment. She took the long way around, careful not to pass by the activity room and chance being spotted by her granddaughter. She knocked on the door. Frank opened it a moment later.

His eyes twinkled as he recognized her. "Hi, there!"

"We did it!"

Frank looked confused. "What?"

"Ginny and Chester! We did it!"

Frank opened the door wider. "Come in, come in. Tell me what happened."

Edith hesitated a moment. She glanced up and down the hallway before stepping inside his apartment.

"Have a seat." Frank pointed to the sofa in the living room, but Edith shook her head.

"I should only stay a moment. I thought you should know. Ginny told me she definitely has feelings for Chester."

Frank clapped his hands together. "I knew we could do it."

"She's getting her nerve up to break up with this other boy." Edith frowned. "But, she's still a little nervous about saying anything to Chester. She's afraid he doesn't feel the same way. I couldn't let her know I knew anything." She shrugged. "What do we do now?"

Frank rubbed his chin. "Maybe I can say something to Chester. Let him know things with the other guy aren't working out."

"That's a wonderful idea."

They stood awkwardly for a moment in Frank's kitchen. Edith turned away. "I should get going."

Frank placed his hand on the door. "I think we should celebrate."

"What?"

His blue eyes sparkled with excitement. "Yes. Tonight. Let's go out to dinner."

Edith caught her breath. "Excuse me?"

"It's New Year's Eve, and we've successfully brought Ginny and Chester together. Let's go out for an early dinner somewhere."

"You can still drive?"

Frank chuckled. "Yes, I can still drive."

Edith's eyes narrowed. "Is your license valid?"

"Yes." He reached for his back pocket. "Do you want to see?"

"No. I believe you." She felt like a schoolgirl. Her heart beat rapidly in her chest. "Dinner?"

"An early dinner. I promise to get you home by seven. That way, we'll beat the crowds."

"Nowhere fancy. I don't have any formal dresses here."

Frank paused for a moment, thinking. "Do you like Italian food? I know a nice little spot in Bellevue."

Edith drew a deep breath. "Sounds wonderful."

"Should I call for you at four-thirty?"

Edith nodded quickly. "I'll be ready."

Frank smiled and opened the door. "I'll see you then."

Chester already had the wet vac out and working by the time I returned to the activity room. He'd also gotten all the bins off the shelves for me so I wouldn't pour more water over myself. He shut off the machine as I walked in.

"Nice shirt. Where'd you find it?"

I pulled at the knot around my waist, trying to make it a little tighter so I didn't look like a whale. "My grandmother." Chester's quizzical look made me giggle. "It was my grandfather's."

When he smiled it lit up his eyes as well, and his mustache curled up at the corners. "It didn't look like something Edith would wear. She's far too classy."

"She's worn her share of jeans and work shirts on the farm. But, yeah, she definitely has style."

Chester turned the wet vac back on. I proceeded to clean out the rest of the closet. It took over an hour for us to complete our tasks. Poor Chester had to empty out the water bucket every ten minutes, and I spent the time ditching ruined cards, paper, and bulletin board supplies. I spread some things out on tables to see if I could dry them out enough to salvage them. I hated to think about trying to restock everything from scratch. At least we had all of Sunday to let the room dry out. With some fans, maybe we could still have activities on Monday. In the meantime, the plumber Susan had called came out and repaired the pipe. I didn't envy her budget this month. An emergency call on New Year's Eve would cost a fortune.

Chester put the wet vac away, then took a load of garbage out to the dumpster. He came back to the tables where I continued to sort through bins. "Can I help?"

I shrugged. "You probably have things to do tonight. Big plans for New Year's?"

His mustache curled downward as he shook his head. "Not really. My sister's having a party."

"Won't you have friends there?"

He carried several cups of Bingo chips over to the sink and poured out the water before laying the chips on some paper towels I'd put on the counter. I brought more cups over and stood next to him. I got up my courage to nudge his shoulder with my own. "So? No one special going to be there tonight?"

He grabbed another cup and emptied it out. "No."

"Really?"

"How about you? You going out?" He turned to look at me, giving me the full intensity of his gaze. My stomach did a somersault.

"I'm supposed to."

His face seemed to drop. "Oh."

"I don't think I'll go, though."

The light returned to his eyes. "No? Why?"

"I don't know." I couldn't look away from him. "I think I'll be too tired."

He took a cup of Bingo chips from my hand, his fingers pausing for a moment on mine. I think I stopped breathing. "Too bad. If you change your mind you could give —"

"Hey, Ginny!"

I jumped and knocked several cups of chips onto the floor. Brad walked into the room and knelt by my side to help pick them up.

"What are you doing here?" I asked.

He laughed. "I kept trying to call to see how things were going. You never answered."

"I guess I didn't hear the phone over the wet vac." I stole a glance up at Chester. I couldn't read the expression in his eyes. *Hurt? Angry?* I looked over to Brad and felt heat rush to my cheeks. *Why am I embarrassed? I haven't done anything.* Brad put the containers of chips on the counter, then turned to Chester. The two men sized each other up.

"Brad, this is Chester."

"Nice to meet you." They looked as if they wanted to arm wrestle each other but they shook hands instead. "What do you do here, Chester?"

"I'm the chef."

Brad smiled. "That's nice." He reached his hand out to help me up. *No tingle.* He kept hold of my hand. "You need some more help?"

"Most of it's done. I'm going to empty out the Bingo chips then get some fans from the storage room to try and dry the carpet out by Monday."

"I can help with that." He glanced at Chester. "I think we can get it from here."

Chester's lips tightened, but he only nodded. He turned to me. "How are you feeling now?"

Brad looked concerned. "Is something wrong?"

I shook my head. "I was telling Chester that I'm a little tired. I'm not sure I'm up to going out tonight."

Brad put his arm around my shoulder. "Don't be like that. I'll finish this for you. You have a seat." He led me over to a chair and forced me to sit. "We don't have to stay out late."

"I'll need to shower and everything. It'll take too long." Chester watched me while Brad finished with the Bingo chips.

"Where are the fans?" Brad dried his hands with some paper towels. "I'll get them set up for you."

Chester pulled his gaze from me. "I'll show you."

Brad drew himself up. "Tell me where they are. I can get them."

"You need a key." Chester walked past Brad, who shot me a glance before turning and following.

I put my head down on the table. *Why am I such a coward?* Now that Brad was here, I didn't have the heart to break up with him. Not on New Year's Eve.

Frank passed Ginny in the lobby. He guessed she was coming from the activity room. A blond young man walked beside her. He sized the boy up and decided he didn't like him. What did they call men like him? Men with manicured nails and hair they got cut by stylists not at the barber shop? Whatever the word, it meant that he cared a lot about appearances, and to Frank that meant the boy liked Ginny for all the wrong reasons.

"Hi, Frank." Ginny grinned. "Happy New Year."

He took her hand and kissed it. "And a Happy New Year to you also." He glanced at her escort. "Going out tonight?"

She nodded. "Frank, this is Brad."

"How do you do, sir?"

Frank eyed her boyfriend while they shook hands. *Too perfect. Reminds me of that kid on* Leave it to Beaver. "I'm fine. How are you?"

"Good. Good."

Eddie Haskill. That was the character's name. A charmer, but a troublemaker.

Ginny eyed Frank. "Where are you headed out to?"

He paused, unsure of what Edith would want him to say. "I'm meeting a friend for an early dinner."

Ginny buttoned up her coat. "You be careful out there tonight. A lot of crazies on the road." Brad took her arm.

"You, too," Frank warned.

She flashed him a tired smile. "Have a good one."

Frank watched Ginny and Brad exit out to the parking lot. They talked for a moment before getting into separate cars.

"What's so interesting?" Chester's approach startled Frank.

"What? Oh, I was just talking to Ginny."

Chester frowned. "Is that guy still with her?"

"Yeah, but not for long."

"What do you mean?"

Frank lifted the right side of his mouth into a little half-smile. "What do you care? I thought you said you weren't interested in Ginny."

Chester went on the defensive. "I'm not. I'm trying to make conversation with you."

"Then I guess you wouldn't care about the fact that she's going to break up with that clown soon." He struggled not to laugh at the hopeful expression on his friend's face.

"Good." Chester nodded. "I didn't like him."

"I didn't like him, either," said Frank.

Chester's eyes swept over him. "Look at you, all dressed up."

Frank straightened his blue sport coat and pulled at his belt. "I'm going for casual but classy. Did I make it?"

The cook stepped back and gave Frank another look-over. He made a face like someone examining a painting and rubbed his chin thoughtfully. "Very tasteful. The blue looks good on you."

Frank tugged on his lapels. "You're jealous because I have a date for New Year's Eve and you don't."

"A date? You're going out with a woman?"

"Well, I'm not going out with a cow! Of course I'm going out with a woman. And, not any woman. Edith MacPherson."

"Wow." Chester nodded. "You aim high, *amigo.* I give you credit."

Frank put a hand on the younger man's shoulder. "If you'd get a little courage up, we could double date."

Chester frowned. "I told you before, she doesn't think about me that way."

"Yes, she does. At least, she's starting to." He shrugged. "Why do you think she's breaking up with this other character?"

"She told you that?"

"I have a source who's in the know. Things have been said in private that may have been shared with me." He leaned in closer to Chester. "I'm only saying, maybe you want to make a move sometime soon, before she changes her mind."

The grandfather clock by the office door rang four-thirty. Frank glanced at his watch to double-check the time. "I'd better go. My date awaits." He slipped his coat on, then stopped. "Would you mind doing me a favor?"

"What do you need?"

Frank pulled his keys out from his pocket. "Could you start up my car for me, get it warmed up while I call on Edith?"

Chester smiled. "Sure thing."

Frank passed him the keys, then made his way to Edith's apartment. Now that the time had come to actually knock on the door, his courage failed him. *What can come of this? Am I really expecting to fall in love again?* His fist hovered over the door. *Who am I kidding? I already have.* He took a deep breath and knocked.

What am I doing? Edith had her coat and purse ready to go as soon as Frank came for her. She'd run to the bedroom mirror to check her hair and lipstick one last time, when she heard the knock. *Oh dear. What was I thinking? I can't go out on a date. Not at my age.*

Edith stopped by the picture on her bureau. She ran her hand along the frame. *You know I'll always love you Lloyd, don't you? Please, let me know that you approve.*

Frank knocked again.

She took a deep breath as she straightened her shoulders. *We're two friends celebrating a job well done. We're celebrating Chester and Ginny. Nothing more.* She slipped on her coat, and grabbed her purse. Opening the door, she smiled as she caught Frank in mid-knock.

"I thought maybe you'd changed your mind."

"A MacPherson doesn't change her mind, Mr. Leno. We're stubborn."

"I'll remember that." He held out his arm.

Edith hesitated. She glanced up and down the hallway to glimpse who might see them. Frank frowned.

"We're already the subject of speculation Mrs. MacPherson. Let's put the rumors to rest." He gave her a boyish grin. "I like you Edith, quite a lot. I think you like me."

Edith's cheeks grew warm, but she looked Frank in the eyes. "I do."

"Well then," he thrust his arm out to her again. "Let's make it official. We're going steady."

She giggled, and put her arm in his. *I'm acting like a school girl.*

"There." Frank patted her hand. "That wasn't so difficult was it?"

They walked arm-in-arm down to the lobby. Chester had pulled Frank's car up to the door. He got out as the couple exited the building.

"What are you doing here?" Edith asked.

"I helped Ginny clean the mess up in the activity room, then Frank corralled me into warming up the car for him."

"That was sweet of you."

The cook stuck his hands in his pockets. "Well, I have to admit, I didn't do it for Frank. I couldn't let you catch a chill, could I?" Chester opened the passenger door for her.

"Thank you, sir."

"You're welcome, ma'am." He shut the door, then gave her a wave. He shook hands with Frank. The older man leaned close, and spoke into Chester's ear before they separated. Frank slipped in behind the wheel.

Edith buckled her seat belt. "What did you say to him?"

"I warned him again not to wait too long to ask Ginny."

Edith watched as Chester trudged through the parking lot to his car. "He has a kind heart, that boy. I hope things work out for the two of them."

"It will. Have a little faith."

CHAPTER EIGHTEEN

I turned down the forty-eighth offer of a beer. Perhaps the latest dude couldn't hear me over the pounding hip-hop music blaring from the other room.

"I've got something," I held up my half-empty can of diet soda. The bearded man who'd made the offer gave me a lopsided grin, before stumbling out of the kitchen into the living room.

I lifted the lid to the cardboard pizza box, then grabbed the last piece. The cheese had congealed, making it easier to pick off the mushrooms scattered on top. I glanced at the time on the microwave. 11:45. From the safety of the brightly lit kitchen, I could see couples dancing suggestively in the living room. Several had made their way down the hallway, toward what I assumed were bedrooms. One couple, unable to find any privacy or too drunk to care, made out on the couch.

I took a bite of cold pizza, tossed the rest into the garbage then set off to find Brad. I found him in what, I guessed, was originally the dining room. Instead, an air hockey game sat under a cheap chandelier.

Brad stood along the far wall talking to another man. They both eyed me as I approached. Brad's friend took a step toward me, and grabbed my hand.

"Wow, I'm Dave and you're gorgeous. Where have you been all night?" I tried to pull my hand away, but Dave dragged me up to his chest. "Are your eyes really that green, or do you have contacts?"

He reeked of beer. I turned my head away, giving Brad a pleading look. He came up behind me, and wrapped his arms around my waist. "Back off Dave, she's with me."

Brad's breath wasn't much better. I wondered whether he'd be safe to drive me home.

Dave let go of my hand. "You are one lucky man." Brad's friend looked me over like a prized cow. "Lucky."

Brad nuzzled my neck. He hadn't shaved, so the stubble scratched my skin. I squirmed.

"It's almost midnight!" someone shouted from the living room.

"Let's go." Dave punched Brad's shoulder as the rest of the crowd around us headed out.

I tried to step away from Brad, but he held me tighter.

"We'll be there in a minute," he called to his friend.

"You don't want to miss the countdown." I put my hands on his to pull them from my waist. "That's what the party is all about, isn't it?"

He brought one hand to my cheek, and pressed my face toward his. His lips crushed down on mine. "I've wanted to do that all night."

"Let's go watch the countdown."

He ran his fingers down my cheek, then placed them behind my neck. He pulled me in for one more kiss. "Okay."

We watched the ball drop in Times Square and blew noisemakers. I'd had enough. As the music volume ramped up again, I yelled to Brad, "I need to get going. Do you want me to call a cab?"

"I'll take you home." He found our coats from some back room I hadn't ventured into, then said goodbye to his friends.

My ears rang as we left the house. I took note of Brad's gait as we walked down the street to his car. He didn't seem drunk. "Are you okay to drive?"

"I'm fine." He pressed his key fob and unlocked his car. "I stopped drinking over an hour ago. I knew you wanted to leave early."

He got into the driver's seat, while I opened the passenger door and slid inside. Brad started the car, turning on the wipers to clear away the raindrops left over from a drizzle earlier in the evening. A song came on the radio that I'd never heard.

I turned to Brad. "Is this the Beatles?"

"Off the *White* album."

"The White Album? What's that?"

"You mean you've never heard the Beatles *White* album?"

I concentrated on watching the lights reflected in the puddles on the road. It looked like a child's finger painting. "Nope."

"It's a classic." His hands drummed on the steering wheel in beat to the song. "Changed the music industry. Like most of their stuff."

"I'm more of an early Beatles fan."

"We're right by my condo." He gestured with his head. "Let me go in and burn you a copy."

"That's illegal."

He let out a frustrated groan. "Okay, then, you can borrow mine."

"Don't worry about it." I yawned. "Let's do it another time."

Brad made a quick turn. "We're right here. Come on up for a second, and I'll get it for you." He pulled into another side street, then parked the car.

"I'll wait here."

He frowned. "I don't want to leave you. It's not the best neighborhood."

I sighed.

"Don't look so enthusiastic." He unlocked the doors. "You'll thank me later. It's a great album."

I followed him into the condominium lobby. He crossed the marble floor to the elevator. "I'm on the third floor. Normally I'd take the stairs, but you don't look like you can walk much farther."

"Sorry." I stepped into the elevator, leaning against the side wall as the doors slid shut. "It's been a long day." The cab lurched up. I grabbed the handrail to keep my balance.

"You want a cup of coffee?"

"No, thanks."

Brad leaned toward me and kissed my forehead. The doors opened a moment later. He took my hand to lead me down the hallway. The muted lights made me feel as though I was in a hotel. Brad unlocked his door, then pulled me inside. He shut the door behind him, but didn't turn on the lights.

"Home sweet home."

I waited for him to turn on a lamp. Instead, he let go of my hand, and ran his fingers through my hair. He slipped my purse off of my shoulder, then reached inside my open coat. I took a step away. His hands pulled me back. He kissed my cheek.

"Come on, Ginny." His warm breath tickled my ear. "Let yourself go." He pushed me up against a wall, holding me there, while his mouth pressed against mine.

I shoved him off. "What are you doing?"

He grabbed my waist. His other hand snaked up inside my shirt. "You came up here. No one forced you."

I seized his wrist to stop him. "To get a CD! Not this!"

He wrenched his hand from mine. "Relax." His mouth was on my neck. "I promise, I'll make it worth your while."

"No!" I tried to escape, my body squirming under his.

"It's okay." His hand came up my shirt again. "You have to let Mark go."

Tears filled my eyes at the mention of his name. "No." *Mark would never have done this.*

Brad kept one hand up my shirt, but the other wiped away my tears. "Relax, Ginny." He tried to force his tongue inside my mouth. When I didn't cooperate, he pulled me into the living room. I made out the forms of a large flat screen TV and a love seat, before he pushed me down onto a leather couch.

This isn't happening.

He started to climb on top of me.

"Get off!" I kicked him hard enough to launch him from the couch. His head hit a glass top coffee table with a loud *thunk* on his way down to the floor. He let out several curses. I took that as my cue to leave. I hurdled over the back of the couch, then ran for the door. I was in the lobby, before I realized I'd left my purse in Brad's condo.

Great.

I couldn't go back up now. Brad would think I'd changed my mind, and jump me again. I didn't have the strength to fight him off a second time. Buttoning my coat, I stepped out into the frigid Omaha night and made my way to the corner to check the street signs. I knew if I followed Dodge down I'd eventually come back to the Old Market section of town. At least there'd be people there. Maybe, I could borrow a cell phone. Cars passed by, spraying puddles up onto the sidewalk where I walked. The rain, which had ended earlier in the evening, started back up again. An icy drizzle that soaked immediately into my bones, making me shiver. I shoved my hands in my coat pockets to try and get them warm. My fingers brushed up against something hard.

My cell phone!

I'd stuck it in my pocket when Brad had called earlier. I flipped through my contact numbers. *Who can I call to pick me up at 12:30 on New Year's Eve?* Not my father, he lived too far away. Definitely not my mother, although if I thought Roger would answer first, I'd have dialed their house. I smiled at the thought of my Marine stepfather beating Brad to a pulp for my honor. *Father Dan?* What time did priests go to bed? Would he get in trouble? What were the rectory rules?

By this time I'd hit 13th Street. Even though I was freezing, I didn't feel like dealing with the inebriated crowds in the bars and hotels. Now that I had my cell phone, I opted for continuing my trek on foot toward home. I turned south. If worse came to worse, and no one picked me up, I'd get home before dawn.

Looking down at my phone, I continued to go through my options. Susan was out of town. I didn't have Patty's number. Karen and Nancy had kids, I didn't want to wake them up. I paused as Chester's name flashed up on the screen.

Chester?

Yes, Chester. I knew that's who I needed right now. A friend. Whether or not he had any feelings for me didn't matter. I knew he'd come and bring me home. I dialed his number. The phone rang. And rang. And rang.

A female voice answered. "*Bueno. Quien es?*"

My heart froze. It wasn't his sister's voice. *Was Chester with another woman?* I struggled to remember my Spanish. "*Yo soy Ginny para Chester's trabajo. Por favor, hablo a el?*" Trumpets blared in the background, some kind of loud salsa music.

"*Uno momento.*" I heard several clicks and thuds.

Up ahead, neon golden arches beckoned to me. I didn't know how long they'd let me stay inside without buying anything, but at least I could warm up. I entered in the back, away from the counter, and slid into a booth. Blowing on my hands, I tried futilely to warm them.

"Ginny?"

I smiled when I heard Chester's voice. "Yeah, I hate to bother you." Now that I had him on the phone, I felt like a fool. "I know you're having a party and all. I'll call someone else."

The salsa music became quieter. He must have moved to another room. "What's up?"

"I'm kind of stranded. I need a ride home."

"Where are you?"

I fought down a rather desperate laugh. "You know? I'm not really sure. Hang on a sec." I walked up to the counter.

The bored teenager behind the register asked, "Can I take your order?"

I shook my head. "Can you tell me where I am?"

The young man looked at me like I was crazy. "McDonalds."

I took a deep breath. "I know that, but what's the address?"

"Corner of 13th and Pierce."

I walked back to my booth in the corner. "13th and Pierce. At McDonald's."

"What happened?" Chester asked. "Should I call a tow truck or anything?"

"No." My voice tightened as I tried not to cry. "Can you come get me?"

"I'll be right there."

∽

Ginny must have been watching for him, because she jumped up as soon as Chester walked in the door. The flush that usually colored her cheeks was nowhere to be seen. Instead, her skin had a chalky appearance. Her red hair lay plastered against her head. The pinkish rim around her eyes indicated that she'd been crying. He rushed to her, and without thinking, drew her into his arms for a hug.

"*A mi corazon, que paso?*" He was glad he'd slipped into Spanish, hoping she wouldn't understand the endearment that had slipped out.

"I'm glad you're here." She sniffled. "Sorry to make you come out so late."

Chester led her back to the booth. "You look like you're freezing. You need some coffee?"

"Do they have decaf?" She wiped her eyes with the back of her hand.

"I'll ask." He walked to the counter and bought two hot chocolates, and two large fries. He carried them back to

Ginny. He pushed a paper cup across the table to her. "It's hot chocolate. Better than coffee."

Ginny cradled the drink in her hands. "Thanks."

"You want to tell me what happened?"

She rolled the cup back and forth. "I feel so stupid."

Chester waited for her go on.

She told him about the party, about going up to Brad's apartment to get the CD. She blinked several times. Tears ran down her cheeks.

He pushed the fries toward her. "What happened after that?"

Ginny put the cocoa down, but didn't take a fry. "It was stupid. I'm overreacting."

Chester's jaw tightened. "What did he do?"

"He thought I went up there to sleep with him. He was all over me as soon as he shut the door."

Chester struggled to keep his anger under control. "Did he hurt you?"

Ginny shook her head. "No. Just scared me." She let out a soft chuckle. "He's going to have a headache in the morning."

Chester cocked his head. *"Por que?"*

"I kicked him off me and into the coffee table."

He was on top of her? Chester clenched and unclenched his fists under the table. "But you're all right? Should you call the cops?"

Her eyes widened. "No. I'm fine. He stopped after that. But I ran out of the apartment and left my purse. I don't have money for a cab."

"I'll get your purse, then take you home."

She looked up quickly. "You don't need to do that. The ride's enough."

Chester surprised himself at how level his voice sounded. "You'll need it tomorrow, and I don't want you alone with him again." He pushed the fries even closer to her. "Don't worry about anything. Eat up, then we'll go." He shoveled a handful into his own mouth.

Ginny sipped her cocoa. "I'm sorry."

"About what?"

"To pull you away from your friends. Your party."

Chester's lips turned up slightly. *Yo quiero nunca pero tu.* Ginny's eyes scrunched up at the corners as she tried to translate. "You want what?"

He hadn't thought he'd spoken aloud. "I'm glad you called."

"I'm sure." Ginny chuckled. "To be pulled away from a party in a nice warm house, to drive around in the sleet and pick up a stranded co-worker. What could be better?" She grabbed a French fry.

He smiled, glad to see she'd relaxed enough to start eating. "It was a boring party. All my sister's friends."

Ginny took another fry, and waved it toward him as she spoke. "Lots of young, single women? You must have been quite a hit."

"I played *Twister* and *Uno* with my nieces."

Ginny raised one eyebrow.

Chester shook his head. "How do you do that?"

"What?"

"The one eyebrow thing?"

Ginny shrugged a shoulder. "When I lived with my grandmother, I watched her do it. I stood in front of the mirror for hours until I got the hang of it." She pointed another fry at him. "But, don't change the subject. I don't believe for a minute you spent the whole night babysitting."

"No." His heart pounded in his chest. He'd waited a year for the opportunity to be alone with Ginny. To tell her how much he liked her. *Not tonight. She's just been attacked.* He ate some more fries. *If you don't do it now, you may never get the chance.*

Ginny stared at him. "What 'cha thinking?"

"Huh?"

The smile she gave him lit up her face. "You're staring at me." The chalky appearance of her skin lessened, as a blush crept up her cheeks.

Tell her. Tell her now before you lose your nerve. "Estoy enamorado de ti."

She cocked her head to one side, concentrating. "*Enamorado?*" Her expression relaxed as she translated. "Enamored? Is that what it means?" Chester dropped his gaze to stare into his cocoa. She wrapped her hands around his. "*Estoy enam...enamorado de ti tambien.*"

He looked up quickly. He hadn't realized she'd leaned closer to him, and they bonked heads. They both cried out, then sat back in their seats.

"That was smooth." Chester rubbed his hand along his hair line. "Sorry."

Ginny giggled as she massaged her forehead. "I don't know if we should start anything. We seem to be constantly in pain whenever we're alone together."

Chester folded his hands. "Is it true?"

"What?"

He watched her face closely. He knew she didn't know *enamorado* meant, "I'm in love." "Do you like me? As more than a friend?"

She gave him a shy nod. She wrapped her hands around his.

He couldn't take his eyes from hers. "I'm glad you called me."

"So am I."

His thumbs made tiny circles on the back of her hands. "I wish I'd told you before how I felt." His looked around the restaurant. "I'm sorry it had to be here."

"But it's New Year's Day. A new start."

Chester tightened his grip. "Are you sure? I mean, are you ready?"

Her eyes darkened for a moment, as if a cloud of sorrow passed over her. Then she lifted her head up. "I'd like to try."

"Okay, then. We'll give it a try."

Chester finished the last few fries in the cardboard container. Ginny pushed hers toward him. "Do you want anymore? I'm not really hungry."

He tossed both into the trash. "You ready to go?"

She took the hand he offered.

Chester took a deep breath. *Don't kiss her. Don't kiss her. Not here. Our first kiss should not be at a McDonald's!* He let go of her hand, then stepped back and waited, while she picked up their cocoas.

"You want to bring yours in the car?"

He nodded. He led her outside, thankful he'd spent some time earlier cleaning out the interior of his Mazda 3. He opened the passenger door for Ginny. She put the cocoas into the cup holders. He had to keep himself from skipping around to the driver's side. *She's actually in my car! Ginny Stafford! Thank you God!* He took a deep breath before getting behind the wheel.

"Where's Brad live?"

"He's probably asleep. I'll get my purse tomorrow."

"I want this jerk out of your life tonight. Where does he live?"

"It's somewhere off of Dodge. I'll have to give you directions as you drive."

He turned the ignition. "You walked from Dodge?"

"Yeah."

He shook his head as he turned onto 13th Street. Ginny guided him to Brad's condominium complex. Chester tried the lobby doors, but they were locked. "Do you have his number?"

Ginny pulled her phone out of her coat pocket. Chester tapped his fingers against the glass door while he waited to see if she could wake Brad.

"Brad? It's Ginny." Anger flashed across her features. She let out a sharp sigh. "No, I didn't change my mind. I left my purse in your apartment. Would you mind bringing it down to me?" She growled under her breath. "No, I don't want to see you naked. Could you please put on a robe, or a pair of sweats, and bring me my purse?" She chewed on her lip. "Thank you." She stuffed her phone into her pocket. "Jerk."

"Why'd you go out with him?"

"He was nice at first. And everyone kept telling me it was time to move on."

Chester pulled her into his chest. "It *is* time. But with me, not him."

He felt her chuckle under his arms. She nuzzled closer to him. "You're nice and warm."

He thought of a number of corny clichés to say, but instead kept quiet. He'd waited too long for a moment like this to spoil it saying something stupid. He rubbed his hands across her back, trying to offer her a little more heat. A few minutes later, he noticed the elevator lights blinking downward. He pushed her away gently. "Brad's coming." Chester took a step back, so he wouldn't be immediately seen when Brad got off the elevator.

Ginny folded her arms while she waited. Brad walked across the lobby, wearing only sweatpants, and swinging her purse from his right hand. He stopped a foot from the door and gave Ginny what was, Chester could only assume, his seductive smile. Chester chuckled at the exasperated little grunt Ginny let out, as well as the large bruise he could see by Brad's left temple. *Good for you, Ginny!*

Brad unlocked the door then noticed Chester in the background. Ginny pushed against the glass, managing to get the door open several inches as Brad tried to get it shut again. Chester stepped out of the shadows. With his hands against the door, he thrust forward, causing Brad to tumble and fall. Ginny ran in to retrieve her purse. Chester walked inside. He towered over Brad. He pointed his finger at the prone man. "If you ever come near her again, I'll pound you so hard, your own mother won't recognize you. *Comprendes?*"

Brad nodded. Chester took Ginny by the arm, and led her out the door to his car. She giggled as he pulled back out onto the road.

"What are you laughing at?"

She giggled harder. "The look on Brad's face when you stepped up to the door. He went from trying to seduce me, to scared out of his mind, in one second." She glanced over at Chester. "It was priceless. Thank you."

"*De nada.*"

Chester turned his car onto the highway, heading toward Bellevue. "You'll have to give me directions to your house."

Ginny nodded.

He smiled at the soft cooing noise she'd made as she yawned, then laughed at himself. *You're pathetic.*

She leaned up against the car door. "Now what's so funny?"

"Nothing. You rest for a minute. I know which exit to get off. I'll wake you up then."

She shut her eyes. "It's been a long day."

He patted her knee. "Go ahead and sleep."

She put her hand on top of his, sighing contentedly.

Chester hated to wake her ten minutes later when he pulled off of the highway. Ginny's eyes struggled to open. She sat up, and guided him to her house. He pulled into the driveway at precisely two in the morning. He jumped out to run and open her door, but she'd already gotten out of the car.

She gave him a tired smile. "And I thought chivalry was dead."

"Not with me." He walked her to her porch.

Ginny fished her keys out of her purse then unlocked the door. She hesitated before opening it. "Thanks again. For everything."

Chester cupped her face in his hands. "Anytime." He caressed her cheeks with his thumbs. "Now, I suggest you put on your warmest pajamas, dry your hair, and go to bed. I'd hate for you to get sick, again."

"Yes, Doctor."

Chester leaned down and kissed her forehead. "Goodnight, *mi amor.*"

She leaned in to his chest and gave him a hug. "Goodnight."

He pushed her away before he let his emotions get the best of him. "I'll call you tomorrow. Make sure you're okay."

"Why don't I meet you at church?"

Chester's heart skipped a beat. "Really? You want to come to church?"

"Yeah. What time?"

"We like the eleven o'clock service."

"I'll look for you in the lobby."

Ginny stepped inside her house. She gave him a small wave before shutting the door. Chester waited until he heard the locks click, then jogged to his car. He slid inside and held onto the wheel. "Thank you, God."

CHAPTER NINETEEN

Edith glanced at the clock again. *9:30 a.m.* Donna would be picking her up in ten minutes for church. *What time is too early to call?* She paced into the bathroom and checked her reflection. *No lipstick smudges on my teeth. The hair looks decent.* She walked back out to the living room. *9:31.* Picking up the phone, she dialed Ginny's number, surprised when her granddaughter answered on the first ring.

"Hello?"

Edith laughed. "Are you psychic? It barely rang on this end."

"Hi! No, I was next to the phone." Ginny paused. "You're calling early. Is everything all right?"

"Everything's good." Edith couldn't suppress the smile that spread across her face. "In fact, it's wonderful. *I* think it's wonderful. I hope you think so too." She thought for a moment. "And Joyce, too. Oh, dear. I hadn't thought about what Joyce would think."

Ginny chuckled. "Grandma, slow down. What's happened?"

Edith sat down at her dinette table and took a deep breath. "I'm dating."

"What?"

"Frank and I are dating."

"When? How? Tell me everything!"

"Last night. He took me out to dinner to Bella Notte's."

Ginny made an approving noise.

"We talked about all sorts of things, and when we got back to Marigold, I guess you could say he walked me home."

"And? Did you get a kiss goodnight?"

Edith's cheeks burned, but she didn't answer.

"Grandma! You let him kiss you on the first date?"

She fanned herself with an envelope from the table. "It wasn't exactly our first date. We've been playing backgammon for a month now."

Ginny giggled. "How was it?'

"Virginia Elizabeth! I'm not going to kiss and tell!"

Her granddaughter let out a short, loud laugh. "A little hint? Did you feel it in your stomach?"

Edith sighed. "All the way down to my toes, dear. Down to my toes."

"I'm glad. Frank is one lucky man."

And I'm a lucky woman.

"Of course," Ginny said. "I'll have to ask him what his intentions are, next time I see him."

"You will do no such thing!"

"Someone has to look out for your best interests, Grandma. Protect you from miscreants who want to take advantage of virtuous women like yourself."

"Ha! At this age honey, men are only interested in one thing."

"What's that?"

"Someone to trim their toenails."

It sounded as if Ginny may have dropped the phone in a fit of laughter. She didn't speak for a long time. All Edith could hear were random bursts of giggles. Ginny sounded winded when she finally did talk. "Grandma, you're the best. You know that?"

"I've heard it said before." She waited while her granddaughter seemed to catch her breath. "Enough about me. How was your night?"

There was a long pause.

"Ginny, darling? Is everything all right?"

"Grandma, I had the worst night, and the best night. How much time do you have?"

"None, actually. Donna's picking me up for church. Can it wait until our ride to Joyce's?"

"Yeah. It'll make the trip go faster."

"Tell me, does it have to do with Chester?"

"Uh-huh."

Edith clutched the phone a little tighter. "Was he the worst part or the best?"

"The best, Grandma. Definitely the best."

Edith smiled at the happiness she heard in her granddaughter's voice.

I hung up the phone with my grandmother, and contemplated what to do with my morning. I finished making the pot of coffee Edith had interrupted, then slipped an English muffin into the toaster.

I realized, as I puttered around my kitchen, that I was looking forward to going to church. For the first time in two years, I *wanted* to go. And it wasn't only because I would see Chester. I was ready to start letting go of my anger toward

God, and looking forward to what he might have to say to me, if I just opened myself up to his voice again.

My muffin popped up. I slathered on the peanut butter. After pouring myself a cup of coffee, I sat down and surveyed the kitchen. I seemed to be looking at everything with new eyes this morning. The sun shone through the small garden window over the sink, a shaft of dusty light danced to the tacky green linoleum floor.

I munched on my muffin, thinking about what color I'd like to paint the walls, and whether to update the linoleum, or go with hardwood floors. The phone jangled. I licked the peanut butter off my fingers before answering it.

"Hello?"

"Good morning, Virginia!"

It was at times like this, I wish I hadn't gone with an old fashioned wall phone in my kitchen, because I had no caller id. The voice *sounded* like Tony's. Only he could say my name in a way that made my skin crawl. *But why would Tony be calling me on New Year's Day?*

"Who is this?"

"I'm crushed you don't recognize my voice, Sis."

"Tony? What's wrong? Why are you calling?"

He laughed. "Nothing's wrong. I wanted to see how your evening went is all." He paused. "With Brad?"

I had a bad feeling about this. "Why? What have you heard?"

There was another chuckle. "Nothing yet. I figured I'd talk to you first." Another pause. "So? How was it?"

"Look, I don't know what you're fishing for, but nothing is going to happen between me and Brad. I'm not seeing him anymore."

"Really?"

"Really."

"So…you didn't sleep with him?"

Ugh. How did a great guy like Roger come up with a creep like this for a son? "Not that it's any of your business, but no. I didn't sleep with him."

"Good to know, Sis. Thanks." Tony hung up.

Weird. I sat down to finish eating my muffin. I couldn't shake Tony's phone call from my mind. It made me feel dirty, like I'd found out someone had been watching me through a peephole. I was putting my plate in the sink, when a thought popped into my head.

He and Brad had made a bet.

I remembered the conversation at the Christmas dinner. That Tony made his friends gamble for his castoffs. My skin crawled as if bugs scurried along my arms. Tony must have offered Brad his old television, if I'd slept with him by New Year's. I wonder what Brad lost when I didn't come through.

My hands shook as I rinsed off my plate. I hurried down the hall to the bathroom. I hoped to wash away my stepbrother's sliminess in a super-hot shower.

Katy had her nose pressed up against the glass of the church lobby. Chester scanned the parking lot as well, hoping to catch sight of Ginny. *Maybe she's changed her mind.*

Nancy strolled over to him, a Styrofoam coffee cup in her hand. "How're you doing?"

"Good." He couldn't stop the grin that crept over his face.

Nancy smiled in response. "What are you so happy about?"

He ducked his head down. "Ginny and I."

"Did you talk to her? Are you guys dating?"

"We're going to try."

Nancy bounced on her toes. "I'm glad!"

Her husband made his way toward them. Chester wondered at the strangeness of their attraction. Luke was so tall and blonde, and Nancy so short and dark, it seemed odd that they would get together.

Luke rested his hands on Nancy's shoulders. "What's up with you two?"

She lifted her head up to him. "Ginny and Chester are dating."

"Really?"

Chester noticed the question in the pastor's eyes. "We haven't had an official 'date' yet. There are still some things we need to talk over. But yeah, we've decided to give this a try."

Luke gave him a cautious smile. "Good. My door's always open, if you need to talk."

"She's here!" Katy banged her finger on the glass.

Chester put his hand on her head. "Okay, okay. Don't break the window." He spotted Ginny walking up from the lower parking lot.

Katy ran toward the front door.

Nancy put her hand on Chester's arm. "Good luck."

"Thanks."

Katy dragged Ginny toward Chester. Nancy gave her a hug, and leaned up to whisper something in Ginny's ear. Luke shook her hand.

"Nice to see you again, Ginny."

"It's good to see you, too."

Luke and Nancy excused themselves, leaving Chester standing awkwardly in front of her.

"How are you feeling?" he asked.

"Really good. I took your advice."

"How so?"

"I put on my warmest pj's and crawled into bed with an extra blanket. I slept in until nine, which is something I never do."

"Good." He helped her slip off her jacket. "Maria and Louisa are saving seats for us."

"Come on," said Katy. "I'll show you where they are." She grabbed Ginny's hand.

"May I," Chester hesitated. "May I hold your other hand?"

Ginny smiled, and held it out to him. "I'd like that."

The three of them walked into the sanctuary together.

The ride to my mother's house went quickly, as Edith and I recounted the events of our New Year's Eve. Edith was suitably shocked by Brad's attack.

"The nerve!"

"Don't worry," I assured her. "Chester made it clear to Brad that he needs to stay away from me."

Edith grinned. "I knew I liked that boy."

I pulled into my mother's driveway. Grandma leaned on my arm as we crossed the icy sidewalk to the door.

Joyce opened it with a smile. "You made it!"

I helped my grandmother out of her jacket. "Sorry we're late, church ran long this morning."

My mother glanced over at me as she hung up Edith's coat. "You went to church? You're starting that up again?"

"I figured it was about time."

"I suppose, if you feel you need that sort of thing." She looked out the window. "Is Brad bringing in the gifts?"

"No, I am." I ducked out of the door again, before she could ask me any questions.

The temperature had dropped since the rain last night, making the walkway as slick as an ice pond. A line of dark gray clouds stood on the horizon, the brisk wind blowing them in my direction. Ice coated the branches of the trees, giving them a less depressing appearance than last month. I risked my mother's ire, opting to walk along the grass, rather than the brick-lined path that led back to my car.

My brother Simon ran out of the house, sliding up next to me like a professional snowboarder without the board. "Hey there! Long time no see." He enveloped me in a hug. His blue cable knit sweater scratched my cheek. Simon and I inherited the same set of ancestral genes—tall with red hair.

I loved the way he smelled. He'd used the same shampoo and cologne since he was sixteen. The result was a pleasant aroma of citrus and spice. "Hey dude!" I hugged him back. "I've missed you."

He kissed my forehead. "I've missed you too." A deep crease appeared between his eyes. "How're you doing?"

I opened the trunk of my car. "I'm okay. I think I'm finely back in the world of the living."

He took the bag of gifts I offered him. "Really?"

"Really." I gave him a second load of gifts to hold, then closed the trunk.

"Is that everything?"

"Yeah." I took one of the bags from his hands. "How've you been?"

"It's been a great year. Terry's teaching again. She's at the same school the kids are at, so we get a discount on the tuition. Actually, her salary all goes to the tuition, but we get medical coverage as well, which is the big draw."

The ice-coated grass crunched beneath our feet as we made our way back up to the house. A flake of snow spun down on the wind. I opened my mouth to catch it.

Simon laughed. "Nothing better than New Year snow."

The cold flake melted on my tongue. "You got that right." We wiped our feet on the mat and opened the door. "I didn't watch the news this morning. Do you know how much we're supposed to get?"

"Maybe an inch. Shouldn't be too bad." We put down the gifts. He helped me with my coat. "I've been watching the weather to see if we need to leave earlier, but I think we'll be okay if we wait until the morning."

He and Terry had been staying with our mother since Friday night. "How's she been?"

My brother lifted his gaze to the ceiling, as if pondering his answer. "For our mother? She's been good. None of the kids are sniffling, and we've kept the sugar to a minimum. They've been pretty well-behaved. All-in-all, she's been okay"

I grabbed the bags of gifts. "Well, I'm here now. I'm sure the fireworks will begin any minute."

We dispensed with the mandatory greetings, hugs, and exclamations at how big the kids had grown. Simon's eldest boy, Joshua, favored his mother Terry with short, dark hair. But he'd inherited his dad's height, and already stood as high as his mother's shoulder. With Terry only standing at 5'5" it wouldn't be long before the boy overtook her entirely.

Hannah, the middle child and only daughter, ran up to hug me, and immediately became my shadow, following me wherever I went. She had our red hair, but had also gotten some of my father's curls, the result being a wild mane that refused to be tamed. With her deep-blue eyes and creamy complexion, I anticipated some sleepless nights when the girl started dating. Hannah and I sat on the couch together, while Joshua, Terry, and Simon sat among a pile of building blocks on the floor. Edith made herself comfortable on the chair in the corner.

"Where's Micah?" I asked, as Roger handed me a diet soda. He sat next to Joyce in the loveseat opposite me.

Terry snapped a pair of wheels onto the car she was building. "We put him down for an early nap, hoping we could eat dinner in peace."

My mother eyed me over her glass of Chardonnay. "Dinner's actually ready now. When will Bradley get here?"

I ran a hand through my niece's hair. "He won't be coming."

"No?" Joyce pouted. "He's not sick, I hope?"

My gaze flickered over to my grandmother. She gave me an encouraging smile. "No. Just couldn't come. Sorry I didn't tell you. It was rather last minute."

Roger stood back up. "Well, then. I'll tell the cook that we're ready for dinner. Everyone head into the dining room."

We trooped in behind him, and found seats around the elegant table. My mother had put out the best china and silverware. Linen napkins in ornate golden rings sat beside each plate. The crystal chandelier glowed overhead. Hannah made sure she sat next to me. I made sure I sat on the end by

Roger. My mother sat at the opposite end with Terry next to her.

The first course was a delicious French Onion Soup. The rich beefy broth warmed me from the inside out, as the tangy smell of the onions filled the dining room. I asked Hannah and Joshua about school, hoping to keep them talking, and prevent my mother from asking more about Brad.

It didn't take long for Joyce to get back to the subject of my love life. She'd poured herself another glass of wine, after polishing off her first during the soup course. The kitchen help swept away the empty bowls, replacing them with plates of roast beef, garlic-roasted potatoes, and asparagus tips. My mouth watered as another server set a basket of fresh rolls on the table then, refilled our water glasses.

My mother took a sip from her wine glass. "So, Ginny. What happened to Bradley?"

"We broke up." I stuffed a potato in my mouth, so I wouldn't have to say anything else.

"Who's Bradley?" Simon asked.

My mother answered before I finished chewing. "He's a friend of Tony's that Ginny was seeing. He seemed quite taken with her when they were here before Christmas."

Terry interrupted me. "You're dating again? That's wonderful."

Joyce took another sip of wine. "She *was* dating, dear. Was. She's not now, although I'd love to know why."

I tried to calm the panic rising from my stomach. *Why did I let her get to me like this?* "He was a jerk, mother. That's why we broke up."

"And how was he a...a...jerk? He's a good-looking boy from a wealthy family. Wasn't he a holy roller like you and Simon? Was that the problem?"

Hannah and Joshua had stopped eating, their eyes wide as they watched their grandmother's anger boil.

"Mother." Simon rested his hands on the table. "Could we discuss this later?"

Roger nodded. "He's right, Joyce."

"Is he, Roger? And why is that? Why shouldn't I know why my only daughter lives like a hermit, and somehow loses the best prospect to come along in...in...." Joyce waved her hands as if trying to grab the word from the air. "In forever."

"What about Mark?" I slammed my fork down. "He was going to be a doctor."

She barked out a harsh laugh. "What kind of doctor? Certainly not one with a thriving practice. He wanted to go to Africa or something, didn't he? What kind of money is there in that?"

"There are more important things than money, Mother," said Simon.

"Oh, really? And what are they?" She cut off his answer with another wave of her hand. "If helping the Africans was so important, then those missionary doctors could make their fortunes here, and send money over to those people. Train their own kind to take care of them, instead of sacrificing their lives for them."

Simon stared at his water glass. "Greater love has no man than he lay down his life for his brother."

"Oh please. Don't talk to me about love. You've had it easy." She gestured to include me. "All my children have had it easy."

"Easy?" My throat tightened. I could barely get the words out. "You think my losing Mark was easy?"

My mother's voice rose another octave. "At least when he died you could believe he still loved you. At least he didn't leave you for some blonde bimbo, young enough to be your daughter!"

My heart jumped to my throat. I'd never realized how much the divorce had hurt my mother. She'd never appeared anything but glad to be away from my father.

No one moved. Even the kids sat silent, staring at the adults at the table.

My mother's face paled. "I'm sorry." Her lower lip quivered. "The holidays seem to open old wounds." She lifted her glass in Roger's direction. "After all, the fates brought me a better man."

Edith picked up her water glass and took a sip. "I'm dating someone."

No one spoke, but everyone shifted their focus to the stately older woman. A little smile played about her lips. She took another sip of water, then cut a bite from the slice of roast beef on her plate.

Joyce blinked. "You're what?"

Edith finished chewing. She looked at her daughter. "I'm dating."

"Who's the lucky man?" Roger asked, with a sly grin.

"He's a gentleman from Marigold."

Simon laughed. "That's great."

Terry beamed. "It's wonderful, Edith!"

"Yes," she nodded. "It is wonderful. I haven't been this happy in a long time."

Joyce bristled, but Roger shook his head when he caught her gaze. My mother's eyes smoldered, but she remained quiet, as Edith told the family about Frank. I wondered why Roger put up with Joyce's temper and insecurities. Maybe the Marine in him liked the challenge. He watched my mother during the rest of dinner, and when he refilled her water glass, I noticed him give her shoulder a gentle squeeze. Edith captured everyone else's attention at the table, but I saw the smile my mother gave him in return. Maybe she wasn't the ice queen I'd always believed.

CHAPTER TWENTY

Edith sat in the chapel, holding Frank's hand. He kept his focus on her fingers, swallowing back his tears. Twenty or thirty people filled the subdued room. A large spray of white and red carnations flanked one side of the altar, while an eight-by-ten picture of Bill Watson, and another bouquet of flowers, sat on the other side. The scent of the lilies nearly choked him. He turned his head and coughed into his shoulder.

"It was nice of the facility to let his son have a memorial here," Edith whispered, as a middle-aged woman struck up the opening chords of a hymn on the small organ in the corner.

"Yes, it was."

They stood and sang, "Amazing Grace." Frank stared at the photo on the altar. *Goodbye, my friend. I'll miss you.* He still had trouble believing Bill had died. It had happened so fast. *What do you expect? Look at where you are. You think the people here are actually living their lives? They're all waiting to die.*

Frank shuddered.

Edith put her arm around him. "Are you all right?"

This isn't what I want, Lord. This isn't for me. I don't feel old. There's a lot I'd like to do yet.

Edith rubbed his arm. She put her head on his shoulder. He rested his against hers. *Life's too short, Lord. Too short to wonder what might come. We have to enjoy it while we have it.* Frank closed his eyes as Bill's friends and family sang the last chorus of the hymn. *Have I waited too long? When will my time be up?*

Edith patted his arm as the song came to an end. "That was a nice service. I think Bill would have liked it."

A stocky man, with only a fringe of hair around the lower half of his skull, approached them.

Frank held out his hand. "Jimmy, your dad will be missed."

"Thanks, Frank. You coming downstairs? Ginny's set up the activity room for us. I brought in some sandwiches and cookies."

"We'll be down in a minute," Frank shook Jimmy's hand. "I want to say goodbye quietly."

Jimmy nodded. "I said my goodbyes at the graveside. I'd better go downstairs and play the host." He shook Edith's hand, then proceeded out the door.

Frank waited by Edith's side until the chapel cleared out. He walked slowly to the altar, staring at the pictures of Bill displayed on a table. *Is that all that's left Lord, when we leave this earth? A bunch of photographs of who we used to be, and some flowers?* He sneezed as the scent of the lilies overwhelmed him.

"Bless you," Edith came up behind him. "What are you thinking?"

"I'm thinking, that I'm not ready to go yet." Frank ran his hand along the wooden altar rail. "For a long time, when my wife was sick, I gave up. I didn't have any desire to go on." He let his gaze fall on Bill's wedding photo. The old black-and-white showed a young man in a coat and tie, next to a woman with a simple white dress, and pill box hat. "But now..." he turned to Edith. "How do you feel about the Vatican?"

Edith stepped back. "Excuse me?"

Frank took her hands. "I've always wanted to see the St. Peter's Basilica and the Vatican. Would you come with me?"

Edith pulled her hands from his. She reached out to lean on the banister. "Frank? What are you asking?"

He smiled at how flustered she appeared. "I'm saying that here I am at my friend's funeral, and it's made me realize how much I want to live. And that's because of you Edith." He ran a hand down her arm. "There are things I dreamed of doing for years, and then gave up on. But, now...."

On an impulse, he struggled to get down on one knee before the altar. "Edith MacPherson, I don't know how much time we have left on this earth, but whether it's minutes, months, or years, I know I want to spend them with you. Please, say you'll come to Rome with me. Say you'll live life with me." He took her hand from the railing, and kissed it. "Say you'll be my wife."

Tears shimmered in her eyes as she stared down at him. "I would be honored, Mr. Leno. Truly honored."

CHAPTER TWENTY-ONE

Chester arrived at my door the following Saturday at three in the afternoon. Katy stood by his side.

"Your carriage awaits, madam," he said with a bad British accent.

Are we babysitting on our first date?

"Come on, Ginny. We have a surprise for you!" Katy took my hand and walked me to Chester's car. Blue-gray exhaust puffed up from the back. Chester ran ahead and opened the passenger side for me while Katy hopped in the back.

"She insisted on coming to pick you up." Chester held the door as I slid into the car. "I hope you don't mind." He shut it then buckled Katy into her booster seat. "You promised to be good, remember?"

Katy gave an exaggerated nod, causing her brown pony tails to bob about wildly. Chester kissed her cheek.

"So, what's my surprise?" I asked as we pulled out of the driveway.

He shook his head. "Can't tell you yet."

"You have to wait and see," Katy's face glowed with excitement. "Mama and Maria are getting it ready."

"It's a family affair then?"

"Uh-huh," grunted Katy. "Maria said she wanted to pick the color, but I wanted to do it."

"Color?" My stomach fluttered. *What were they going to color? A picture? A cake? A room?*

Chester glared into the rearview mirror and made a face at his niece. "No more. We don't want her to guess before we get home."

I think I would have been more nervous if Chester didn't look so pleased with himself. "What are you up to?" I asked.

"You have to wait and see." He turned for a moment giving me the same look as when we danced at Marigold.

Any fears I had melted away.

∽

Maria pounded a drum roll out on the table. "Ladies and Gentlemen. Or just gentleman I suppose. I now present to you, after an afternoon of primping and pampering, the new, the improved, the gorgeous Ginny . . . ." She leaned back in the doorway and Ginny whispered "Stafford." Maria resumed her announcement. "The new and improved, the stunning, Ginny Stafford!"

Ginny paraded into the kitchen with her hands held out in front of her showing Chester the deep burgundy color the girls had painted them. Her toenails, he noticed, were painted the same color. Her hair was stunning. Louisa had cut it shoulder length and layered it so it framed her face. Ginny did a little twirl in the kitchen to showcase how it moved.

Chester nodded appreciatively. "Wow."

Louisa leaned against the doorframe. "What do you think?"

"Wow." Chester mumbled again.

Ginny raised an eyebrow and looked at his sister. "Do you think he likes it? Or is the shock too much for him?"

"I think he likes it." Louisa grinned. "He hasn't taken his eyes off of you."

Chester turned back to the stove and stirred the Alfredo sauce he'd been making. "Are you happy? That's the important thing. I wanted you to have a day where you were pampered. Where people took care of you for a change." He glanced back over his shoulder, surprised to see Ginny's eyes welling with tears. "Do you like it?"

"I love it." She gave Maria a hug and kissed Katy on the top of her head. "Thank you all, so much. This has been," Ginny wiped her eyes. "No one's ever done anything like this for me. Made me feel so special." She waved her hands in front of her face as if trying to blow dry her tears. "Look at me! I'm all *verklempt*." She walked over to Louisa. Ginny opened her arms wide. "Can I give you a hug as well?"

Louisa smiled. "Sure."

His sister looked Chester's way as she embraced Ginny. She gave him the thumb's up sign and mouthed *I like her.* He mouthed *I like her too.*

"I like her, too!" Katy shouted, causing the kitchen to erupt with laughter. Ginny broke away from Louisa and moved to the table.

"All right girls." Louisa clapped her hands. "Time for us to go to Tina's house for dinner. Get some shoes and your jackets on."

"Can't we stay here?" Katy whined. "I like *Tio* Chester's food."

Maria swatted her sister lightly on the head. "They want to be alone, stupid."

"Don't call your sister stupid," scolded her mother. "Let's get going."

For several minutes the house seemed to burst at the seams with the energy of the two girls as they ran about getting ready. Chester poured Ginny a glass of ice water and then turned back to the stove to finish up the meal. The girls and Louisa yelled their good-byes and the kitchen abruptly went quiet.

"Peace at last," Chester said as the oven timer buzzed.

"Not quite." Ginny giggled.

Chester pulled two salads out of the refrigerator and placed them on the table. Next he brought out a wine bottle.

"None for me, thanks." Ginny put her hand over her glass.

He held the bottle out for her to inspect. "It's non-alcoholic. Kind of a sparkling grape juice. I thought it would make things seem more special.

He filled two wine glasses then sat down at the table. "What should we toast to?"

Ginny appeared thoughtful for a moment. "To the hope of a new year. To old friendships and new relationships."

"Sounds good." He tipped his glass toward hers and they clinked together. "Cheers."

"Cheers."

Ginny gave Chester the details of Frank's wedding proposal while they ate their salads. It helped to take Chester's mind off his fear about the conversation he knew they had to have before the end of the night. *Should we eat dinner first? Or would it be better to have something to distract us a bit?* He stood up and pulled the bread out of the oven and gave the Alfredo sauce one last stir.

"Are you all right?"

The spoon dropped from Chester's hand then clattered to the floor. "What?"

"You seem really nervous. Is it me?"

He threw the spoon in the sink before plating the shrimp and crab Alfredo pasta he'd made. "I need to talk to you about something."

Ginny frowned. "Something bad?"

Chester shook his head. "Not bad." He paused. "But serious. Something you need to know before we get too involved."

Worry crept in behind Ginny's eyes. "What is it?

He brought the plates over to the table and went back to the oven to get the bread. "Do you want dinner first?" He sliced the bread into thick pieces and tossed them into a basket.

"I don't think I'll be able to enjoy it without knowing what's on your mind."

"I'm sorry." He sat down. "I shouldn't have said anything yet." He lowered his head and spoke quietly. "Ginny, I've waited a long time for this chance. I mean, I thought you were pretty the first time I saw you coming in to visit Edith. But when you started working at Marigold..." He stole a glance at her face. "When you started working at Marigold, I found out how beautiful you are. Inside and out."

Her mouth curled up in small smile. "Thank you." She waited for him to go on but he remained silent. "Was that all?"

He shook his head. "No, but we better start eating before the sauce gets cold and clots up." Ginny picked up her fork but Chester stopped her. "Do you mind if we say grace first? "

She blushed. "No. I'm sorry. I've gotten out of the habit."

Chester took her hand. *Lord this feels right. Please let this work out.* "Father God, we thank you for this new year, a time of hope and new relationships." He looked up at Ginny. She had her eyes closed. "I pray Lord that you guide my words tonight and that you would open our hearts up to your will. That all we do and say tonight would be pleasing to you. Now bless this food into our bodies and our bodies into your service. In Jesus name we pray. Amen."

Ginny opened her eyes as she whispered "Amen." He waited as she twirled some pasta onto her fork and took a bite. She chewed for a moment then stopped, her eyes getting wide. She chewed again then swallowed. "That's amazing! Chester, this is fantastic!" She eagerly twirled another forkful.

"I'm glad you like it."

They ate in silence for a few minutes before Ginny finally spoke again. "All right, fess up. What do you need to talk to me about?"

Chester took a deep breath and a sip of water. "I wasn't always such a nice guy."

"What do you mean?"

"My parents were very strict as I grew up. They had a strong Catholic faith and they were all about hard work and discipline. We towed the line or dad took off his belt. It wasn't like abuse," Chester explained quickly. "We deserved to be punished for breaking the rules, but that's not how I saw it when I was young. I left, as soon as I could."

He took a piece of bread, buttering it while he spoke. "I joined the Navy at seventeen so I could get away from them. For the next nine years, I saw the world, and did whatever I wanted." He wanted to look at Ginny, but couldn't. "I mean it. I turned my back on every value my parents had taught me. I was your stereotypical wild sailor, drunk and with a girl in every port." He stared at his fingers, unable to lift his gaze. "I used women, Ginny. I used them to fill a hole I didn't understand I had." He risked a glance at her, but shifted his focus away when he saw her watching him intently.

"I lived with two different women during my shore tours. The first girl, Sheila, got me hooked on drugs. We started on marijuana but soon we were doing coke on the weekends. She tried to get me onto heroin, but somehow I resisted that. I threw her out when I got put on probation after a random urine test. The Navy made me go to a rehab center and I cleaned up."

Ginny had stopped eating. "But you're clean now?"

He traced the faint jacquard pattern on the table cloth with his fingertip. "It didn't stick right away. But yeah, now I'm clean. Going on six years."

"And the other woman?"

"That was Julianne. She got pregnant." Chester picked up his wine glass and swallowed the rest of the juice. *It's been a long time since I wish I had a drink, but tonight is one of those nights.* "She wanted to get married. I didn't." He couldn't meet Ginny's frank stare. "I told her to get rid of it. I told her to kill our baby." He put his head in his hands. "That's when I hit bottom. I left her a check for a thousand dollars and moved out of the apartment. I didn't do the drugs anymore, but I drowned my guilt with alcohol."

He ran his hands over his face. "Everything my parents had told me about being a good man, about God, it all came back to me. I was lucky . . . no," He shook his head. "Luck had nothing to do with it. It was God. He arranged for the captain of my new ship to be a Christian. The atmosphere was totally different than my first tour. Captain led Bible studies for anyone interested. I started going, mostly because I wanted someone to take off their belt and beat me for what I'd done, like my dad used to. But Captain wasn't like that. When I finally told him what I'd done, he helped me to ask God for forgiveness. He mentored me as I got my life turned around."

Chester struggled to take a deep breath. He turned to face Ginny. "I got out of the Navy and came out here to help Louisa. I'm not the man I was anymore. Honestly. I haven't slept with a woman since I gave my life to Christ five years ago."

Ginny played with the stem of her wine glass. "The woman. Julianne. Did she have an abortion?"

"I think so. I tried to find her a few years ago. I wanted to apologize, but she'd moved away. None of her friends knew where she'd gone."

Ginny nodded but didn't say anything.

"There's one more thing."

Ginny puffed out her cheeks and let her breath out slowly. "Okay."

"Sheila, the first girl I lived with? She tracked me down." Chester wished he could see Ginny's face but she'd lowered her head and played with her wine glass. "She wanted me to know that she tested positive for HIV."

A small groan escaped from Ginny's throat. She finally looked at him again. "Do you have it?"

"I've been tested for the past three years and I'm negative. I don't have it."

"Thank God."

"I do." Chester nodded. "I thank him every night for giving me a second chance at life." He watched Ginny's eyes

closely, trying to read her expression. "And that's why...
Ginny, I can't let myself fall into that temptation again. I have
to be careful."

"What do you mean?"

"I mean, just like I don't drink anymore because I can't
always control my behavior, I've made a promise to God not
to have sex again. Until I'm married."

Ginny stared at him blankly.

"Do you understand? If you need . . . if you want a
physical relationship, I can't be the one."

Several seconds past before she finally responded. She
lowered her head and chuckled softly.

"What's so funny?"

"That's what all this was about?" She waved her hands
over the table. "You don't want to have sex with me unless
we're married?"

Chester shifted uncomfortably in his chair. "I guess so."

She leaned forward and placed a hand over his. "I'm sorry,
I don't mean to laugh, but I can't help thinking Edith had
something to do with this."

"What?"

"Now it's my turn to be honest." She took a deep breath.
"I didn't go to church until I moved in with my grandparents.
Other than Christmas, my family never talked about God so
Edith and Lloyd had a lot they had to catch me up on. It
almost killed her to talk to me about sex, but she did it."
Amusement danced in Ginny's eyes as she reminisced. "She
made it clear that I should do everything in my power to stay
a virgin until I was married." Ginny mimicked her
grandmother's voice. "It's God's purpose for sex."

"Did you believe her?"

"Not really, but I loved her so much, I didn't want to hurt her by doing something I knew she wouldn't approve of." Ginny poured herself another glass of juice. "It was Mark who made me see sex for what it really could be."

Chester looked away, uncomfortable with the image of Ginny and the man from the photo in her office that crept into his imagination.

Ginny reached over and touched his arm. "I never slept with Mark."

Chester turned back, his eyes searching hers.

"We had a talk like this on our third date, and Mark explained how he felt." She took a sip from the wine glass. "He said it wasn't about us remaining 'pure' as a gift to each other. It was about us abstaining so that we honored God. And God in turn, would bless our marriage. Somehow it made more sense that way."

"You knew?"

"What?"

"On your third date you knew you wanted to get married?"

The familiar sadness he'd seen so often in her eyes clouded her face. She nodded. "Yeah. We knew." Ginny shrugged. "I think I knew the first time I saw him."

What about me? Chester knew his feelings for Ginny ran deeper than anything he'd ever experienced before, but he had no idea how she felt. "Does it matter? Does it bother you that I didn't wait?"

Ginny stared at him a moment, then looked up at the ceiling before facing him again. She furrowed her eyebrows. "I don't think so. It's like you said. You're not the same man you were before. This new Chester, the Chester I know, he *is* waiting. I think God will honor that."

The knot his stomach had been in all day loosened. "Thank you." Chester looked down at his plate and realized he was famished. He took a forkful of pasta then shoveled it in his mouth. He nodded with approval at the taste. "I'm a pretty good cook, aren't I?"

"I'd say you're better than good." She stabbed at a shrimp on her plate then waved it at him before popping it in her mouth. "I'd say you were great."

∽

We'd barely finished dessert when Louisa and the girls returned home. Katy burst into the kitchen to greet us, but Louisa looked in cautiously. She smiled when she saw me.

"Oh, good. You're still here."

I took the last bite of chocolate torte as Katy hugged her uncle. "He bribed me with the offer of chocolate. I couldn't resist."

Louisa laughed.

Chester stood. "You guys want some?"

"Yes!" Maria and Katy yelled in unison. They ran around the table, grabbing the two empty chairs. Louis wheeled in a computer chair from the living room and sat down across from me. The girl's chattered about their evening.

Louisa remained silent, her eyes watching me as Chester served up the torte. She got up to pour herself a cup of coffee. Stopping by my shoulder she bent down and whispered, "Did you guys...talk?"

I looked up at her and smiled. "Yeah."

"And everything's okay?"

"Yeah."

Louisa breathed a sigh of relief and made her way around the table to sit down. Chester refilled my coffee cup and offered me another slice of torte.

"No thank you. I'll pop!"

We joked and talked while the girls ate their dessert. Once the plates were cleared, Maria pulled out a deck of Uno cards. We spent another hour in cut-throat competition. As nine o'clock approached, Louisa insisted Katy get ready for bed. The little girl gave me a fervent kiss on the cheek.

"Will you come to church again tomorrow?"

"I will if you'll sit next to me."

Katy ran off happily to put on her pajamas. Maria waved good-by and went to text her friends.

Louisa got up to supervise her youngsters' bedtime routine. She paused in the doorway. "I'm really glad you stayed." She glanced over at Chester who stood with his back to us filling up the sink with water. Her face grew serious. She spoke quietly, "Try not to hurt him. Okay?"

"I'll try."

She watched me for a moment before nodding and leaving the room.

Chester turned from the sink. "I suppose it's time to get you home, no?"

"Yeah."

He got our coats as I found my purse. I called out good-night to the girls and promised Katy again that I'd see her in the morning at church. Chester and I walked out to the car. A full moon shone, casting its blue-silver light over everything. Chester opened up the car door for me, but I paused before getting in.

"What is it?" he asked.

"The trees."

"What?" He looked around at the few trees that lined the street. The moon's glow reflected off their barren limbs. It was as if they bloomed with soft silver buds.

My chest filled with warmth as I heard Father Dan's voice in my head, *You remind me of one of those winter trees. But there is hope Ginny, if you allow God to fill your heart again.*

Chester put his hand on my shoulder. "What do you see?"

My eyes filled with tears as I whispered, "Hope."

ACKNOWLEDGEMENTS

To John, Ian, and Anna – the best family a girl could pray for! I love you all so much, and appreciate your encouragement and sarcasm.

Becky – because your constant validation keeps me motivated.

All the women at Grace Bible Church, but in particular - Laura Horak, Julie Sweet, Linda Dunlap, Gwen Mueller and Cheryl Hauge. I am honored and humbled to have such sisters in Christ to support me. You are blessings to me!

My sisters – Vicky and Lorraine, because without you as role models and confidants, who knows how I would have turned out? Thank you for your constant support and help with publicity.

Minna Lonsdale, Pat and Doug Stokely – Thanks for your encouragement and all the talks over cups of tea.

The members of the Nebraska Writers Workshop – I learn so much every time I'm able to attend. You guys rock!

The Nebraska Writers Guild – An awesome collection of writers who inspire me with their talent.

For the prayers, opinions, and support of my fellow writers, including but not exclusive to – Steve and Janet Parlato, Shannon Smiley, Angela Prussia, Chuck Grossart, and Cher Powell. Thanks so much for all you do.

To God be the glory great things He has done!

ABOUT THE AUTHOR

Born and raised in Connecticut, Kim has found herself
transplanted to the geographic center of the country,
Nebraska. She still wonders how it happened.

She's worked at everything from Microfiche photographer to
Assisted Living Recreation Assistant. She's grateful to be
working from home now and writing!

Her favorite color is green and she loves all things chocolate
(except for chocolate covered garlic peanut butter cups. Some
things should never be mixed.)
Please visit her website: www.kimstokely.com
And her Facebook page:
https://www.facebook.com/kimstokelyauthor

CPSIA information can be obtained
at www.ICGtesting.com
Printed in the USA
LVOW10s2003281216

518995LV00010BA/849/P